Thunder on the Mountain

Graeme K. Talboys was born in Hammersmith. In between teaching in schools and museums, he has published eight works of non-fiction (on museum education, drama, and matters spiritual). He has also written more than a dozen novels. The first (written when he was seventeen) was lost on a train. The next two (written in his early twenties) he wishes had been. Thankfully, he's had considerably more success with writing since then. His previous jobs have included stacking shelves, pot boy and sandwich maker, and sweeping factory floors. As an adult his first job was teaching Drama and English. Some of his pupils still speak to him. You can follow him on Twitter @graemeKtalboys and visit his website: www.graemektalboys.me.uk

Also by Graeme K. Talboys

Shadow in the Storm
Stealing into Winter
Exile and Pilgrim
Players of the Game

Charlie Cornelius
Thin Reflections
Stormwrack

Wealden Hill

Thunder on the Mountain

GRAEME K TALBOYS

Book Four of Shadow in the Storm

MB
MONKEY BUSINESS

MONKEY BUSINESS
An imprint of Grey House in the Woods

www.greyhouseinthewoods.org

This paperback original 2018

A catalogue record for this book
is available from the British Library

Paperback ISBN: 978-1-909295-13-1
ebook ISBN: 978-1-909295-14-8

This novel is entirely a work of fiction.
The names, characters and incidents portrayed in it are
the work of the author's imagination. Any resemblance to
actual persons, living, dead or yet to be born, events or localities is entirely
coincidental.

Set in Times New Roman.

2 3 4 5 6 7 8 9 0 1

For Leslie Gardner

PART ONE

Transfer

Chapter One

There was pain. Deep. Leaden. Sickening. It was the only thing of which she could be certain. The rest... She tried to make sense of it, but that just made the pain worse so she let go and drifted back into the comfortable numbness of the silent dark.

When she came to again, the pain was still there. So were all the uncertain things. She ignored them and spent all her energy focussing on the pain.

When she came to again it was with a feeling that it had all happened before. She explored her small world step by careful step. There was pain in her torso, her arms, her legs, her head. She tried to move.

When she came to again the initial feeling of déjà vu was soon swamped by a wave of dread. Of what, she could not even begin to understand. That level of effort was still beyond her. So, in the end, she tried moving one of her hands. It seemed to be trapped. The other one she could not feel at all. She no longer had the energy to worry.

After resting a while, she moved her head a quarter turn to try to see her surroundings. Even after everything had stopped spinning, she could make no sense of the dim space that had been revealed. It remained stubbornly out of focus, which did not help with the nausea in which her pain freely swam.

Closing her eyes, she rested again. The fruitless moments she had just spent had exhausted her. As she drifted into sleep she became aware of the hardness of the surface on which she lay, of a swaying motion that may just have been her, of...

A steady vibration drifted into her senses as she surfaced again. She wished it would go away as it made her head throb in sympathy. After a period of time she could not measure, but which seemed close to infinite, she thought it might be a good idea to move, pondered a while on whether this was the first time she had considered such a thing, then thought about it again. The thought was not accompanied by action and for a good deal longer she puzzled over this. She felt her strength going and began to panic.

Determined not to slip back into darkness, she made an effort to move one of her arms, the one with the trapped hand. It was like trying to push a recalcitrant mule she could not feel. Sweat formed on her face and her head began to swim. As fuzzy lights began to pop in the backs of her eyes, something shifted so she kept going until she was aware that a dead weight was moving freely.

Relaxing, her head went back and hit the floor. A brief explosion of bright red pain pushed her over the edge into darkness once more.

The pain in her head throbbed in time with the droning as it vibrated through the hard surface on which she lay. It made no more sense than it had before, but as it had clearly continued unchanged and, as far as she could tell, done her no damage, she set it to one side. For a moment she was distracted as something behind her gave out a soft, prolonged creak. More immediate concerns demanded her attention however. Like the hand she could not feel; and fear, peering out from the entrance of the dark cave where it was normally pushed away.

With a considerable degree of caution, she moved her head. It wasn't caution enough. Sickening pains exploded in the muscles in her neck and shoulders. A faint red haze blossomed in her eyes and faded as she settled into a new position. It was still dim wherever she was; barely light enough to see the ground was smooth. Which meant, she realised with a flood of relief, that her vision was no longer blurred.

Moving her head again, she discovered the wooziness, discomfort, and nausea had not gone away. She closed her eyes for a moment. Opened them on the same smooth floor. Was aware that somewhere off to the left her arm was moving, lowering her hand to the flat surface in front of her eyes. She knew it was her arm because she felt the pain.

Limited by something she couldn't yet understand, her hand moved about the surface not far from her face. She watched it edging its way along, trembling, like a small sick beast. A small sick beast that had bled. Horrified by the dried streaks of gore, she missed what the hand was telling her until the persistence of sensation finally made itself known.

With the dam breached, more messages began trickling in from beyond her tiny world and began to form little pools that edged closer together and joined, one by one. The ground was smooth. She already knew this, but it had not, until now, had any meaning. It was smooth. It was flat. Artificial. She stared at it stupidly for a while, felt a wave of lightness and heaviness followed by nausea, as if the whole floor had dropped and risen, taking her with it.

Through the dullness in her head she choked back a sob of frustration – that she could not move, that she could not understand. And in that fog of uncertainty, some part of her became angry and lent her strength.

The trembling hand before her face shifted into a position with fingers splayed and took the strain as she pushed. Every muscle protested, but with the leverage she turned her body and began to free her other arm.

With several stops and slight shifts of position, she finally pulled the other limb out from where it had been trapped under her torso and lay nursing the agony as feeling returned. As she waited, tiny whimpers escaping her lips, she once more had the sensation that the floor had given beneath her just a little before pushing up again. Vague memories of being on board a ship came back to her. Memories of sickness and fear. She shivered.

Pulling herself from mental agony with the same slow painful progress as her fight for a semblance of physical control, she began to look again at her surroundings. This time she had a marginally better view. Although the space was still dim, she could at least now see a wall of some description.

Her vision was still apt to go out of focus if she expended too much energy, so she went back to sorting herself out. She tried and failed to ignore the dried blood that was on her hands and soaked into her sleeves. There seemed to be a lot of it and it no doubt explained the state she was in. Yet... the pains didn't seem to match. She swore mightily inside her head, hating such lack of control and understanding. She was in an alley. It hit her suddenly. She had not long found her way into the city. There had been a group of unsavoury youths who had set on her. Beaten her. Kicked her. And then... No. No. That was a long time ago. She swore some more.

After what seemed an age, she found enough strength to drag herself along the ground. Inch by agonising inch, fighting both nausea and the desire to curl up and rest, she made her way to the nearby wall. Inch by agonising inch, she slid her back along it until she reached another wall. And there, in the corner, in a swirl of dizziness and hurt, she pushed herself into a sitting position.

Forcing her head upright, she felt the floor give beneath her, had a panicked image of sand. It dropped again and before she could brace herself, it lifted, throwing her head against the wall with a bang that pushed her off the ever crumbling edge of consciousness.

There were noises. There had always been noises. That droning vibration. The gentle creaks. Her own breathing, gasps, and groans. This, however, was new. And the light. It was brighter out there on the other side of her eyelids. She wondered if she dared to see just how much brighter.

A shuffling noise, somewhere just beyond her feet. Could be anything. Self-preservation forced the issue and she opened one of her eyes just enough to allow the lashes to act as a filter.

It wasn't bright light, but it pierced through to the back of her brain and she closed her eye again, suppressing a groan. Not before she had seen a shape. A pale grey moving shape that was, somehow, comforting in its familiarity. If only she could work out...

She opened both her eyes this time, bracing herself mentally for the shock, but the door was closed and the person had gone. It was gloomy again. There was enough light, however, to see that the person who had been in the room had left something on the floor by her feet.

In her condition that was a long way away, but she wanted to see. Taking the time to co-ordinate her movements, she began to shuffle round and across the floor. Her head didn't feel quite so much that it might come loose, and her eyes focussed more readily on the things close to her. It still left her exhausted.

When she drew near enough, she could see that the object left behind was a tray on which there was food and drink. She stared at it for a while and then decided she was hungry. It was too precarious out there away from the wall, though, so by careful increments she dragged the tray along with her back to the corner.

Keeping her head forward, she picked up a bowl and began to eat, pushing cold oatmeal into her mouth with her fingers. Her jaws ached and her throat felt like it was stuffed with grit when she swallowed. With sticky fingers she lifted a wooden mug of water and sipped. Warm and stale with a metallic tang, she had never enjoyed a drink so much.

Somewhere in the back of her head was a faint voice scolding her for eating and drinking like that and she stopped, frowning. It made her head hurt.

"Shut up," she croaked.

The voice went away and she finished her meal in silence, ignoring the rest of the world until the bowl was empty and her fingers were licked clean and dried on her tunic.

It was then that a number of events, past and present, crowded in on her. The tunic on which she wiped her hands was also covered in blood. A great patch of it, dried and stiff, down the left hand side. There was some on her trousers as well, splashes on her boots. Despite all the pain, she knew it couldn't be her own, yet whatever it was that had caused such massive bleeding eluded her, always just out of sight no matter where she searched through the dense fog inside her head.

As she looked down at herself she caught sight of the tray that had been left and it dawned on her that there were two bowls and two mugs. She stared at them for some time as the fog inside her head began to lift a little and images emerged. They had no sequence or sense, but the more she saw, the greater was her feeling of dread.

That was when she saw the third boot.

On the other side of the small, dim space in which she sat, she could see a pile of what appeared to be blankets. They had been there all along, so she had paid them no heed. Until recently she couldn't even focus on them. Now they formed an amorphous and untidy mass in the meagre light. And from the far end, a boot protruded.

Other images flashed through her mind and, ignoring the pain and dizziness, the threat of her stomach to reject her hasty meal, she crawled on her hands and knees across the space. By the pile, she sat back on her heels and began pulling at the blankets. Several came away easily and she pushed them to one side. The next one seemed to be stuck, the coarse wool stiff and sticky.

With care she lifted one corner, peeling it away from what lay beneath, grabbing at clothing to part the one from the other. When it was free, she cast it aside with some violence and sat waiting for the room to stop moving round her.

In the gloom lay a man; dirty, pale, silent. She stared down at him. Dislocated memories emerged. There had been that carefree ride down the coast; a peaceful moment making camp. Seeing to the horses, gathering wood for a fire. The noise. The darkness.

The man that lay there. Alltud. She thought he was dead and the tears ran freely down her cheeks as the fog lifted and exposed every last memory to the harsh glare of recollection.

She leaned forward and with a shaking, grubby hand stroked his bristly cheek. As she did so, she felt the faintest breath of air against the side of her thumb. With tears still streaming, she tore open his tunic and laid a hand on his heart. She could feel nothing and in a panic laid her ear to his still warm breast.

It was the faintest of sounds and, to her, the most glorious. A tiny thump, slow and defiant.

Twisting, she reached back for the tray and pulled it slowly across the floor so the water was within easy reach. She turned back to Alltud. Her hands trembling with the pain of gripping, she lengthened the tear in his tunic, desperate not to disturb him or make any worse what must surely be a terrible mess beneath the cloth.

The material parted with difficulty and would not move at all around what she assumed was the site of the wound. There was precious little water in the mug, so she dribbled some with care on the centre of the blood stain, watching it soak into the gory mess.

It would not peel away the first time, pulling flesh with it as she lifted. More water soaked in and blood stained her fingers, made them slippery. She wiped them on her own tunic and went back to work, slowly peeling the cloth away from Alltud's side.

As she worked, revealing torn flesh, she cried, had to keep wiping her face with the back of her hand; angry at the throbbing in her head and her vision going in and out of focus, angry at what had been done to Alltud, angry that it was because of her.

In the dim light she picked away at the cloth, cleaning as best she could, turning the dead weight of his body to examine the smaller wound in his lower back, praying to all the gods and goddesses she had ever heard of that she was not doing more harm than good. And as she worked and prayed she also cursed, made a solemn vow.

Chapter Two

In the still, quiet moments that followed her initial ministrations, Jeniche felt all the borrowed strength drain out of her. The very thought of moving from where she sat was tiring. Forgotten aches in her neck and arms reminded her of their presence, echoed by the creaking in the structure around her. The throbbing in her head picked up the faint rhythm she could feel through the floor.

Head bowed, she remained motionless and fought other battles. Out of a bleakness, she had discovered a future, only to have it snatched away. And now it lay there before her again and she did not know if the future she had rediscovered would survive. It had been bright, despite the darkness from which it was born; now she saw it had been a false dawn, storm light rather than sunlight.

And from the darkness of her despair, a different vista emerged. A dim vision in a dark place. It was short, brutal and, for the moment, the only future she could see.

Alltud was still unconscious, his breathing unchanged. The clean blanket she had placed over him barely moved. She checked the pulse in his wrist, slow and weak. Wiping her eyes, she turned, picked up the other bowl of food, and ate the cold, congealed oatmeal. Far better that the food be put to use before it was taken away. Even so, she felt guilty.

As she ate, she looked around the ill lit space into which they had been thrown. Long, thin, and high. The wall against which Alltud lay curved inward as it rose so that the ceiling was narrower than the floor. The upright walls were lined with doors of different sizes. Cupboards she assumed, apart from the large one set back in an alcove close to the corner where she had propped herself earlier.

Leaving the empty bowl on the tray, she shuffled sideways to the nearest wall and climbed to her feet. It was not easy. She had to keep her head upright. When she had tried to bend forward, she was thrown off balance by an alarming dizzy spell. Even after the dizziness had passed, she still felt unsteady on her feet as if the floor was pitching gently.

She rested against one of the cupboard doors for a moment, holding fast to the handle and eyeing the curved wall. It was a puzzle to her why it should be so disorientating. She had been on ships before. Straight lines rarely figured. With a shrug she turned her attention to the nearest cupboard and opened it. What she most wanted was something to store water so that whatever was left over wouldn't be taken away. Anything else she could find would be a bonus.

A click behind her made her turn too fast. Her legs gave beneath her and she slid down the wall to sit with her back in the corner. Light flooded in from the opening door. Squinting, she gathered herself.

Shadow filled the bright space and into the storeroom stepped a young man, stocky, tanned. He was hesitant, wary, peering into the gloom. With him came noise, the drone she had heard all along but clearer now. And with it came realisation. It was not a boat they were on. It was an airship.

The young man stared at her for a moment, his eyes quickly adjusting to the lack of light. She saw them move, taking in her, the open cupboard, the man on the floor. After a moment he took a step further into the room, bent down and picked up the tray. As he was leaving, Jeniche found her voice.

"Water," she croaked. "We need more water."

The door had closed as she spoke, but not before she had seen a guard in Occassan military uniform standing outside in a narrow corridor. She counted a hundred and then pulled one of the bowls out from behind her. It wasn't ideal but it held water and she had saved enough to dampen a bit of her tunic torn from the hem. Bending over Alltud, she moistened his lips, cleaned his face as best she could.

And then she could do no more. Curling up beside him, wrapped in the other clean blanket, she let herself sleep.

The light hadn't changed when she woke. Nor had the low level droning. She might have slept for five minutes or five centuries. Either way she was stiff and sore and struggled to get into a sitting position. Once there she used the last of the water to moisten Alltud's wound. If they were flying, it would be much the same as being in the mountains and there, she knew, you had keep a wound moist or it would not heal.

She woke with a start to find herself cross-legged beside Alltud. Five minutes? Five centuries? This couldn't go on. She needed to be fit for what was to come, needed to assess her own hurts.

She stood and stripped and examined herself as best she could before dressing again. As far as she could tell her only serious injury was the extremely tender lump on the back of her head. There was nothing else a long soak in a warm bath wouldn't cure. But all the same the activity had exhausted her and she sat down again alongside Alltud, her back to the wall and her legs stretched out.

There were shadows she could not understand, clinging like cobwebs. She tried brushing them away but they simply clung to her hands and made it difficult to shape the sand. The wind was against her as well, picking away at the structures grain by grain, blowing them across the surface in a sinuous layer that streamed from the dune tops. As far as the eye could see.

"Dreaming?"

She turned her head, still half-asleep, to see Alltud looking up at her.

"It's darker," she said.

Alltud's brows flickered.

"Sorry. Not making any sense."

He smiled for a moment but hadn't the energy to sustain it. "Bad?"

She refused to cry again, but moved round onto her knees so he could see her more easily.

"Bad," she replied after taking a deep breath. "I don't know if anything vital is damaged. Something went through your side below your ribs. You lost a lot of blood."

He lifted his right forearm and she gripped his wavering hand. There was no strength in his fingers as they curled round hers.

"You get a chance to go. Go."

She looked at him.

"Did you hear?" he asked. "I'm serious."

15

"When have I ever listened to you?"

He bit back on pain. When it passed, he said: "Now would be a good time to start."

Half smothered and unable to move she woke to momentary panic. She could see nothing, heard the ever present droning, felt a weight across her shoulders. Turning over carefully, she felt something slip and remembered the cold in the night, remembered the blankets.

She reached up and gently lifted Alltud's arm, slipping out from underneath. They must have slept like that the whole night through, tangled together beneath the blankets. For warmth, she told herself. So that she would know straight away if something was wrong. She told herself.

With a blanket round her shoulders to keep the chill air from her aching joints, she bent over Alltud and inspected his wound. It had dried out in the night and showed no signs of healing. Not that it was easy to see in the ragged mess of flesh in the dim light.

She was still sitting wrapped in the blanket when the door opened and the same young man entered with a tray.

"We need extra water. For his wounds."

He said nothing, looked startled at having been addressed in an attempt at Occassan.

"And if you're not going to do that, we need somewhere to... to..." she groped in her memory for the words, "relieve ourselves. Unless you want to be cleaning that up from the floor in here." She was shouting the last bit as he fled.

Having woken Alltud, she fed him his oatmeal and was eating her own portion when the young man returned. A guard crowded into the room with him. The young man, clearly embarrassed, put an old pot down beside Alltud before he turned to Jeniche and said, "You have to go with the guard."

She stood, angry.

"Jen," Alltud said quietly in Makamban. "It's all right. I'll manage. Now is not the time."

The bright light in the corridor made her blink and she let the guard push her in the right direction.

At the end of the corridor which was short and had five doors in it, she found herself in a slightly wider corridor.

"That way," said the guard, pointing to the left.

She followed his instructions, keeping her eyes wide open, until she opened a door to which she was directed and found herself in a small room with a seat and a bowl fixed to the wall. Cramped and of a design she had to work out when she'd rather just be using it all, it was an improvement on squatting on the other side of the nearest rock or bush. And there was as much water as she needed for washing. She was swilling her mouth and gulping down handfuls from the tap when the guard banged on the door.

She emerged considerably more comfortable and was escorted back to the store room that was their prison. Much to Alltud's embarrassment, she was immediately ordered to remove his pot and make the journey again. This time she had to keep the door open whilst she disposed of the waste, noting with relief that he had passed no blood. She swilled out the container and washed her hands thoroughly with the block of rough soap.

"This is one of five rooms on this corridor. I'm assuming they are all store rooms, but I could be wrong."

He winced before answering as she dabbed at his wound. "Why do you think that?"

"Narrow corridor. Identical doors with identical spacing. It leads to a wider and longer corridor. It's noisier out there. Not loud, but it must be closer to whatever is used to move us along."

"And you're certain it's an airship."

"We're not at sea. My stomach stands witness to that."

"Anything else?"

"We must be near the outside. Curved wall in here. Didn't see that anywhere else. And it's big."

"How so?"

"I saw at least a dozen different people when I went back and forth. They were all in military uniform. Different types. Some I've not seen before. And other people must be steering it. Our food comes from somewhere, so there's a kitchen. We've been in the air at least a day."

"Are we in the air? It feels very smooth to me."

"It has been for a while, but when I first came to there were a few moments..."

"You think they're taking us to Occassus?"

She sat back. "Something that Mord Kint said..." Her voice faltered and she cleared her throat. "Yes."

They dozed and talked quietly through the long morning. Alltud had seemed fairly bright on waking, but he was clearly fading. He managed to smile for her, but it did nothing to hide the pain.

Food and water came and went at what she assumed to be midday. Alltud tried to eat, but could only manage a couple of mouthfuls. He pushed his bowl over to Jeniche. She knew she should, but it was hard to eat when she was holding back the tears.

She was woken by another meal being brought in. Climbing to her feet she caught the young Occassan by his wrist.

"He needs more than oatmeal and water."

The young man tried to pull away, shaking his head.

"He needs help."

The young man broke free and scuttled out of the door. Jeniche tried to follow him, but the guard outside slammed her against the door jamb and then pushed her back inside the store room.

As it grew darker and colder, she sat nursing Alltud. He was becoming agitated, the pain overwhelming his strength. The only time he seemed to find any rest was when he slipped into unconsciousness. He did not stay there much to begin with, but each drop into oblivion was longer than the last and Jeniche began to feel the first cold touch of fear for him.

For a while she paced up and down, but three steps one way and three steps the other did little but wind up her anger. A cry from the prone figure triggered her and she tore open the door, hurling herself at the startled guard.

She was not sure what she was shouting, but all it earned her was more bruising and a violent return to the store room where she sat once more beside Alltud and rocked herself to sleep.

Bright light. Voices. People crowding into the small space as she woke. She tried to fight but was pushed aside and, still disorientated, dragged along several of the bright corridors. Rooms came and went, people standing aside in open doorways. She saw startled faces peering out at her from cramped rooms; saw ladders and hatches; felt blasts of icy air; was pushed finally into a room with large, dark panels along one wall. There she was made to stand just inside the door.

A table filled much of the room, the remains of a meal being cleared away by several young men. She recognised the one who had brought their meals. He looked away and kept his head down.

Sitting round the table were several men in one of the uniforms she did not recognise along with one she most certainly did: the black with silver trim of the Bureau of Reports. Mord Kint watched her with pitiless eyes. They were easy to read. He would have been happy to kill her where she stood and throw her out of the nearest door. But something...

The others watched her as if she were some after dinner entertainment laid on by the BoR. She stood straighter and tidied her blood-stained sheepskin waistcoat.

Mord Kint sneered. "You don't stop, do you. A savage little bitch out of some backward country... You know what you've cost me?"

The anger had gone out of her. "What do I care about you? Alltud is badly wounded and needs proper treatment."

"Why should I waste resources on him? Do you know how many Occassans died at Anka'a? Do you?"

She could see him trembling, wondered why he didn't get up and strike her. She shifted slightly as the floor beneath her canted; saw the thick dressings on one of his legs.

"If he dies," he continued, "it's one less mouth to feed."

"You flatter yourself that you know me, Mord Kint. You have chased me round the world for some reason known only to your particular madness and lost an army in the process. So think on this. I know you need me alive otherwise I would not be here heading to Occassus. That's my advantage. And this is my promise. If Alltud dies – so does everyone on this vessel. And you know, no matter how you restrain me, I would find a way to do it."

It had become very quiet in the room. She noticed the dark panels were decorated with horizontal streaks of moisture, realised they were windows onto the night. Somewhere nearby someone dropped something with a loud clatter.

"You would give up your own life? For that man?"
Jeniche smiled. "For that man? Yes."

Chapter Three

Alltud had almost bitten through the thick leather strap before the surgeon had finished and Jeniche felt she wouldn't have full use of her left hand again for some while. Her hand would get better and she would soon forget the crushing it had received from Alltud whose pain had lent him strength. She wasn't so sure about what she had witnessed, whether that would ever fade from her memory.

The irony was not lost on her. She had fought face to face with people, maimed them, killed them, and learned in her own way to live with it, learned to sleep most nights. Yet holding a person's hand and using the other to help whilst someone cut them open, methodically explored their insides, cleaned them, and stitched them back together was something she hoped never to see again. Unless someone was doing the same for her.

Before he had started on Alltud, the doctor had examined Jeniche.

"Don't want you passing out on me half way through," he had said, just before his prodding of the lump on the back of

her head had shown her once more to the edge of unconsciousness and given her a few moments gazing into the spinning
darkness.

She took it with a degree of equanimity that surprised even
herself. Perhaps because the man was about to treat Alltud.

"You'll do," he had said when he'd finished checking her
ribs. "Bruising, but nothing broken. Now, I need you alert. If
I ask you to do something, you do it. These aren't what you'd
call ideal conditions, but when the Bureau issues orders..."

She tried to work out if he was treating them against his
better judgement or whether his coldness was reserved for his
own people. It didn't seem like a good idea to ask.

When, after several hours, he'd finished and wrapped the
wound, he gave her instructions about keeping it clean. She
had then followed as Alltud, strapped to a long board, was
carried through the narrow corridors and into a new room.
Food was brought in by the same young Occassan who had
brought it before.

"Service room next door," the doctor said. Before she had a
chance to thank him, he left along with everyone else. Despite
that initial coldness he had been thorough and careful, not once
scolding her when she'd hesitated.

In the sudden quiet she felt lost and exhausted, sitting on the
edge of the bunk gently flexing her left hand. The room they
were in was smaller than the store where she had first woken,
but decidedly more comfortable. Two beds, one above the
other, took up half the space. The floor area was reduced by a
tall, narrow cupboard at one end and the door at the other. The
cupboard, she discovered, was empty.

Not knowing what the doctor had meant by 'service room',
she opened the door onto the corridor. There was a guard to
her right. He had been leaning against the wall, but stood up

straight and watched her. She shrugged and turned in the other direction. There was a single door there, and she suddenly knew what was on the other side.

It was basic, purely functional, and the lock had been removed, but to have their own toilet and wash basin and to be able to use it when they wanted would make things so much easier. There was even a chamber pot in a cupboard, held in place with straps.

Refreshed and washed she returned to their new cabin with mugs filled with water and settled on the floor beside Alltud. He slept deeply and with a clearer face than she had seen for... she tried to reckon the hours, was surprised at how few had passed since they had started to make camp and been ambushed.

She sat with her legs curled up beneath her and picked at the panel along the side of the lower bunk. It was for something to do rather than anything else, although she argued with herself that it wouldn't hurt to know if there was a space and where it led.

"I used to do this in Antar," she said, glancing up at Alltud to make sure he still slept. "When Palna wasn't watching. I'd take things apart and try to find ways in and out of rooms. It's where I learned to climb. The Dhalar was a vast building. Ancient. Perched on a rocky promontory across the river from Jhilnagar. We lived in just a small part. Me. And Palna."

She brooded, as lonely now as she had been then.

"At least you don't try to keep me away from the others," she whispered, following her own train of thought. "She knew, of course, but there was nothing she could do except go and look for me, then haul me back inside when she found me. Usually down by the river, playing in the sand."

Endless corridors lit by shafts of sunlight striking down through holes in the roof, nailing the darkness in place. All those flaking murals, so badly decayed they were meaningless, more fungus than paint. Hundreds of blocked up doorways, the chronology of their permanent closure marked by the deteriorating quality of the stonework; the most recent filled with unmortared boulders dragged up from the river bank. Places even she feared to explore, in the heart of the building and down in the tunnels beneath.

She had gone once, after long months of gathering courage, and lost her way; sat in the deep soundless shadows until her candle was burned up. Even down there Palna had found her. Long afterwards she wondered whether she had been left in the dark to frighten her into staying away.

"None of it ever made sense to me. She kept me away from the other children until I grew to ignore the need to be with them, taught me herself in that room that was painted to look like it was somewhere outside. I grew to hate that room."

The images were still vivid. Mountains and a lake with houseboats, greenery, brilliant flowers, all out there beyond that painted rail with its strange stone balusters that made pictures of the spaces between them.

It had been the only time she had ever seen Palna smile. That day she asked if they meant something.

"It wasn't long after that I started looking for a way out. Not just of the Dhalar, but of Antar. I started crossing the river and visiting the city. Jhilnagar is a lot like Makamba. Perhaps that's why I settled so easily when Trag took me in. They're both built around a steep hill, one on the side of the lake, the other by its river.

"That's when the stealing started. Clothes. Money. Maps. I even—"

A tremor in the floor made her stop and she became aware of a subtle pressure against her body, pulling her away from the side of the bunk where she rested. It didn't last long, but she listened to the visceral creaking of the machine and wondered if the ever present background noise of the airship hadn't undergone a subtle change.

There was no doubt about it by the time their next meal arrived. The floor had dropped from beneath her several times although not in a way to which she could find a rhythm and thus anticipate. Alltud had groaned each time but had not woken. She was just tucking him in after checking his bandages when the door swung open and the young Occassan wedged himself in the doorway with a tray in his hands.

"Does it take long to get used to it?" Jeniche asked, taking the tray from him.

He shot a glance at the guard then shook his head.

"What's happening, then? Why is it getting rougher?"

Another glance along the corridor. Jeniche put the tray on the bunk beside Alltud's legs.

"We had to change course. It's storm season." Yet another glance. "We wouldn't normally cross the ocean at this time of year. Too risky. But we were attacked and..."

Jeniche picked up her bowl.

"I'm not your enemy," she said quietly.

He didn't seem wholly convinced. No doubt word had gone round the crew of what she'd said to Mord Kint. She had threatened their lives, after all. And there was no way of knowing what lies Mord Kint had since told about her. At the same time he didn't seem in a hurry to leave.

"I... I have to go," he said eventually and backed out, closing the door behind him.

Flailing wildly, her hand made contact with something she could hold onto. And hold on to it she did, trying to wake, trying to remember where she was. A faint light filled the room. As she began to sit up, she was thrown back, wrenching her arm and hitting the back of the upper bunk as it lurched in the opposite direction. She kept tight hold of the edge of her own bunk, felt everything drop, braced herself for it to rise up again, except it didn't and she hit the mattress with a breath expelling thump.

"Jen?"

"Hang on."

"Trying."

She began to untangle herself from the blankets, conscious of the noise around her. The drone of the airship had gone, submerged beneath louder sounds, a scary groaning, distant drumming, and the roaring of the wind somewhere not very far away just outside of what suddenly seemed a fragile and ridiculous form of transport.

Sitting now, her legs over the side, she edged forward. Although the motion was similar to a ship in a storm, something she tried not to think about too hard, it was subtly different and she had no experience on which to draw. Chancing to luck, she edged further forward, intending to drop to the cabin floor. The whole room rolled first one way, pitching her back into her bunk and cracking her head, then rolled the other so that she was thrown feet first down to the floor.

Buckling at the knees, she managed to prevent her face hitting the wall, but was too dazed to do much else but remain braced in position whilst the room steadied itself.

"Are you all right?"

Reaching behind her, she felt a hand grip hers and she risked turning. Alltud looked drawn, even in the small amount of light in the cabin. His blankets were loose and he had been thrown around as much as Jeniche.

She wanted to shake her head to clear it but didn't dare.

"I want soft pillows under that apple tree," she said.

Bracing herself with a foot against one wall and one arm stretched over Alltud to the opposite wall, she peeled back Alltud's blankets. The dressing on his wound showed spots of blood, but nothing major. All the same she wanted to check.

When she had redressed the wound, she rather wished she hadn't spent the last few minutes bent over in a confined space with the floor dancing beneath her feet. Still, she consoled herself, it's nothing as bad as that storm was when they travelled down the east coast of Tirmawr.

She smiled for the benefit of Alltud.

"It's fine. Those stitches the doctor put in have held. A tiny bit of bleeding, but nothing to worry about."

"Nothing to worry about?" he asked as the room shuddered and something nearby groaned. "The last time I heard a sound like that was when the top of that tower began to collapse beneath Aros as he grabbed Gwyan."

"Thank you for the reassurance," said Jeniche as she straightened his blankets and tucked him back in.

She just had time to get herself settled in the other end of the lower bunk, a blanket behind her head, when the storm hit.

What they had heard before was nothing compared to the screaming rage that engulfed them, the bangs and groans of the airship, the crashing of objects that had worked loose, the duller thuds of people trying and failing to stay upright.

For a few seconds they had time to see the fear on each other's faces and then the lights went out completely. They were cast into a plunging, howling darkness that threw the room around and tried to dislodge them from the bunk.

In a brief lull in the noise from outside, they heard what they assumed must be the guard giving it his all in the service room next door. More shuddering followed and the room felt like it was swinging around. They heard no more from next door after that, but Jeniche didn't feel inclined to risk the short journey outside to see if the guard was all right.

After what seemed an age, the shuddering and groaning settled down although the screaming of the wind continued somewhere close by. Jeniche had known fear, but nothing like this, not even in the desert; never so helpless in the face of forces she could not possibly stand against. She hoped that despite the vulnerabilities of the Occassan vessels, they had been built to take a storm or two, that it all sounded and felt worse than it really was. Because if the wind didn't tear them apart where they were, it was probably a long drop to the ocean beneath them.

"So," came a weak voice from the darkness. "Tell me more about Antar."

It took a second to register.

"More? You heard?!"

"Some." A hand grabbed her foot and squeezed. "Now talk, desert girl. Take my mind off the... scratch in my side for a while."

Chapter Four

As she was directed through the maze of narrow corridors, Jeniche had time to reflect on the fact that everyone she saw looked in worse condition than Alltud who was snoring quietly in his bunk. The two flight crew who had turned up for her had given her time to finish her food, sneered at the military guard in the corridor who was still green in the face, and then pointed her in the right direction. Also facts on which she was able to reflect. In the end, she put them to one side as she didn't have enough information from which to draw any conclusions.

The man who led the way had a recent tear in the back of his pale grey uniform jacket, grease and possibly blood staining the frayed material. She was convinced that the one behind her was limping.

As they negotiated the corridors, she saw the damage that the storm had inflicted. Much of it was loose debris, personal possessions, small bits of equipment, but one corridor was blocked by the shattered remains of a wall through which a metal spar had been forced. To avoid that, they went up a ladder in a small alcove and through a hatch in the ceiling where she encountered parts of the airship she little imagined existed, let alone expected to see.

Up there, the complex, angular innards of the beast were laid bare. Jeniche shivered and saw her breath form clouds. Her sheepskin jacket would have been welcome but it was so badly stained with blood she had thrown it away along with Alltud's.

Her escort stepped onto a walkway that, she guessed, followed the line of the corridor below. It was laid across a sturdy framework and she could see others crossing the dim space as well as ladders that clearly led back down into the enclosed world she had come to know. Other ladders led up into an incomprehensible latticed framework that contained what must be the bags containing the gas that kept them aloft.

She stumbled several times as she gaped up into the shadowy, cold space; stopped when she saw several figures higher up on a small platform from which other ladders climbed even further. They were so small that she realised she had completely misread the scale of the space. She had known it was big. She had seen some of the larger airships crashing and burning at the Battle of Anka'a. But this must be something on an altogether different scale.

A gentle nudge pushed her on the way to another ladder. They descended into a corridor much like all the others. Jeniche welcomed the warm air as it touched her face.

Disorientated for a moment, she found herself being led into a large space with windows along one side. It took her a few moments to realise it was the room in which she had faced down Mord Kint and won for Alltud the treatment he had been given as well as the room they now shared. Now, thanks to her recent, diverted journey, she knew just where she had to go if she ever wanted to bring an airship down from within. She shivered again.

Tucking that piece of information away and wanting to speculate no more on such a terrible death, she looked around. The room was a mess. Furniture had been thrown about, broken, and caused more damage in the process. One of the windows had been covered over with what looked very much like a door, a cold draft hissing through rags stuffed around its edges. Scattered across the floor were all sorts of bits and pieces that had rolled and fallen from the many cupboards that filled the space beneath the bench seats and which lined the walls.

A face popped up from behind an overturned table at the far end. It was the young Occassan who brought them their food. He looked surprised.

"The Captain says you should work your passage," said one of her escort. "The apprentice there'll tell you what needs doing."

They left and the young man stood, watched her uncertainly. He didn't look too good himself, pale, moving as if he walked on eggs, although he too was in considerably better shape than the guard on their room. Given what they had been through in the night, she doubted she was much of a picture herself.

"I'm…" It was all he said before his eyes moved from her to the corridor behind her. "We have to sort out what is broken from the rest. Start at this end and if you don't know, just ask."

She picked her way over splintered furniture. "Wouldn't it be better to clear the big stuff first? Give us more room?"

"Oh. Er… Yes. I suppose. Broken stuff on the pile at that end. It might be of use for repairs."

They worked in silence, picking through the debris and straightening the undamaged chairs. The large table was more or less in one piece although one of the brackets that fixed a leg to the floor had broken.

"That'll be someone else's job."

Every time she had the opportunity, Jeniche stared out of the windows. It was difficult to comprehend that all she could see was water; grey, chopped, cold water. Fascinating. Horrifying.

She drew her gaze away from the view. "How high up are we?"

He looked briefly through the window. "About three hundred feet."

"It seems a lot more."

They worked on. Jeniche tried now and then to engage the young man in conversation. Every time she asked a question, his eyes would flick toward the corridor where someone stood. So she kept quiet for a while and then, when they were at the end of the room farthest from the door, she said: "My name is Jeniche."

Again he looked up, but there was no protection any more. She had spoken quietly and no one could have overheard. "Kenak," he said in the end. "Kenak Zonador. But I'm not supposed to talk to you in case I give something away."

"Like what? I know we must be heading for Occassus. I know that my friend and I are prisoners."

"The Captain told me to guard my tongue. That..." he lowered his voice even further, "...officer of the Bureau, the Duke of Lant—"

"Mord Kint?"

Kenak nodded. "He said that I was to say nothing just to be on the safe side."

"I bet he was a lot ruder than that."

A slight smile appeared on Kenak's face and was immediately suppressed. "Did you..." He was whispering now.

"Go on."

"Is it true you would have brought us down? Killed us all?"

She sat back on her heels, an object of indeterminate nature in her hands. She passed it to Kenak. He looked at it, shrugged, and threw it on the pile of damaged objects.

"I wanted treatment for my friend, Alltud. Mord Kint knows what I am capable of. I know how I would have felt if my friend had died."

They worked in silence for a long while after that; Kenak brooding, Jeniche quietly putting items in the right piles when Kenak placed them incorrectly.

When they had more or less finished, Kenak left without saying anything. The guard who had been loitering in the corridor stepped into the room. Jeniche noted that he was in light grey as well. She carried on tidying, putting undamaged items into one of the cupboards under the bench that ran beneath the windows, keeping an eye open for anything that might prove useful.

A short while later, Kenak returned carrying the familiar tray.

"I've taken some in to your friend."

"How was he?"

"Awake. I told him you were all right."

"Thank you."

The guard, who had taken a bowl for himself, frowned but said nothing. Jeniche and Kenak settled on the bench and ate their stew and flat bread in silence.

As they stacked the empty bowls, Jeniche took the cuff of his grey jacket sleeve between thumb and forefinger and tugged gently. "Are you wearing this by choice?"

Kenak looked puzzled. "Of course. I'm apprenticed to be a Navigator. Ever since I was little I wanted to fly. We live near Amparo and I saw the first airships. They were small. Buzzed around. Even the accidents… I shouldn't talk about that," he finished in a whisper.

"Was it just the thought of being free?"

"I wanted to discover the world."

"It's been discovered already. By the people who live there."

Kenak sighed. "I don't think they're in any danger from me. Since I signed to the *Trepaharos* all I've learned is how to find my way to the kitchen and the broom cupboard."

Jeniche almost laughed. "Yes. Well. That's better than the weapon store."

They both ducked instinctively at the explosive crack from behind them and were then thrown from the bench to the floor as the room tilted and twisted beneath them. A loud, metallic, heart-stopping scream filled the air. The sound stopped as quickly as it started, shudders running through the cabin. A few seconds later the room levelled out.

"We're descending," said Kenak.

Jeniche felt the telltale lightness of a sudden descent, the momentary heaviness that meant they had levelled off.

"Why would we do that?" she asked.

Kenak had climbed up onto the bench on his knees so he could look out of the window. His body was twisted and he was looking upward.

"Because of that," he said.

Jeniche joined him at the window and peered up at the curve of the envelope where it swept outward above them. And there, fixed to struts holding it clear of the airship, was one of the large pods that contained a machine which turned one of the giant oars used to propel it through the air.

The pod should have been level, but one of the struts was broken and the others had buckled so that it hung away from the ship at an odd angle, vibrating in the flow of air around the hull. At its rear, the great, double-ended wooden blade had stopped turning. Jeniche went cold as a shiver danced along her spine. The last time she had seen one of those oars was in the valley on their way up into Tundur. It had been broken, lying in a bush. They had found it not long before they had come across the rest of the airship, torn apart and scattered over the length of a mountain meadow.

She looked down for a moment to see that the waves were much closer now, tall peaks, racing in one direction, their flint grey tops breaking occasionally and sending off spray ahead of them. The sky was none too inviting either – cloud-filled and heavy.

There was no time to see more as a number of senior crew members strode in, several that Jeniche recognised from her recent encounter with Mord Kint. At least he wasn't there. Indeed, the black uniforms had been conspicuous by their absence. Kenak cleared out of the way and stood to one side. Jeniche saw him salute but no one paid him any attention. She moved as well to give the newcomers full access to the windows.

They talked softly, rumbling at each other, pointing, discussing in measured tones. She could understand nothing of it. Her grasp of Occassan wasn't that good and they were no doubt using a lot of technical jargon that was beyond her. She sidled up to Kenak where he stood at attention.

"What are they talking about?" she asked in a whisper.

Kenak frowned for a moment, leaning forward to catch the discussion. He looked pale.

"One of the struts that hold the engine pod has broken. The others are bent out of true by the weight of the pod. There was damage before we left Arbiq, apparently, but it wasn't thought serious. The storm has made it worse. If something isn't done, the whole thing will continue to vibrate until it falls off, tearing a hole in the port side of the envelope."

His explanation wasn't that much clearer, but she got the gist of it based on what she had seen for herself. "Can't it be fixed?"

"The internal companionway that gives access to that pod has collapsed and the weight of the engine swinging back and forth has buckled the superstructure there. There isn't any safe access from inside."

She was still struggling to make sense of what he said. "Can it be fixed?"

"I don't know. I couldn't hear properly. It can't be left loose. The more it moves, the more damage it will cause to the hull. They may just try to cut the other supports without damaging the envelope."

"Drop the whole thing into the sea?"

Kenak shrugged. He didn't look happy.

"Are there people in that?"

"Two engineers usually. There might be more. If it had been damaged, they would have been making repairs."

Jeniche edged between two of the airship's crew and peered out.

"The broken... struts," she said. "Can they be fixed back?"

Conversation stopped and the senior members of the crew turned to her. There was more than one raised eyebrow.

"If it can be..." she searched for the right words. "If it can be put back where it belongs, can it be fixed?"

The crew turned to the one she recognised as the Captain. He shrugged. "In theory. But we cannot get to it. I thought I heard Apprentice Zonador explaining it to you."

In any other situation it would be funny as all heads now turned to Kenak who went crimson at the attention.

"Can you not send someone outside?"

"The only hatch—"

"Why have we stopped?!"

It was Mord Kint hobbling into the room, using a makeshift stick for support. Another member of the Bureau was at his back.

"Storm damage. If we continue under power it could cause irreparable damage to the superstructure along this side. Fatal damage. Another storm would tear the ship apart."

"So what are you doing about it apart from standing around like a bunch of nervous hens?"

The Captain looked at Mord Kint for a moment as if he had suddenly worked out what the terrible smell was.

"I believe your... guest was about to suggest a possible solution."

Jeniche suppressed a smile. From the corner of her eye she saw Kenak's eyes widen. It must be his first real introduction to the power struggles that Jeniche had surmised existed between various elements of Occassan society.

"You would take ideas from... from this butcher? She who led the armies against us at Anka'a?"

"She succeeded, Duke. Which means she is smart. I'll listen to anything that might keep us safe."

"Safe? You heard her yesterday. In this very room. She threatened to destroy us all."

"And you, I recall, backed down in the face of that threat. Which suggests to me that you also believe she is a capable person."

"You will face the Order for this," said Mord Kint quietly.

"Only if we reach Amparo," the Captain replied.

Mord Kint stood his ground although he clearly had nothing more to say. After long, uncomfortable seconds he turned and hobbled away.

The Captain turned and faced Jeniche, searching her face for a moment as he retrieved the thread of their interrupted conversation. "Hatch. The only hatch to the exterior is on the upper surface of this outrigger. We can send people down, but wind and stability means we are just as likely to lose them. And even if they get to a point above the pod, they will hang too far out from the envelope."

"What about climbing up from below?"

The Captain frowned. "Have you seen the outside?"

"The bands that run upwards. What are they?"

He gestured to Jeniche to join him at the window. "Do you mean these?" he asked, pointing up to a narrow band of metal that ran around the outside of the envelope.

Jeniche nodded. "Yes."

"They are part of the external skeleton. They hold the three main sections together from the outside."

Jeniche shrugged. She didn't really understand. "They'd take my weight?"

The Captain looked at her and back out of the window. "Well, yes. But—"

"Then I'll need a rope around me and anchored in here in case I slip. I'll need a coil of rope for… just in case. And a length of cord. If I can get up to the pod from here I can loop the cord round where that strut is fixed to it. Will that hold?"

After a whispered conversation with someone in stained overalls, the Captain turned back to Jeniche and said, "Yes."

"And will I be able to get the ends of the cord to someone inside from up there?"

"A long pole," said Kenak. "With a hook?"

The Captain turned. "Good lad."

Kenak reddened again.

"Well? Go on. Get it organised."

Kenak ran from the room. After that it was all bustle as ropes were brought, the boarded up window unboarded, one end of the rope anchored to Jeniche's satisfaction, and all the rest laid on.

She didn't give herself too much time to think about what she was doing. It was certainly no worse than the time she had climbed out over the river in Kodor. Better. Here she had a rope and there was no ice to contend with. Yet everything she had ever climbed before had been fixed to the ground, had been, to a degree, solid. Best just get on with it and not think of the ocean below.

The structure that contained the room was fixed, in part, to the first of the metal strips so it was an easy move to climb out of the window and test whether she would be able to get her fingers under the band where the envelope was not held close by internal ribs. It was a tight squeeze, but gave her sufficient hold to continue.

Almost immediately, Jeniche felt the wind. Even though the airship was moving with it, it curled around the curve of the hull, pulled at her and began to suck away the heat from her flesh. They had offered her one of the heavy padded jackets she had seen some of the crew wearing, but it would have made climbing difficult. So, it would have to be a quick job. No stopping to think.

The bands covered the exterior of the midship section in a diamond pattern. She climbed up one to where it crossed another and then climbed back down until she was hanging almost from the very bottom of that part of the airship, looking between her dangling legs to where an even larger bulge blocked her view. It was the first time she had been scared on a climb.

40

If she ever got back inside with her arms still in their sockets, she would have to ask Kenak just how big the vessel was. For now, though, she must move on to the next band and work her way up otherwise she would freeze there.

A pattering sound stopped her for a moment and she felt water on her hands and face, tasted salt on her lips. A quick glance down showed gigantic waves racing past fifty feet below. It was all the impetus she needed to move on up the band, crabbing across the surface of the envelope at an angle until she was close to the pod and the torn opening to the interior.

For Jeniche, much of the rest was a blur. Her muscles screamed at a growing consciousness of the race between accuracy and tiredness. There was also the dispiriting knowledge she had the climb to do again in reverse, even though she was so close to what had once been an entrance to the interior. Close to the juddering pod, she managed to hook her legs round a twisted end of broken strut so that her arms were free not just of the weight of her body but to throw the cord.

The first attempts failed. The wind caught the line and blew it away from the target. Each attempt cost her energy and heat. In the end, she hung by one leg and reached up to remove a boot. With fingers already half numb with pain and cold, she secured it to the cord as best she could. Praying the boot wouldn't be lost, she began to swing the cord. The weight helped and she was able to cast the line straight into the hole torn in the side of the pod. There was a cheer; faces peering at her from within followed by a signal she assumed meant that the cord was secure.

When the long pole appeared in front of her with a large metal hook on its end, she looked at it blankly for several seconds before remembering what to do next. With increasing difficulty, she managed to hook the other end of the cord securely into place and saw it being drawn in through the tear in the envelope.

At that point she knew she had nothing left. She was no longer the agile young thief she had been in Makamba. Fear, beatings, hunger, and the passage of time had taken their toll. And now the wind had sucked all the heat from her body, her fingers were numb, and she had started to shiver uncontrollably. The journey back would not be possible. It was a relief to let go and feel the cold air rush past as the waves approached, leaping up to greet her.

Chapter Five

"What in the name of all the gods and goddesses were you thinking?"

"Not much towards the end."

He glared at her. "Not much at the beginning, either."

She was unmoved. "You know I can climb. You've asked me to do it on your behalf in the past."

"That was different."

"Explain how."

"Well, for one thing, I was there to catch you."

She couldn't help but manage a smile at the memory of landing on him when she fell those last few feet after climbing out of their rooming house in Alboran. Just after she'd dropped a bag on him.

"By accident."

"And you've never done anything like this before."

"I was attached to a rope."

"Held at the other end by your enemies."

"They're not my enemies, Alltud. Not all of them. Now lie back and take it easy. You're supposed to be resting."

"How can I rest knowing you might be out there swinging from the end of a rope again?"

"I'm fine. Truly. I didn't even get wet. The doctor said it's just some bruising on my midriff and rope burns. They'll fade. And I soon warmed up. Besides it was for the good of us all. There's another storm chasing us and if that pod thing had been torn off the side of the airship it would have let the storm in. You're in no state to be swimming just now."

Alltud slumped back with a growl, his face bearing the marks of tiredness and pain.

Jeniche placed a hand lightly on his shoulder. "I know you hate all this lying around—"

"I can cope with that. It's worrying about you that gets to me."

There was a long silence.

"Just don't do anything unnecessary," he added, putting his hand on hers. "Please. And if you must, just don't let me know about it afterwards. At least, not until I'm fit enough to put you over my knee."

"Oh, the things you say to a girl."

She could see him blushing and smiled.

Alltud was asleep when Kenak tapped lightly on the cabin door. Jeniche stepped out into the narrow corridor, where the tired looking guard leant against the wall.

"The Captain wants you in the ward room," said Kenak, keeping his voice low.

"More cleaning?"

Kenak shrugged.

She followed him along the corridors, now cleared of debris, squeezing round crew members busy repairing walls and refitting furnishings. They waited for several minutes whilst

44

two crewmen manoeuvred a heavy frame through a narrow door.

"Is all this worth it?" asked Jeniche. "With another storm on our tail."

Again Kenak shrugged. He seemed in a sombre mood.

"Bad storm?"

"Yes."

"Scared?" For the second time that day she had made someone blush. "It's nothing to be ashamed of."

"That's easy for someone like you to say."

"Someone like me?" He didn't answer. "Never mind. You think I wasn't scared out there?"

"Maybe, but you did it."

"Or what? Let the wind tear us apart? We all have things we can do that others can't. I learned those skills, the climbing, the fighting, the thieving, because I was running away from things. Did you run away from anything?"

"Well..."

"No. I bet you went to your father, knowing how it would cause all sorts of upset, and told him that instead of working on the family farm you wanted to fly, to become a... a navigator. Bet that wasn't easy."

"It took me months."

"And you did it. You didn't run away from it; didn't end up watching the airships go over wishing you'd had the courage."

"But it's not the same."

"Isn't it?"

They entered the ward room. There was boarding back over the broken window, properly shaped and sealed this time. The table was repaired. The pile of broken objects had gone. Someone had even washed the bench along the side and swept the floor.

Jeniche went over to the window and looked out. They were much higher now. The wave tops still raced along, flecks of white bright against the deep grey, but they seemed remote.

"More speed at this altitude," said Kenak.

"That engine... is that the word? It isn't working."

"They have to make sure the whole structure is stable before daring to start it up. And the propeller needs to be checked as well."

"Is that the great oar?"

Kenak didn't answer because two men came into the room, shuffling their feet by the doorway.

"Don't stand there," came a voice from the corridor behind them.

They shuffled further in and the Captain appeared behind them. He smiled at Jeniche. It reminded her of Kenak. Perhaps he too was an enthusiast, maybe one of those pioneers whose flights had so captivated the young apprentice. Despite the uniform and the easy air of command, he didn't seem much like a soldier. Which was just as well, as someone who thought like a soldier would not, she thought, make a good airship captain.

"They wanted to offer their thanks," prompted the Captain. "And now seem to have lost the power of speech."

Jeniche looked at Kenak.

"They are the engineers who were in the pod," he explained quietly.

"Oh."

One of them stepped forward. The sheepish grin on his face died as Mord Kint pushed his way into the room, still limping on his bandaged leg.

"What is this? Not content with endangering us all by placing our lives in the hands of an enemy of the Order and an enemy of the State, you are now encouraging your crew to fraternise."

"Out," said the Captain, his voice calm.

The engineer who had approached Jeniche had his back to Mord Kint. He mouthed a quick 'Thank you' and, with his companion, left the room.

"You too, Navigator Zonador," added the Captain. "And please take our... the prisoner with you. The Pilot has things that need tidying."

Kenak led Jeniche into a part of the airship she hadn't seen before. Behind them, they could hear the Captain explaining some of the realities of life on board an airship over the ocean during storm season. Jeniche would have loved to loiter and listen, but it was heartening to know there were Occassans even at the Captain's level who were less than enamoured of the BoR and the Order that Mord Kint had mentioned.

So many questions. Time to be careful.

"How big is this airship?" she asked after they had been set their new task and stood looking into the room that needed sorting.

"One of the biggest in the fleet. A triple-hulled transport."

Jeniche looked bemused. "I understand the transport bit."

Kenak smiled. "It's like three airships fixed together. The central bit is the main lifting body and has the large cargo holds. Then there's a smaller airship fixed on either side, the outriggers. They are for lift, stability, contain all the engines, crew quarters and smaller cargo stowage."

Jeniche nodded politely. She had understood only half of what she'd been told, filled in the rest with guesses. "And what's all this?" she asked looking into the room.

"The chart room. Each chart belongs in its own pigeon hole."

Each chart was now on the floor, mixed up with every other chart.

"So this is your area, then."

"Charts? Yes. Not that I'm normally allowed near them."

"There's hundreds of them."

"One thousand and thirty-two of the B series. They cover the world beyond Occassus. As much as we have explored, anyway. And there are two hundred and seventy-nine in the A series. That's Occassus, some of the Great Salt Waste, and the territories to the north and west."

"Are they all different?" She was thinking of the library on Pengaver and how they would love a collection like this.

Kenak sighed. "Yes. And we have to get each one in its right place or there will be trouble. It's one of the things you have to learn as an apprentice, the number for each chart..." His voice tailed off and he stood for a moment grinning at Jeniche.

"What?"

"The Captain."

"What about him?"

"He called me Navigator Zonador."

"Aren't you?"

"No. Yes."

"Both? At the same time?"

"No. Yes."

"You're not making any sense."

"I'm an apprentice. I shouldn't be called Navigator until I've earned it."

"Can the Captain make that decision?"

"As long as the Chief Navigator agrees."

"Seems like he did then."

Kenak kept grinning.

"The charts?"

"Oh. Yes. Right. So some of them from the A-series will be on the bridge for the flight ahead, but all the rest are here. On the floor."

"Come on then."

It was a simple task if somewhat tedious. Each pigeon hole was numbered, each chart marked with the same number. It was a matter of making floor space and then putting each chart in its appropriate home. Before long they were having a look, unrolling them part way to see if Kenak's memorising was any good.

It made the task more bearable, especially when they came to charts for parts of the world that Jeniche knew. The first one had been for part of Gyanag. Jeniche had seen it. The writing and the other annotations were beyond her, even though her command of spoken Occassan was improving. It was the way a series of lakes were spaced along a river that had made her unroll the chart further.

Kenak was envious. Seeing the world was his ambition. Jeniche shook her head, pointing out places she had been ambushed, robbed, beaten, places where she had learned to plant rice, places she had nearly frozen to death. He lapped it up like a kitten who had found the cream dish. Easy enough, she supposed, when it hadn't happened to you, when it was all annotations on a map.

They worked through what was left of the morning until Jeniche had to stop. Her arms and torso ached. It hadn't helped that she'd fallen thirty feet on the end of a rope. Kenak apologised and disappeared to get some food.

"Make sure Alltud gets his first," she'd said as Kenak left the room. "And tell him I'm safe and warm, not dangling above the waves on the end of a line."

As soon as Kenak had gone, she began to look for a chart of Occassus. She now understood the principle of the numbering system and knew he had said the charts for the voyage ahead were on the bridge, but there might be something.

In the end she had to content herself with a kind of index, a book with outline sketches of each chart in their storage order plus maps that gave an overview. She picked out Rajan and Makamba, worked through to Tundur, Gyanag, Azak and Sova, Arben and Arbiq and finally found Occassus. It was a large country, long and relatively narrow with a mountain range forming a spine in the northern reaches. To its east was the ocean and in the west what appeared to be wilderness.

It was all she had time to take in before Kenak returned with their food. They ate in silence, completed their task, and made sure the locking bars were firmly in place across the front of each column of pigeon holes.

By the time they had finished, Jeniche was looking forward to going back to the cabin and checking on Alltud. Kenak had other ideas. He asked her to wait whilst he returned the bowls to the galley. She shrugged. Alltud wasn't going anywhere.

Kenak was gone some time and she began to wonder if he'd forgotten her. When he did return he apologised.

"I had to run a couple of errands and couldn't very well say no."

"So what's the big secret?"

"Follow me."

They left the chart room and Jeniche followed him through more corridors. Given time she would probably make sense of it all, but everywhere looked the same and there were few signs – all in a language she could not read. At a junction they stopped and he turned to her with his finger over his lips. Gesturing to her to stay, he disappeared round the corner. A few moments later he was back and beckoned her to follow quietly. Anyone watching would have known straight away they were up to something.

Once they had turned at another junction, Kenak relaxed. "The BoR commandeered those cabins," he whispered. "It's the only way at the moment to get where we're going."

The corridor they were now in appeared to be a dead end. Kenak reached down and lifted a hatch in the floor and stood aside. Jeniche peered down the hole where a ladder dropped at an angle into the gloom.

"Go straight down and through the trap at the bottom."

She smiled but felt that he could have used a different word for hatch had he wanted to put her at her ease.

It was cold in the space and grew darker when Kenak closed the hatch above them. She peered into the deep gloom but could see little beyond the struts that held the ladder even though she was conscious of a large void. Once she had found the handle, the hatch at the bottom of the ladder opened easily enough and light flooded upwards. The ladder continued down into a small space surrounded with small windows.

"It's the landing observatory." He pointed to an apparatus toward the front. "There are signals and speaking tubes there. We're right underneath the central hull."

"And why are we here?"

He pointed to the windows and Jeniche looked out. All she could see was the sea.

"We've crossed the ocean."

She looked at him and then back down at the dark waters.

"We're heading north now which means that is the Gulf of Remola."

Jeniche stared down trying to see some difference. Perhaps the water was a bit muddier looking, but that was all.

Kenak stood beside her and stared down as well. "They say—" he stopped and looked round to make sure the hatch above them was shut. Even then he lowered his voice. "They say there used to be land down there. A whole country. When the sea is calm you can see the ruins of cities beneath the surface. We're not supposed to talk about such things."

"Why? Who says you mustn't?"

Another glance at the hatch. "The Order."

"Who are they? I've heard them mentioned."

"The rulers of Occassus. The BoR is their hand in the world, their voice."

"Why don't they want you talk about such things? The world is littered with ruins. Hard to keep them a secret."

"All the same."

"And that is what you wanted to show me?"

He looked crestfallen.

"I'm sorry," said Jeniche. "It must have taken courage. A shame it wasn't calm. I would love to have—"

"Oh. Look."

Kenak was pointing off to one side. Jeniche squinted, trying to see anything other than waves. She shrugged.

"Close to the horizon. Something else we are encouraged to pretend doesn't exist."

"Those dark patches?"

Kenak nodded and Jeniche looked harder. "Are they ships?" she asked.

"Sort of. Huge rafts. They are like towns floating on the sea. The Gulf has an almost circular current and they follow it round. There are several large collections and lots of smaller ones. It's unusual to see them this far west at this time of year."

"What do they do? How do they live?"

"Fish mostly. The Gulf is rich in fish. And they dive in the shallows."

"Into those ruins that don't exist?"

Kenak nodded. "It's not safe, though. Not now."

"They seem to have survived the last storm."

"But maybe not the next."

Pulling her by the sleeve, he took her to the back of the cabin. The underside of the vast hull filled the upper part of the window as it stretched away, but beyond it, in the far distance, the sky was black, so dark it could only be seen because it was shot through with flickers of lightning.

Chapter Six

"I am beginning to develop a real dislike for this room," he muttered as he edged back through the door, right arm bent across his abdomen.

"And good morning to you," said Jeniche.

Alltud squinted at her in the gloom, shot out his left hand to the wall to steady himself as everything tilted. He grimaced. The trip to the room next door had tired him and his side already hurt like fury. Being jolted about did nothing to help.

"The water seemed a bit reluctant when I washed."

"Tanks must be low."

"More information from your boyfriend?"

Jeniche climbed down from the upper bunk and stood beside Alltud in the confined space. "Not wise to tease someone who is about to prod your wound."

She helped him onto the lower bunk and supported his back as he lay down so he didn't put too much strain on his stomach muscles.

"The dressing is clean, which is good, but that wound looks a bit sore."

"Oh, very funny."

"Red. Inflamed. Have you been scratching?"

"It itches."

She sighed. "Because it is healing."

"Well, it's driving me mad."

"It didn't have far to send you, did it."

"Are there no books on this forsaken vessel? Anything to take my mind off things."

The room shuddered.

"You won't have time for reading, even if there were something in Ketic."

"This going to get worse then?"

Before she could reply, the door opened with a bang. The guard stood there, holding on to the door frame. He already looked less than happy, a pale almost green tinge to his flesh.

"If you want food," he said, his face clearly demonstrating the unsettling nature of such an idea, "you'll have to get it yourself. The young un's busy."

They heard him blunder into the service room and slam the door, exchanging grimaces at the sounds that followed.

"Stay put," said Jeniche, ignoring the look of annoyance on Alltud's face. "I'll be back as soon as I can."

She staggered along the corridor, bouncing from wall to wall as the floor canted beneath her feet. At the end, she braced herself and waited for a calm moment so she could turn the corner and head toward where she thought the galley was situated.

Retracing her steps, she bumped into Kenak.

"Sorry," she said as she helped him to his feet.

"It's all right," he replied with a grin. "I'm beginning to get used to it."

"They keeping you busy?"

"The speaking tubes aren't much use when the wind gets this loud. I'm running messages."

"Galley?"

He pointed. "Left and then right."

"Thanks. Take care."

"At least we'll be over land soon."

"Is that before or after the storm reaches us?"

He shrugged. "Better go."

She watched him climb a ladder, pausing half way as the airship slewed and righted itself. He pushed up through a trapdoor that slammed shut behind him. And then she was alone again. For a few moments she held on to a rail and listened to the bangs and howls, the slow grinding creaks as the wind assaulted the machine in which she rode.

With a slow shiver, she pushed on in search of the galley, following Kenak's directions. It was a surprisingly small, well-ordered room, spotlessly clean. The cook had stowed everything and was putting locking bars across the cupboard doors, checking as he went to make sure nothing was loose enough to fly around and cause damage.

He looked up when he noticed Jeniche and pointed to a small sack that was sliding back and forth on the counter beside the door. It fetched up against a low rail before heading back toward the side of a cupboard.

"Not able to cook anything," he said. "Not in this. There's salted meat in there, biscuits."

"Need any help?"

"No. Thanks. Nearly battened down here."

The floor pushed up at them and Jeniche fell sideways, grabbing the rail beside the sack. The cook watched with a smile, seemingly untouched. He nodded.

"You're getting there," he said.

"Seems like a hard way to learn."

"Isn't it always?"

She conceded the point, picked up the sack, and left him to his work. With one hand in use holding the sack, her return to the cabin was somewhat more diverting and she collected more bruises to add to her already considerable collection.

There was no sign of the guard when she arrived. "Is he still in next door?"

"No. He was called off to help somewhere else."

The small Occassan lantern fixed to the wall flickered and dimmed before finding its former strength. They looked at each other for a moment before Jeniche decided it would be a good idea to wedge herself in at the other end of Alltud's bunk. She helped him sit and braced him with pillows before she climbed into the narrow space and tipped out the contents of the sack.

Trying to guide food to their mouths was an interesting experience and occasioned more than a few smiles. With memories of the previous storm still very fresh, however, it was difficult to keep their worries at bay. Last time had been bad enough not least because they were helpless in the face of such power. And it was worse for Jeniche as she had seen the dark, angry monster that was bearing down on them.

When they had finished, Jeniche put the plates back in the sack and clambered out of the bunk. As she was leaving, the lights dimmed again. She wondered if she'd be able to find her way back in what little natural light made its way into the corridors. It was doubtful and the urge to stay put was strong, but there were things she wanted to do.

Banging back and forth between the walls and taking a tumble in the passage to the galley door saw her back where she wanted to be. And, as she had hoped, the place was empty.

After a quick search, she wedged their plates into a crate with other dirty pans and utensils, securing the lid when she'd finished. Then, after checking there was no one outside, she went to the drawer where she had seen the cutlery go. Minding her fingers, she sorted through and found a wicked looking knife. After she wrapped it in a napkin, it went into the small sack followed by food. More biscuits. More salted meat. A small round of cheese. Some carrots. Whatever happened now, she doubted it would be missed. All she had to do was get it back to their cabin without anyone seeing.

It was almost inevitable that, in an airship where everyone should either be wedged in somewhere out of the way or busy with whatever aircrew needed to do, she would hear voices approaching. Returning to the kitchen would have been too risky, so she tried the nearest door. It was unlocked and she stepped inside the dark room.

Even before she could close the door, the floor went out from under her and she fell. Kicking out she slammed the door and held it shut with the toe of her boot.

"Was it this one?" she heard a moment later, grimacing as cramp bit her foot.

Shuffling over she pushed a second foot against the door just as someone tried the handle.

"It's locked. Whatever went over will have to—"

There was a clattering from outside as the airship lurched again.

"I'll be glad when we get to Amparo." The voice faded as the crewmen walked away.

Not taking any chances, Jeniche climbed to her feet with her back to the door, flexing her toes until the muscles came out of their painful spasm. As she listened she looked round, her eyes having adjusted to the gloom. It was not unlike the room she had first woken in. The walls were lined with cupboards. Piles of canvas sheets that had been neatly stacked were already leaning and unravelling; from a series of hooks, coils of rope and cord swung back and forth.

She was tempted to go through the cupboards, but decided not to risk it. Instead she helped herself to a coil of cord, slinging it over one shoulder.

Bracing herself against the frame, she opened the door a fraction and pressed her eye to the crack. The corridor seemed clear and she could hear nothing but the protests of the great machine as it was assaulted by the leading edge of the storm it was trying to outrun. She stepped out, closed the door behind her, and headed off toward her own cabin.

"What the...? Where have you been?"

"I went to the galley to return the plates. Remember?"

Alltud made a point of looking at the full sack and coil of cord in exaggerated fashion before he raised an eyebrow. Jeniche looked down at them.

"Goodness," she said. "Where did they come from?"

"I suppose you want to hide them in my bunk?"

"I thought you'd never ask."

Alltud shook his head and then rolled to one side.

"Under my feet."

Jeniche hid the items and tidied the bunk again.

"Are you all right?" she asked.

"Oh—" he gasped as a particularly sudden drop caught him unawares and he wrenched the muscles in his side. "Never better."

"It's deserted out there. Everyone's busy securing things and holding on."

"Meaning?"

"I'm going out for a quick look."

"Jen."

"I'll be careful."

"That'll make a change."

She poked out her tongue and then stepped out into the corridor.

Quite what she hoped to achieve was uncertain, but the opportunity seemed too good to miss. The aircrew didn't seem to take her any more seriously as a threat than did the lone soldier in dark blue who guarded them. Sensible really, especially now. The Occassans needed everyone to help with doing whatever needed to be done during the storm. She couldn't go anywhere very far. Even if she hid, there was little point. At some stage she would have to emerge.

Yet the place was, to all intents and purposes, deserted and who knows what opportunities might arise from a quiet nose around, especially now she wasn't carrying a stolen knife. She had learned from a very early age that the better prepared you were and the better you knew your surroundings, the better were your chances of survival. All those years exploring the Dhalar had made it easy to escape when the idea and the time came. All those years getting to know Makamba...

In the end, she found her way down to the viewing room where Kenak had taken her. Most of the journey involved falling, although she was getting better at keeping her feet. As she opened the hatch, the room below was flooded with light for an instant and she was left with vivid coruscations dancing before her eyes. By the time she reached the bottom of the ladder it was in darkness again although she was fairly sure it must be mid morning, if not later.

The windows were streaked with rain, even there beneath the central part of the airship. She peered out, her hands cupped either side of her eyes and pressed to the window so she could see clearly. Below them, swamp sped past. It was difficult in the darkness to gauge how high they were, but it was considerably lower than when they had been at sea. She hoped the pilot knew where they were. She thought of that long line of mountains on the map; consoled herself with the scale. They must be hundreds of miles away to the north.

More lightning, fierce and spreading across the horizon, lit everything in stark detail. Trees on the patches of dry ground were bent almost horizontal, grasses were laid flat, and water was whipping at an angle to their line of flight. Something that looked uncannily like the front of a house cartwheeled past and exploded into myriad fragments that were torn out of sight. She wasn't sure she wanted to know more. But, of course, she could not stop herself from crossing to the other side and peering out into the face of the storm.

The last time she had looked out, it had been distant and dark on the horizon, shot through with lightning. Now she could see down its violent, seething maw into its very heart and she thought, with what felt even to her like an unnatural calm, that they were probably going to die.

Even in the very face of death she refused to go without whatever fight she could muster. Racing up the ladder and hurtling along the corridors, she picked up more bruises and ended up in their cabin out of breath.

Alltud looked up, alarmed. He was having a bad enough time as it was, what with all the jolting on his wound and the thought of another storm. He didn't need a panicked looking Jeniche bursting in.

She didn't stop to say anything, but stepped up on the edge of Alltud's bunk and began pulling at her bedding. A protesting Alltud disappeared under a pile of blankets, pulled them off his head in time to see Jeniche's mattress drop to the floor.

She stepped down onto it, kicking it flat. As he watched, she fished out the coil of cord from beneath his legs and unwound it. The knife appeared as if from nowhere and she cut the cord into two more or less equal lengths, threading them under each end of the mattress on the floor.

"Out," she ordered.

He knew not to argue with that tone of voice. With an arm over her shoulder he let her help him into a sitting position. From there he climbed out of his bunk and knelt. The scale of what was to come was beginning to sink in.

"Lie down."

Again, he did as he was told. She took his weight and as soon as he was lying down on his back, she put a pillow between his head and the door and began packing blankets around him. When his own mattress came out of his bunk and was lowered on top of him, he guided it into place and burrowed a small passage through the blankets to allow a passage for air.

In the darkness he could hear Jeniche moving around, felt the mattress tighten down as she tied the cord at the end mearest the door. How she manoeuvred after that, he could only imagine, but he felt her feet push carefully up alongside him and then felt the other end of the mattress move as the other length of cord was tied off.

Somehow, unable to see, muffled by blankets, they managed to find each other's hand and hold on tight.

Chapter Seven

There was a moment after all the mayhem when the violent gyrations and tumbling had ceased, the assault on their senses had stopped, and normal levels of fear had been restored, when they both thought it might be over. It was an almost blissful moment in which everything seemed to be still and the only sound was the shrieking of the wind. They should have known better, but they each mistook the slightly weightless feeling for the natural adrenalin induced euphoria of someone who survives a life-threatening event.

When the first collision occurred it was far worse than anything they had so far experienced. Until that moment, no matter how savage the irresistible force of the storm, it had simply hurled the airship forward on its tumultuous flight. Now it had found an immovable object against which to drive the vessel with all the fury it could muster. Alltud cried out, a sharp explosion of pain in his side. Close as she was, Jeniche did not hear him above the rending of metal and splintering of wood, the arrhythmic concussions of all the small objects that formed a lethal blizzard in the confined space of their tumbling cabin. Afterwards there was a succession of anonymous and dreadful sounds close by caused by the shuddering and bumping, the twisting and turning and rolling. There were other moments of weightlessness, but they grew shorter and further apart and they both knew now what would follow.

Into the chaotic nightmare, into the cacophony of howling sound, a scream began, loud and agonised, hurting their ears. It went on and on, long after they had come to an abrupt halt and felt a succession of objects falling on top of them. It yowled into the dark and the storm, a great beast dying, wailing at its own demise, defiant in the face of the raging tempest.

And then the energy went out of it. The howl faded and was submerged by the roar of the gale that swept away the sudden feeling of suffocation that had enveloped them. In their darkness the world shivered and trembled, spasms and thrashing of the nearly dead beast. Now and then little flashes of light reached into them, with thunder pressing into their ears.

Shivering and uncertain, they did not know whether to fight their way free or stay in the cocoon that had so far preserved them. The storm still roared, but the airship was clearly on the ground. They might now be safe; or some new peril might be about to descend on them.

Unable to untie the knots at hand, Jeniche retrieved the stolen knife from her boot and cut the cord. Pushing out of the blankets, mattresses, and a collection of anonymous debris, she was met by the full volume of the storm. For a moment she couldn't work out where they were. The dark space seemed far too narrow.

A muffled voice and movement of nearby legs had her scrambling all the way out. She caught her head a glancing blow and stooped as she scuttled toward the other end of the top mattress to cut the second cord. It parted easily and Alltud, already pushing from the inside, emerged and drew breaths of cool, damp air.

"While we have light enough," she said to forestall what she knew he was going to say, "I want to check your wound."

"I'm fine."

"All the same, it needs to be checked."

"I don't know if you had noticed, Jen, but the world is falling apart around our ears."

"Let it."

He held up his hands in surrender. She didn't often have that edge to her voice, but when she did he knew it was wiser to give in straight away.

It didn't take her long. In what light was available, Jeniche ran her fingertips over the scarred flesh. She could see neither fresh tearing nor bleeding, so she wrapped the bandaging back around and fastened it with a practised hand. Almost before she had finished tying the last knot she was looking about the dim space to work out where they were and to avoid Alltud's eye. It was this, perhaps, that made her miss the effort Alltud put into hiding just how much pain he had suffered as a result of the crash.

What she did see was that they lay in a small space that was the bottom bunk tipped at an angle. Once she understood that, the rest of the enclosing shadows made sense. Everything shuddered, but it seemed to be the shivering of a structure rooted firmly to the ground. Cold, damp air continued to push its way around the remains of their cabin, bringing in the sound of the wind and rain. Occasionally a deep rumble of thunder rattled their very bones.

Jeniche clambered out, careful to avoid Alltud, and stood unsteadily on a sloping floor slick with water. The cupboard that had stood at one end of the floor space had completely disappeared and there was a ragged hole through to where the service room had been next door. In the flashes of lightning that penetrated whatever debris was out there, she could see torn, muddy grass and deeply rutted earth.

Alltud had levered himself up, ignoring the pain in his side. He was looking over the edge of the bunk and had seen the grass as well.

"Now's your chance," he said.

She shook her head. When it came to it, she didn't want to go, didn't want to leave Alltud.

"Don't you dare," he said, leaning back against the end wall. "You promised."

"I can't."

"You can and you will. They haven't brought you all this way to hold a feast in your honour. Nor have they kept you alive with your best interests in mind. And this crash will not improve their feelings toward you. I'm fine. This... scratch is healing, just like you said, but I'd only slow you down. I'm weak and I've walked no further than the room next door for days. You have to go now."

She hesitated. "I'm not ready."

"Jen!"

She could hardly believe herself, feeling suddenly tearful.

"Please. You have to go, Jen. For my sake if nothing else." Still she didn't move.

"Who is going to rescue the old man if you aren't free?"

To put the moment off, she clambered up to the door and pushed her way out into the corridor. It sloped up and sideways, the far end choked off with splintered wood and twisted metal. She hauled herself up to the next cabin and fell in through the door. It was a tangled mess of bedding and other belongings, none of it of any use.

She repeated the exercise with the next cabin and in the dim light found a long dark blue coat that probably belonged to their guard, wherever he was. It was too big for her, but if she was going out into the storm, she needed more than the clothes she stood up in.

Back in her own cabin, she found Alltud wedged into a corner with a blanket round his shoulders and the sack of food on his knees.

"Just get as far away as you can, Jen. And don't worry about me."

"I can do the first, but I'll never stop doing the second."

She bent to him and kissed him on the lips. He took her hand and held it a moment.

"Go safely."

"I'll find you," she said.

The storm may have finished with the airship for a while, but it was still ravaging the land. Crawling sideways out of the cabin and along the ground toward where she could see flashes of light, she felt everything above her shivering in the wind. She was glad she was alone, wiped away tears with the back of an already muddy hand.

It did not take long to realise just how fierce the storm still was. Pushing under a loose, sagging, and waxy smelling fold of the airship's envelope, she found herself out in the open. Despite the fact that part of the aerial behemoth's structure curved up above her, she was hit full in the face with rain and struggled to stand upright.

Leaves and twigs and other bits of unidentifiable windborne debris whipped into her face and caught round her legs so she turned her back to it, bracing against the gusts. Working sideways along the wreckage, a sudden blast pushed her over and she saw the enormous segment of airship lift and move away from her.

A huge section of the envelope began to undulate wildly and ripped loose, flapping with loud cracking sounds until the wind tore it completely free. It was gone into the gloom in an instant, swallowed by the storm which began looking for other morsels to tear from the carcass.

Climbing back to her feet, Jeniche saw some of the debris that had spilled out when the airship had been pushed along the ground. A long trail of metal shards, shattered timbers, sodden blankets, broken chairs, clothing, and thousands of anonymous fragments plastered to the ground by the rain and sinking into the mud. It diminished in the distance by virtue of darkness, revealed now and then in stark detail when lightning ripped through the clouds.

Close by and face down, partly covered by a branch stripped bare of all but a few wind withered leaves, was a body. Her head told her to leave it and get away, but she didn't always listen to her head. Besides, this someone was in the grey uniform of the airship's crew. It could be Kenak for all she knew.

Pulling the branch away she knelt and felt for a heartbeat. It was an older man, someone she hadn't seen before, his face a picture of fear endured. There was something there, trembling uncertainly in his chest, but she knew it would not last long in the open. The cold wind would drag the remains of his life from him if flying debris did not crush him first.

She rolled him over and, grabbing his wrists, dragged him across the sodden turf, back to the spot where she had emerged from the wreck. Much of the cover had been torn away, but there was enough shelter there to give him a chance. As she straightened she saw his eyes watching, saw a weak hand grip the nearly dry blanket she had found and wrapped round him.

To her surprise, she saw no other bodies as she fought her way through the wind and round the wreckage. Remembering those they had found in the mountains on their way to Tundur, she hoped the size of the airship had helped most of the crew to survive. She did not care what had happened to the members of the BoR.

The structure still groaned and creaked loud enough to be heard above the howling storm and as she neared the nose of one of the hulls of the vessel, a large section broke away and slumped down beside her. Even before it had settled, the wind tore up inside and pulled at the exposed innards. A blizzard of small items whipped into the dark, fluttering and falling to the sodden ground.

Jeniche staggered along, fighting to stay upright, and in the lightning that still shot through the wild cloud she saw what had brought the great airship to a stop. A steep slope rose directly in front of her, covered in vast, mature trees. The airship must have hit the ground and bounced along the flat until it fetched up against the wooded scarp. Torn to shreds and no longer buoyant it had crumpled against the earth. Having seen them burn and explode she was thankful for the relatively soft landing.

The slope was slick with sodden leaf mould. Trees thrashed and shed branches as she fought her way upwards. Under-growth whipped into her face as she sought anything to hold onto. Everywhere she looked there were bits of the machine and belongings of the crew. Trapped in a bush she found the remains of a chart, soaked through and fast turning to pulp. Wrapped around a fallen branch was a section of the envelope, the edge frayed and flapping.

With care, she untangled it and folded it, fighting the wind for possession. The fabric was light and waterproof and though an encumbrance now in the wind and rain, it might come in useful. Retrieving it had, however, been exhausting work and climbing the rest of the slope was a battle.

At the top, she rested against the lee side of a tree and squinted back round it into the storm. Below her she could see the whole of the broken-backed leviathan stranded against the base of the slope, the remains of the triple-hulled vessel trembling in its death throes; its entrails stretched back along the path of its flight across the flooded fields.

In the distance was another line of hills and she could see, when lightning permitted, a swathe cut through the trees where the airship had first been brought down by the wind. She remembered that moment of weightless euphoria, imagined those last seconds of the beast as it bounced free of the crest of that first slope only to hit the meadows below. With a farewell blessing to Alltud whispered under her breath, she turned away.

The slope on the other side of the crest was gentle and she walked for a long time before she began to feel a lessening in the effect of the wind. The trees still swayed and creaked, the branches still caught the wind as it roared overhead, but down at ground level it was no longer battering her along or trying to push her over, no longer mazing her with its incessant howl.

She kept going for as long as she could, wondering all the while about the crew and the others on board. Alltud had come through it more or less intact. Kenak? The rest? Who could tell? She didn't even know if the airship was expected, if Mord Kint's people would be looking for her if he did not survive.

When she had fallen for a third time, tripping over tree roots in the dark, she decided to stop. Wrapped in the torn section of envelope, she burrowed her way in beneath some thick under-growth and fell fast asleep with the wind still screaming its triumph high above her.

Chapter Eight

Great rags of black cloud, edged with silver by the light of the moon, raced across the dark blue sky, chasing one another to the horizon where lightning still flickered. In the high canopy, through which the night sky was visible, the susurration of damp leaves kissing as branches moved back and forth was a gentler sound than the shriek that had accompanied her plunge into exhausted sleep.

She watched the dizzying display for a minute or more, still not fully awake. At some point, earlier in the night, when the storm still roared overhead, she had crawled out of the under-growth and shed the damp coat, spreading it over a thorny bush before returning to her lair, too tired to care that it might rain again. It had been discomfort that had woken her then. Now she was dry and warm inside her wrapping, as snug and as comfortable as you could be on the ground beneath a bush, beginning to wonder what had woken her this time.

A gentle footfall, barely audible above the sound of the whispering trees, something moving with easy stealth across the leaf litter. Curling sideways in slow motion, she reached down to her boot top and pulled the knife free. In doing this, she rolled onto her side and could see along the ground.

In the gloom beneath the nearest tree, a shadow moved and then stopped. Clouds parted again and it grew light enough to make out a form, distinctly feline, muscular and lean, head raised, ears swivelling. A flick of the tail and the cat moved a few more steps, head still high, mouth open, tasting the air.

It was a large creature, powerful, silent but for the weight of its paw on the layer of dead leaves on the ground. Breathing as slowly and as quietly as she could, Jeniche watched as it tried to work out what was new in its territory. She doubted it would attack her, but she was in a poor position if it chose otherwise.

Two more steps and its head turned to the bush where Jeniche had spread the coat. The cat reached out an impressively broad paw and dabbed the garment, holding it in place as it leaned forward to smell it. Another flick of the tail was followed by a casual bit of scent marking as it strolled away.

Jeniche watched the darkness into which the big cat disappeared for some time before she lay back and breathed more easily. Even then, she listened, her thoughts trailing back through the woods to the hill below which the airship lay, to Alltud, and into her sleep. Dark dreams of trying to drag someone out from under... a bush, a tree, a flapping, howling, elusive form that wrapped around her, tighter and tighter, until she woke in a pale grey dawn with the torn piece of airship envelope tangled around her legs.

The coat reeked all day. It had, though, dried in the night and now kept her warm. When she had set out, she'd tried to convince herself the stink would fade. As the day progressed, she resorted to consoling herself that most other predators, such as wolves, would probably give her a wide berth.

Superficially, the area she found herself walking through resembled Ynysvron. Rolling hills, woodland, fields, small communities tucked away and building their enclaves against the dark. Somewhere in the south of Occassus if she had understood Kenak's explanation of their intended flight path. But it was dangerous to think of it as anything other than a surface likeness. Because this was Occassus, home of a people that had cut a wide and indiscriminate swathe of destruction through every country in which they had hunted her.

Beyond that, she knew next to nothing about the place or its people. For most of her life, Occassus had been a myth. It had been used by fireside storytellers when people wanted a change from tales of the pre-Ev world and the Evanescence; a handy fantasy realm where all manner of wonders existed and strange events occurred. The reality was very different. Mundane. For here she was tramping through the mud of what might once have been the back lanes of a rural community with no way of knowing how its people would react to her. If she ever encountered any. Because for a country that had revived secrets of the ancient world it seemed particularly empty and neglected. Perhaps, she mused, they had all been sent overseas.

Judging by those she had met on her own travels, they weren't all like Mord Kint. That was some comfort. But how to tell them apart? How to survive? What else to do so far from home and so alone?

She foraged as she walked, trying to eke out her own food. There was no doubting it was a fertile land but it had become unkempt, untended, and her searches didn't come to much. The hedgerows along the track she followed were thick, tall, and overgrown yielding just a few early berries. There were some nearly ripe ears of wild cereal from the beaten down stems in a small field. And she found some mushrooms, but delicious as they looked, she was unfamiliar with them and did not dare take the risk.

She was in no danger of dying of thirst. The day stayed dry as she walked, but she kept to an overgrown path that followed the spring line along the hills and came across any number of small streams, clear, pure, running swift and swollen over beds of sand and gravel.

All day the path had taken her more westward than north where her ultimate destination lay. For now, though, she was content to follow it, simply wanting to put distance between herself and the wrecked airship. The time to think on what she had done and what she must, in consequence, set out to do would come soon enough.

When the sun began to set ahead of her, she gave up trying to follow the increasingly obscured track and climbed up into the tree laden hills to look for somewhere safe to spend the night, somewhere a touch more secure than a bush. She had been lucky the night before. Luck was not something she wanted to rely on.

The western horizon was shot through with angry reds and bruised looking clouds were spreading to the sky above when Jeniche came across the remains of the cabin. It was a crude, single-roomed, timber construction on the edge of what had once been a sizeable clearing in the woods. Long abandoned, the glade was now waist deep in wild growth and saplings. She skirted the overgrown open space with careful, silent steps and came round to the cabin from the rear. It was just as deserted and decayed, but she hadn't wanted to take any chances. Happy that no one had been there for some considerable time, she approached through long grasses and fireweed. Rotting as the structure was, it seemed to offer somewhere secure to rest.

Shutters hung askew from the single window which was no more than a square opening in the front wall. She managed to jam the slimy panels of wood into the open space and prop them up with lengths of timber pulled from a pile at the side of the building. There was no door, so she collected a series of scratches and puncture wounds by uprooting a young blackthorn from the back edge of the clearing.

Grateful for the shelter, and with the doorway blocked, Jeniche retreated to the driest spot and settled on the floor, her back to the wall. The place reeked of decay and cat urine, but she was too tired to care and before she could even think of eating what little food she had left, she fell into a deep sleep.

It was a bleak awakening. Stiff, cold, and hungry, with an ache deep in her bones and deeper in her heart, she climbed to her feet and shuffled to the doorway. It had rained in the night and water dripped from the surrounding trees, pattering softly in the undergrowth. The air was chill and damp, lifeless. For a few moments as she gazed out through the blackthorn, she felt like sitting down and giving up. She didn't want to walk any more; she didn't want to fight. She had nothing left. Somebody else could do it. She would stay here and someone passing in the future could bury her bones.

But then there was Alltud. If it hadn't been for him, she very likely would have let go. Yet she had to find and rescue him. Wherever he was. Get him out of the trouble she had caused for him. It was a bridge of swords she crossed, edging away from despair and balancing over a beckoning pit of self-recrimination. Somehow she found her way to solid ground. Of a sort. A place where she knew that, at the very least, she had to find out what had happened to him. So, chewing on the last of her biscuits, she left the cabin and made her way up through the trees to look for a suitable vantage point.

Trudging up the long slope through the woodland cleared some of the shadow from her mind, although it left her tired. She didn't go all the way to the top of the hill. Instead, she chose the tallest tree she could find, a magnificent elm. With slow, cautious movements, she climbed high enough into the crown to see over the surrounding trees and down to the valley beyond.

In the still, early morning air, thin trails of smoke marked out the widely scattered homesteads and villages all the way to the western horizon. They rose out of a low, pellucid mist that lay like a silvered grey veil waiting for the dissolving touch of the sun. Jeniche waited as well, watching the drear scene transformed by a pale, fresh, shining orb that imbued it with a sense of breathless anticipation.

By the time she had found her way down to a track across the valley, the mist had gone and the sun was warm on her back, drawing the pungent smell of big cat out of the heavy coat. As she passed one field, a nearby cow looked up, shied, and lumbered across to the far side where it turned and watched her with reproachful eyes. There must have been a farm somewhere close by as the beast looked well cared for and its udder was empty, but she saw no buildings and carried on her way.

Although foraging kept her going, by nightfall she was hungry. Dusk was deepening when she came upon a small village. She approached with caution. Dogs began to bark and people appeared, watching her in silence. Hunger and fear battled it out. In the end, she lost her nerve and headed off toward the nearest piece of woodland, reaching through a gap in a hedge and helping herself to a handful of carrots when she was sure no one was watching.

It had been a good half hour since the last person had left the long, low building and closed the door, ambling along the veranda in well worn work clothes, before clattering down the steps. Jeniche had watched him collect a long-handled hoe from a shed and wander off in the same direction the others had taken earlier. No one else had appeared and the thin smoke from the chimney of the building had died away. With that many people in one building, Jeniche reasoned, there must be food. Hoping they had left some behind, she edged forward from her hiding place.

The previous night had been long and restless, plagued by dreadful dreams she could not recall each time she woke, simply filling her with a sense of loss that left her sobbing herself back to sleep. The early morning march through fresh, open woodland had dispelled something of the hollowness in her heart; it had done nothing to fill her belly.

Even though she was certain there was no one around, she moved with extreme care. There were other buildings beyond the one she was making for and someone might appear at any moment. She also watched the surrounding fields, moving short distances and checking all round each time she got to a new hiding place.

It felt like it was taking forever, and she had no way of knowing if it was worth it. However, she knew she didn't have the strength for a confrontation, let alone running away, so she continued her stealthy approach.

The hedge line took her from the shelter of the trees to a spot some half way to her objective. That had been the easy bit. After that she walked from one cover to the next as if she had a right to be there. At a wagon, she bent and checked the wheels, leaning against one end of the footboard for a moment to rest. At the corral where an old horse stood at the fence whisking away flies with its tail, she took a few moments to stroke its nose and share her last carrot to calm its suspicion of the human who still smelled of big cat. At a stack of boxes she spent a little time pretending to check the symbols branded into the wood, all the time keeping an eye on her surroundings. There was nothing between the boxes and the building so, once she was as happy as she could be that no one was in sight, she simply strolled across the open space and mounted the steps to the veranda.

Here she was in shade and screened from most of the farm as well as the other buildings. There was even a handy pile of boxes and sacks on the far side of the door that meant she could approach the entrance with little risk of being seen.

After a last look round and a moment's silence so she could listen, she tried the door. It opened and she slipped inside. Like the rest of the farm it was tidy and well maintained. The floor was bleached pale with regular scrubbing, the windows were clean, and there wasn't a cobweb to be seen. The furniture looked to be of good quality as well and for a moment she wondered if there was work to be had. It must be the hunger talking, she decided.

Bunks filled the far end of the large room, each set in an alcove formed by portable screening. She moved toward them with quick steps to make sure all the beds were empty. Back by the door, she cast an eye over the long table with its benches down either side. It was clean. And empty. But she didn't despair. Against the end wall was a large, low dresser and by an open window a locker consisting of a framework with muslin screening. She opened it to find a large jug of milk and a stack of cheeses. Beside it, under a cloth, were several freshly baked loaves and a pile of oat cakes. Under another cloth was a bowl of apples.

She bit into the crisp, juicy flesh as she filled her sack, wrapping the bread and cheeses in cloths she found in a drawer of the dresser. Her stomach wanted more. She knew, though, that she dare not linger, knew that even if she walked away the theft was a clear pointer to her presence. However, she couldn't get much further if she died of starvation and Alltud would never thank her for that.

Smiling at herself and the change in her mood since first thing, she slipped across to a window by the door and froze. Approaching the building were two men. They did not seem to be in any hurry but they were clearly making straight for her. With a quick glance round she looked for somewhere to hide, although given how thoroughly she had looked the place over on first entering, she knew there was nowhere that would keep her hidden for more than a few seconds.

Peering back out of the window to look for somewhere to run to outside, it was to see the two men walking off in a different direction. With a frown she moved round the table to a window on the far side. The two men came into view, walking at the same steady pace toward one of the barns.

Weak at the knees, she crossed back to the door. With a trembling hand, she opened it a fraction and looked out. Now that it was clear, she stepped out onto the veranda. She had just closed the door and stepped to the rail when a deep, quiet voice stopped her in her tracks. Her heart leapt into her mouth almost choking her.

"They catch you, boy, starvin' or not, they will beat you. They catch you in that coat, anyone catch you in that coat, a beatin' will be the very least of your problems. Cos for all you reached for a sword just then, you ain't no soldier. And there's no love for those colours here in the south."

Jeniche turned slowly, hands visible. She frowned and then started as one of the sacks by the door began to move. It was pulled down to reveal an old man sitting on a low stool, stumps of legs jutting forward with thick leather pads on the ends. He folded the empty sack that he had thrown over himself and put it on his lap, laughing quietly.

"It's all right, boy. Don't you fret. I watched you all the way from them woods over there. You're good. I'll give you that. But I'm better. I get plenty of practice watching things these days," he said gesturing at what was left of his legs.

"Get that coat off." He lifted the sack from his lap and threw it at Jeniche. "Cut yourself a neck hole and some arm holes. That'll help keep you warm. Storm season is near over and nights'll be getting cold." As he spoke, he slipped down off the stool and, using his hands for balance, hobbled into the bunkhouse on his stumps.

Jeniche did as she was told. She was far too tired to try to run away and it was a relief to shed the smelly dark blue coat.

The old man returned after a few minutes with a loose bundle under one arm. He dropped it at her feet and made his way back to the stool, climbing up and seating himself.

"Now." He squinted. "Boy? Huh. Not so sure any more. Don't matter. Close that door."

Jeniche closed the door to the bunkhouse and, at a gesture from the old man, leaned down and picked up the bundle. It unrolled to reveal itself as a heavy poncho. There was also a thick felt hat.

"Sheep's wool, that poncho. Tight weave. Keep the damp out."

"Thank you," she said finding her voice at last.

"Yeah," he said, his eyes clearly seeing more than she would ever willingly reveal. "Well, my name's Jankoot and

I'm an old fool. A sucker for a hard luck story, which I'm sure you could tell if I was inclined to listen. Besides, that was my horse you gave what I'm guessin' was the last of your food on your way in. So listen to me and listen good. First thing you do when you get well clear of my land is bury that coat. Deep, cos it stinks, and you don't want it being dug up again any more'n I do. Now get gone."

Chapter Nine

Having managed to avoid coughing when the first billows of smoke reached her, she now had to endure the smells of cooking that drifted up toward her perch. It was enough to make her cry, although she would have put that down to the smoke had any-one been there with her.

It had been a day since the supplies from the farm had been finished. Cheese harder than biscuit which had softened to the consistency of old leather after giving her jaw ache, and bread from which she had picked the mould with the tip of her knife.

There was, she knew, one last apple in her pocket, but it was bruised and only half of it edible. She rather wanted to eat it right there, but that would mean moving and she didn't dare risk alerting those below to her presence. Instead she made her-self sit back against the trunk of the ancient beech and settled in to wait.

The most annoying aspect of it all was that she couldn't hear what any of them were saying. Her grasp of Occassan was basic, although it was good enough for everyday. Being able to eavesdrop might at least have made up for the discomfort of balancing on a particularly gnarly branch. However, in her bid to remain unseen she had climbed high and all she could hear were murmurs and occasional bursts of laughter. She just hoped they didn't decide to make camp for the rest of the day. Or longer.

From her position, she watched them like a carrion bird, noting where all the scraps of food were, noting all the points she might investigate once the soldiers had gone. It was clearly a good perch because a crow appeared as if from nowhere and settled on the far end of the branch where she sat. It cocked its head on one side as soon as it noticed her. She kept perfectly still and prayed it would not protest at her presence. It watched her with a dark, calculating eye as if listening to her silent plea before flapping off to look for a less crowded spot.

Below, most of the troop of soldiers had gathered in a loose circle round the fire and were sitting and eating. Even in their own country, she noticed, they kept pickets who slowly walked a perimeter, guarding the temporary camp. Which told her a great deal. And it gave her a chance, finally, to count them: twenty-six in all.

There hadn't been much opportunity earlier. Lost in thought she hadn't even noticed that she had emerged from the woodland let alone that she was following a broad, neglected path. She supposed that on some level she had realised, but her mind was elsewhere. She was worrying about Alltud and feeling guilty at having abandoned him, she was worrying about food, about where she was, where she was going and how she was going to get there.

It was a kind of chanting that had alerted her. A marching song, she guessed. She had stopped and speedily taken in her surroundings. A wide grassy track between woodland and a broad strip of meadow sloping down to a shallow, meandering stream. The track curved out of sight ahead of her and it was from that direction she heard the voices.

A second of indecision was followed by a dash into the woods. She had intended to find some undergrowth and hide until they passed. Once amongst the trees, however, she heard what she thought were other voices, other noises, so by an instinct developed from an early age to climb away from trouble, she had headed for the nearest substantial tree and clambered up as high as she dared.

It hadn't been an elegant climb or particularly quiet, twigs and leaves falling to the ground in her wake, but it was clear no one had noticed and she managed to get herself securely seated by the time the soldiers came to a halt beneath her. They were joined by compatriots who had obviously been making a sweep on their flank through the woodland.

From the safety of her hidden vantage point they seemed an amiable enough bunch. All men, mostly young, perhaps conscripts enjoying a few days away from all the things soldiers normally do. She realised how vague her under-standing was despite all the time spent with Tohmarz and his cavalry troop in Arbiq. Affable as they seemed, however, she doubted whether she would have got very far if they had found her on the ground. Assuming it was her they were looking for. It seemed arrogant to think so, but they wouldn't be the first of their kind.

With them were two older men. They wore the same dark blue uniform. Although they bore no obvious insignia, they were clearly senior to the others. They gave the orders; the others deferred to them. The only good thing, as far as Jeniche could see, was that they weren't wearing the black and silver of the BoR. That and the fact she now knew the military were on the lookout. Even if it wasn't for her, they were looking for someone or simply patrolling and she had no desire to fall into their net.

It was true she wanted to head north to the capital, find Alltud, and get them both out of this benighted country. It was equally true she wanted to do it on her own terms. And her own terms included freedom. Food was also something of a prerequisite and she hugged her stomach as it growled, convinced someone down on the ground must have heard it. But no one came to investigate.

Eventually, the troop packed up their things, extinguished the fire, formed up, and moved on along the road, a small party disappearing into the woods to comb the undergrowth. Jeniche counted slowly to a thousand to give the soldiers time to move off to a safe distance. Safe for her to descend and take care of other priorities before scouring the site for scraps of food.

As she began her descent, an unusual sound made her stop. Twenty feet above the ground, stretched between branches, she listened and, as best she could, she looked. There was nothing more, but it had made her doubly wary so, with all the stealth she could muster, she continued on down.

At ground level, she headed for the nearest thick clump of bushes and came face to face with someone doing the same from the other direction. Her heart pounded painfully and she forgot about all the other bodily discomforts as she felt herself preparing to run.

In that heightened moment she took in the fact that his clothes were dirty, marked by bark and moss, that his skin with its reddish bronze cast, was dark though nothing so richly brown as the legless farmer who had been so generous, that his face was frozen in that instant with a mixed expression of surprise and fear which very likely mirrored her own.

They stood facing each other across the undergrowth. Jeniche didn't worry about being mistaken for an Occassan soldier or scout, but she couldn't be certain about this stranger. The fact that he was wearing a patchwork of leathers that made for effective camouflage told her nothing about his allegiances.

He raised his hands slowly, palm out. "I'll... I'll find a different bush."

Jeniche watched him scuttle off into the undergrowth, noting how silent he was as he crossed the leaf litter. Once he was out of sight she went to find somewhere else of her own, waiting until she was absolutely certain she was alone. And when she was comfortable again, she made for the road, keeping to the fringe of trees with an ear open for the soldiers and both eyes watching for the newcomer.

At the snapping of a dead branch further ahead, which must have been deliberate, she stepped into the nearest cover.

"Best keep off the roads for now," said the man when he emerged onto the track.

She stepped out and approached him, cutting the bruised portions out of her last apple so that her knife was to hand. "I was thinking that might be wise."

He watched her for a moment. "Not from these parts."

She shook her head. "Are you going north?"

"A way."

She started in that direction in the shade of the trees and as she passed him he fell into step beside her. "If that's all right?"

She assented warily with a slow nod of her head and carried on along the grassy road. They hadn't gone far when he pointed across the way to a narrow track in the lee of an overgrown hedge.

"Farm here once," he said.

"You knew it?"

87

"Worked there a few seasons."

"What happened to it?"

"Really not from these parts, are you."

"No."

He looked at her with a thoughtful expression. "Same as happens to most places round here eventually."

She didn't push the point. Trusting strangers was not easy at the best of times, but as a fugitive in a foreign land she felt especially vulnerable. Perhaps he did as well.

The path they followed led up into yet more hilly woodland and had clearly once been a wide cart track. Now the surface was breaking up, saplings pushing through the compacted soil and shrubs spilling over from choked ditches along the bounds. Toward evening, Jeniche had lost sight of it altogether, but her new companion seemed to know where he was going and seemed to know how to keep up a solid pace all day. He also knew how to keep his thoughts to himself which suited her. Small talk would have been pointless and anything else was out of the question.

"Not far," he said as they dropped over a ridge and headed down a slope. It was the first thing he had said for several hours.

"To where?"

"Somewhere dry for the night."

After standing still for a moment watching the meadow before them, they passed out from under the trees and began crossing the grassy lea in bright evening sunlight. They went in single file and had just reached the small stream that ran down its length when a faint sound reached Jeniche's ears.

"Company," she said, pointing to the sky.

"Too far," said the man, looking for cover

"Lie flat. Less shadow."

They both dropped into the long grass by the water's edge and lay on their backs. Jeniche hoped their path to this point wasn't too obvious, hoped it might be mistaken for the track of a deer going down to the water to drink. She knew from experience you could hope for all sorts of things in tight situations and that you could rely on none of it. As it was, a cloud trailed shadow across the valley and a slight evening breeze began to move the grasses, filling the meadow with rippling shadow just as the airship passed over them.

They watched the machine, seeming no bigger than a forefinger, as the silver grey of its hull caught the sun. It kept to its course, north and east, and before long was obscured by the tops of distant trees. The moment it was out of sight they were on their feet and heading on across the meadow. In under the trees, they stopped a moment to gather their breath.

"You have good ears," he said.

"It helps."

He nodded and turned, picking a way up the slope. Jeniche followed and had never felt more alone. The airship had reminded her of Alltud. She ached for his presence, wishing it was him up there ahead of her, desperately afraid she would never see him again.

"I'm sorry. Did you say something?"

Jeniche looked up the slope. The man had paused and was looking back at her. She was glad that dusk was thickening beneath the branches.

"No. Sorry. Perhaps. Just thinking of someone."

"Come. Not far now."

He waited until she caught up with him and they walked side by side through the woodland, higher and higher until the ground became rocky underfoot. It was as if the bones of the world had pushed their way through, broken and worn by the weather, colonised by trees. They followed narrow paths that wound like a maze between outcrops covered with moss and late blooming flowers, wove their way into deeper twilight.

"Smoke," said Jeniche. "I can smell smoke."

It was the faintest tang of wood smoke on air growing cold.

"I hope so," said the man. "A fire and food will be most welcome."

Almost immediately she heard another voice, a challenge out of the dark: "'I sit and look out...'"

"'...upon all the sorrows of the world'," replied Jeniche's companion. "The words of a poet from ancient times," he explained.

Intrigued, she followed on until they emerged into a natural, rocky amphitheatre, the mouths of caves lit by flickering light.

"Welcome to my home."

Chapter Ten

Jeniche looked at the piece of cloth again turning it one way and then the other as she tried to match the markings on it with the landscape around her. Nothing tallied. It was a well made map, there was no doubting that, and detailed as well. The trouble was, she began to suspect, her hosts had imagined her prowess matched theirs. Yet they were used to the woods and knew the land. For them, the river was two days walk from the caves. This was her fourth day and the only water she had seen was a lake in the far distance. Or something that shone like a lake. It was too far away to tell. And if she was really honest with herself she didn't much care.

After a last attempt at reconciling image with reality, she folded the map, pushed it into her pocket, took another rough bearing, and decided to add a bit more east to her northerly course. It would take her closer to the mountains she thought she could see. There had been mountains on the map she'd studied in the airship's chart room when Kenak was getting food. A chain of mountains that led all the way to the capital, Amparo. Unless they were just clouds on the horizon.

Walking was now a habit, despite her stay with the cave people. She had done it yesterday, so she would do it today. And tomorrow. And the day after that. On her own. Through a broken land that had been destroyed more than once. It was the only thing that reached through the dull wall of her despair, all the signs hidden beneath the trees and the grasses. The further north she travelled, the more prevalent they became, a vast swathe of countryside abandoned in the Evanescence, colonised, abandoned again in the punitive aftermath of a vicious civil war, and now trying to find its way again despite the jealous, prying eyes of the Order and the murderous hand of the Bureau of Reports.

She could have stayed back there in the south. They had invited her. It would have been easy to disappear from the world under the very noses of those who were looking for her. The settlement had been peaceful and self-sufficient and the people there, all of them fugitives or misfits, had made her welcome. They had fed her, clothed her afresh, let her rest and cleanse herself, and taught her something of their country's painful history.

Even then she had not been able to settle, fretting over the fate of Alltud, desperate to move on and find him, find out what had happened to him even though it now seemed a task with no hope of resolution. Besides, how long would it have been before she brought down the destructive wrath of the BoR on her hosts?

When the river appeared below her as she crested the next rise, she sat and cried. There was no need to look at the map again as she knew she was back on course. It was a hazardous route, they had explained, but it would take her through to the populated lands beyond and put her within reach of Amparo. The stupidest place to go, they had argued, but if she had a fight then she wanted to take it to the very heart, to the very people with whom she had an argument.

Her leaving had been like a funeral. They clearly considered she was on her last journey. Despite that, they respected her decision, had lined the way out of their enclave and watched her go in silence, some with heads bowed.

After a celebratory meal, she set off for the river. There would be no need for maps now she had the watercourse to follow, winding its narrow way between the interlocking feet of the steep hills. And as the days progressed, the season brought her more to forage, keeping hunger at bay. For all that, it was not an easy journey. The land was wild and if there had ever been roads or paths they had long since been submerged by the tide of trees.

At night, she chose camp sites from which she could see the sky. When it was clear she would let the stars sing her to sleep, watching for the wanderers as Teague had taught her all those years ago in Makamba. The Moon, she noticed, seemed to have acquired a moon of its own, but the nights became cloudy before she could observe it properly.

The moon went from quarter to full before she noticed a change in the world around her. It was nothing drastic. A different mood in the landscape and a realisation that the old familiar feeling of nausea had returned. It was clear she was approaching what she had been told was the epicentre of that second war, the struggle that ended with the Order taking control and pushing the heel of its boot into the face of the people. Mostly people in other countries judging by what she had so far seen. But perhaps they had perfected the art here in the south of Occassus before moving on to spread their misery elsewhere.

Several days later, the sparse woodland finally gave way to rough scrub on a poor sandy soil. The terrain was cut through with narrow ravines created by rainwater, all running down toward the river which now ran broad and dark. A bird hovered away to her right, its wings and tail shifting as it rode the wind running up the side of the valley. She stood and watched, fascinated by the subtle ways it worked with the elements; gasped when it folded its wings and fell. It didn't re-appear so she assumed it must have made a kill.

The ravines grew in size the closer she got to the river making progress increasingly difficult. In the end she chose one, scrambled down into it, and followed it down the slope. Although she had seen no one about, she had spent so long in the forest that open ground left her feeling exposed. In the ravine she could relax a little and move more freely.

Some distance from the sluggish, dirty waters of the river, the ravine opened out onto a rough, gravely slope. There was a similar bank on the far side of the water. The top edges, lined with patchy scrub, were probably the winter high water mark. She stayed close to the top of the slope where the scrub offered some cover, peering warily into each ravine as she passed. The nausea grew stronger.

It wasn't long before the first signs of what lay ahead became apparent. Sticking out of the sandy bank to her right was a culvert made of that same cast stone she had seen in other sites. Badly cracked and abraded, it was of great age. Having a river pound it with stones each winter over the centuries seemed to have done most of the damage.

Culverts began to turn up at regular intervals, all worn and broken, all choked with silt and debris; all with the familiar aura. She pressed on against the queasiness and a growing vagueness in her head. As she rounded a bend in the river, she saw another broad flow of water joining it on the far side, the surface churning as the two currents fought then merged. Impressive as it was, it didn't much hold her interest. She had seen more rivers than she could remember. It was what sprawled all round the confluence, stretching along the banks of both rivers as far as the eye could see that made her stop and stare.

An immense, ruined city, the bleached bones still visible, stark against the sky. Everywhere else she had encountered ruins they had been underground, buried by mounds of soil or sand blown there over the centuries, covered with vegetation. This was different. In normal circumstances she would have taken the opportunity to go exploring, but the place was bare of greenery for a reason. It made her cautious.

Scrambling up the loose gravel of the bank and onto the higher slopes, Jeniche began looking for a way to skirt round the ruins without losing sight of the river. She wasn't able to stay completely clear as she kept coming across piles of rubble, the debris of fallen bridges, and the remains of strange structures buried in the soil. The place was vast and she wondered how many people must once have lived there, what had happened to it, why it was so devoid of life.

The blow, when it came, took her completely by surprise and she rolled a long way back down the slope in a cloud of dust and gravel, hands instinctively grasping for swords that were no longer there. Dazed and disorientated, she staggered to her feet, tears streaming from the grit in her eyes. A hand grabbed at her arm and she lashed out. There was a satisfying thud, but other hands held her and she was dragged, kicking out, back up the slope to where she had first been attacked. There she was dumped on the ground.

A moment's silence was followed by laughter. She blinked furiously to clear her eyes. It wasn't the sort of laughter you were encouraged to join in with. It became more raucous as she wiped the tears away.

Looking up as her vision cleared she saw two men, large, dirty, definitely not in any kind of uniform. Beyond them, in a stand of withered trees, two horses and a number of mules were tied to a picket line. On the ground by the animals were piles of objects the men must have scavenged from the ruins; poor stuff by the look of it but it was probably their living.

"Keep your eyes off that," said the one on the left.

"Or you'll feel my fist again," said the one on the right.

"Now let's see what you got in that bag of yours. This is our patch." The one on the left indicated the ruins. "We don't like people stealing from us."

Jeniche climbed slowly to her feet, staggered just a little. No point in letting them think she had recovered from the attack.

Her bag was a sack with a cord tied round the neck and the other end attached to one of the bottom corners. She lifted the cord over her head and threw the bag down half way between her and the nearest man. He stepped forward, lifted it and, with a long, very sharp knife, cut into the hessian.

The contents spilled out onto the ground. Half a stale loaf. Two apples. The remains of a cheese. Some salted meat. A spare tunic given to her by the people in the caves. He shook the sack to make sure everything was out and then threw it behind him whilst he looked at what had spilled to the ground. After a moment, he picked up the apples, threw one to his companion and then kicked the loaf of bread down the slope. Jeniche didn't take her eyes from him, marked the position of the other. And then smiled.

"You know," she said. "For a moment back there, I thought I was in trouble."

The man nearest her frowned, didn't even have time to react before Jeniche had stepped forward, shedding her coat as she went. It hadn't even settled on the ground before she leaned back on one leg and let the toe of her other boot find the side of his kneecap. His yell was shut off as she followed the kick through with a twist to the body that brought the heel of her other foot up to catch him beneath the chin.

He hit the dust unconscious and Jeniche landed in a crouch with his knife firmly in her hand as the other man rushed her. Something in her face made him change his mind. He tried to change direction as well, but it was far too late. There was a deep well of anger in her, fed by springs of despair and desperation. He was a lucky man. She wanted to hurt and she wanted to kill. She settled for a minimum of the first knowing he had seen in her expression what she really wanted to do.

She stood over the unconscious forms for a moment, coaxing her anger back into the cave from which it had sprung. One of them was breathing raggedly, a trickle of blood from where she had hit him on the temple with the handle of the knife. She knew that she should cut their throats and leave them for the carrion birds. If she didn't they would doubtless go running to the authorities just as soon as they could. That type of bully boy always did. But bodies can speak as loudly as living men and killing in cold blood was a step too far.

One after the other, she dragged them roughly by their feet up to where the animals were tethered. There, she proceeded to strip them and then tied them to a tree. They were beginning to drift back into consciousness as she unhitched the last horse and led the string of animals away from the cover.

As she had no use for the objects they had foraged from the ruins, she left the pile alone. The rest of their belongings, including their clothes, she took with her as she rode away, picking a route across the slope and up to the distant tree line, ignoring their calls and curses. It looked like it was going to rain and she wanted to be as far away from the ruins and the loose slope as possible when it did. If the two she had left tied to the tree should catch cold or worse, she would shed no tears for them.

Eventually the bare ground sprouted wiry grasses and thorny shrubs as a precursor to greener land. She led the animals up across increasingly softer ground to the trees beyond. The river became harder to see, yet she did not worry. She knew her direction now and kept going until a small clearing in the trees tempted her to rest. It had stayed dry in the end. The cloud cover had broken and she sat in a patch of moonlight to rest. The animals stood patiently while she looked through the saddle bags for food. All she found was a half-full water bottle. She picked the grit off her own cheese and nibbled a bit of that.

It was clear to her that, as the two who attacked her must have a camp within a day's ride, she ought to keep moving. The horses and mules didn't seem to mind. It was a pleasant night, cool and refreshing. And as a chorus of bird song greeted the dawn, they dropped down a gentle slope out of the trees into a long narrow meadow. A small stream ran down one side. She smiled.

One by one she stripped the harness from the animals and turned them free. While she sorted through all the bits and pieces, tried on the riding coats, strapped on the knife that had been used to threaten her, the horses hovered in her vicinity, wandering back and forth but never too far away. The mules also seemed reluctant, but in the end they all decided that it was rather a pleasant place to be and made no attempt to follow her when she left. They were happily cropping the grass when she last saw them.

Chapter Eleven

The late summer days had long since blurred one into another. By the time the sun set she could no longer remember clearly how long it had been since the encounter with the scavengers. One part of her said a day and she could recall it vividly; another saw it as if from a great distance, like the time she had looked the wrong way down one of Teague's smaller telescopes. And then the incident faded into her own private mythological landscape as something that may or may not ever have happened. Either way it wasn't happening now so it was no longer important.

Her only real priority to which she devoted most thought and energy was finding food so that she could keep heading north. It reminded her of something else that lay in that mythical past of hers, something that went back even further. Something to do with Alltud. She surveyed her memories. It was a fruitless exercise as they were a misty, twilit landscape so she kept walking, passing the dead campfire before she realised what she had seen.

With weary steps she retraced her path. The small circle of stones, enclosing charred earth and burned sticks, had been constructed in a sheltered spot that would have shielded the flames from breeze and onlookers alike. It looked fairly recent. She went down on one knee and placed her hand over the ashes. They were cold. A day perhaps. No more. The ash was still dry and fine.

The mist that had descended in her head was dispelled and she listened for sounds of soldiers. It wasn't a big fire so there wouldn't have been many. If it was soldiers. And studying the layout with greater care, she had her doubts. It was too much like the sort of fire pit she and Alltud used to make. In exactly the sort of place they would have chosen.

Pulling her thoughts away from that melancholy backwater, Jeniche looked around. There were no other signs of a camp, but she did find footprints in a piece of soft ground and she decided that, in the morning, she would follow on in the same general direction. Perhaps there would be food to beg or steal.

She set off early and kept up a fierce pace. It ate into what limited reserves she now possessed. By late afternoon she began to slow yet would not let herself rest. As it began to grow dark, she became conscious of movement somewhere up ahead. It was quiet and steady and she tried to gain on it without giving herself away. No matter how hard she tried to catch up, she could not close the gap and was on the point of giving up when the sound she was following stopped. She crouched against the nearest tree and rested as she listened.

The silence lengthened and she was beginning to think she had lost whatever it was, beast or person, when a familiar clinking was followed some moments later by the flicker of a flame. Using the tree, she pulled herself up and took cautious steps toward the light, stopped when soft voices drifted through the intervening gloom. After waiting for a while, she took several more steps, waited again, closed in a bit more. And then her strength and her courage failed her. In the deepening dusk she hunkered down again, half dreaming, listening to the voices she could not understand, a liquid sound peppered with one or two words that seemed familiar without having any recognizable meaning. She watched from behind the bole of an oak, peering through the darkness at the two people sitting by their fire, the light flickering on the pale flesh of their long, thin faces, the bare flesh of their elongated heads.

Waking was a slow and fuddled climb out of deep oblivion into all-embracing pain. She was barely half way there, the place where memories emerge, when she began to think it would be pleasant to slide back into the darkness. Instead, she peeled the side of her face away from the bark of the oak against which she had fallen into an exhausted sleep.

Circulation returned to her left leg after she managed to pull it from underneath herself and swing it round. At least it distracted her for a while from all the other bone deep aches and pains. Her chest hurt as well and she tried to sit up straighter, feeling the trunk of the tree pushing at the creases in her spine through her nearly empty pack.

Like a drunk with a hangover, she clambered onto her feet using the tree for support and stood there awhile letting everything settle into new patterns of discomfort. Her head throbbed with the effort and she shivered in the cool dawn air. With a sinking feeling of déjà vu, she stared into space gathering whatever thoughts she could find. A leaf drifted in front of her eyes to remind her it was early autumn. Winter... She wouldn't survive that without food and shelter and a good fire.

First things though came first. Once she had made at least one part of herself comfortable and was settled back into her clothing, she made her way to where she had seen those two... She frowned. Were they really Pilgrims or had it been a combination of their firelight and her hunger? She shook away the doubt. Their faces had been clearly visible, the shape of their heads unmistakable. Yet, as she wandered about the clearing she could find no sign of anyone ever having been there. No pit. No stones. No suggestion the leaf litter had ever been disturbed.

Had she dreamt it? All of it? Even those footprints she had followed? Weary, hungry, reluctant to leave, not wanting to stay, she stood staring at the spot where they had sat warming themselves, knowing she had heard their soft voices. There were even words, repeated, that she remembered.

But then what was the point. Dream or chance encounter it was over, done, gone and made no difference to the here and now in which she drifted with a goal she was too tired to pursue and a desire she knew she could never fulfil.

Deeper than her despair, however, were her instincts and the instant she heard the noise she was moving. There were people in the woods. A voice had called out. In the moments that followed she could hear people walking in the leaves. No point in trying to ascertain how many. No point in climbing a tree and hoping they would pass beneath. Instead she put what energy she had into walking as quickly and as quietly as she could in the direction of away.

Before she had gone very far the familiar irritating sound of an airship drifted down to her through the forest canopy. Up there beyond leaves that were just starting to change colour, eyes surely watched for a fugitive. Behind her, a line of soldiers were advancing noisily as if to flush her out into the open. Or maybe it wasn't her they hunted. She frowned, hoping the Pilgrims had started early enough to be clear of the search. If they had stuck to the same direction, they must be somewhere up ahead of her.

Perhaps she should have approached them, made herself known, asked the thousand and one questions to which she wanted answers. Perhaps. It was not lack of courage that had stopped her. As she had sat and watched and listened, trying to pick out words from their conversation, waiting for the right moment to approach, she had simply fallen asleep. So all she could do now was change direction and use what reserves she had to pull the search after her.

Why she chose to do this she could not fathom. It went against everything she knew to be sensible. All the same, she headed for the nearest patch of open, damp ground and crossed it at an angle, making for the east and leaving behind her a clear line of footprints. When she came to the next open space, she half expected to see the airship floating above, but it was nowhere in sight. So she pressed on, crashing through underbrush and dropping the empty pack in the next stretch of woodland, kicking a few leaves over it as if she had tried to hide it completely.

As the day progressed she stopped wondering why she felt the need to protect the Pilgrims, stopped planning, let the mist descend in her mind and concentrated solely on putting one foot in front of the other. The first time she fell, she climbed back up to her feet and continued on her way. It barely registered on her consciousness and she made no effort to brush away the dirt and leaves.

The second fall came an hour later. She lost her footing whilst crossing a steep slope and slid down between the trees for a considerable distance, fetching up against a young pine.

The ground had been rocky, but although she saw blood it didn't really register that she had hurt herself in any way.

She lay against the trunk for a while, breathing the clean, sharp scent of the sticky resin, drawing a little strength. When she stood, she looked for a way forward and managed the few steps that took her to the crumbling edge of a narrow ravine full of scrub. Too tired to think of finding a way round, she clambered over the edge and slipped down, the scrub oak and deerweed breaking the worst of her fall.

Again, she lay for a while before the deeply ingrained habit of movement took over. She struggled and pushed until the undergrowth gave way and let her through to the ground where she began to crawl, her direction dictated by gravity.

Stones and small rocks joined her downward scramble and piled up round her when she could go no further. Dust settled on her prone form and she dropped into the darkness she had desired for so long.

When she woke, it was morning. An old one. A new one. The same one. She no longer knew. Above her, through a lattice of branches, was a pale blue sky. Within her was pain and exhaustion. All still there.

Gathering herself slowly, she stood up and, turning her back on the rocky slope with its scattering of pines and scrub, she faced the prospect ahead. Directly in front of her was a sandy beach. It had been many centuries since water had lapped there and washed over the rocks further out, but even with eyes blurred by hunger and tiredness, she could make out the level shoreline curving away into the distance both left and right.

Slithering down the loose sandy slope, she reached more solid ground as the sun rose over the hill behind her. Following her own shadow for want of some better direction to travel, she stumbled across the cracked saltpan. After a short distance that seemed to take forever to cross, her knees gave way and she dropped down onto them, easing slowly back until she was sitting on her heels.

Morning sunlight was bright on the salt, a luminescent mist of exhaustion engulfing her. She sat there for an eternity, devoid of thought. When the shadow of the airship passed over her, she didn't even notice.

PART TWO

Attachment

Chapter Twelve

There was pain. Deep seated. Pervasive. Sickening. In all the world, it was the only certain thing. As for the rest... She tried to sort it out but it just made the pain in her head worse so she gave up.

Like flotsam rising and falling on gentle waves climbing a deserted strand, she drifted in and out of consciousness. As her apprehension of the world flowed and ebbed, she was assailed by an undertow of hopeless misery, a sense of terrible loss. They threatened to overwhelm her, and there was little she could do to fight against them so she forced herself to concentrate on the protests of her physical body.

Try as she might, looking elsewhere did not make those other pains go away or in any way diminish their effect. The scars inside her head and on her heart, the grief, the dreadful feeling she had been through all this before and would likely go through it all again were too deeply gouged into her being. It was enough to make her cry, tears that ran in thin streaks across her grimy face. She had no energy for anything more.

After dozing a while, some unseen part of the world intruded. She moved her head in an attempt to see what it might have been. Once everything had stopped spinning, she could see the dim space was still there before her. It remained stubbornly out of focus which did nothing to diminish her sense of dislocation.

Closing her eyes, she rested again. The simple movement and its resultant dizziness had exhausted her. She let go and allowed herself to be pulled back into the dark. As she drifted into sleep she became aware of the hardness of the ground on which she lay, of a swaying motion that may just have been her, of...

A low, pulsing vibration was the first thing she noticed as she became conscious. It made her head throb in sympathy and she wished it would stop. When it became clear it was unlikely to do so, she thought that moving might help. The thought was not accompanied by action and for a while she puzzled over this, until the pain of it and the confusion it induced made her stop.

Determined not to slip back into darkness, she tried once more to move. This time she started small, concentrating on one of her arms. Sweat formed on her face and fuzzy lights began to dance in the gloom. Clenching her teeth, she increased her effort. Nothing seemed to happen. She was on the point of giving up when she became aware that, by some method she did not understand and had not felt, her arm was free.

Some time later, she woke into the same nightmare. With a degree of caution that experience taught her was sensible, she moved her head and looked along the ground. It was still dim wherever she was but there was light enough to see the ground was smooth. Moving her head a bit further, she discovered the dizziness, pain, and nausea had not gone away. She closed her eyes for a moment. Opened them on the same smooth floor.

Was aware that somewhere off to one side her left arm was moving, lowering a hand to the flat surface. She knew it was her arm because she felt the pain.

Limited by something she couldn't yet understand, her hand moved about the surface not far from her face. She watched it edging its way along, trembling, like a small sick creature. Two messages finally broke through the mental fog, almost simultaneously. The ground across which the five-fingered beast tottered was smooth. Flat. An artificial surface. A floor. She embraced the familiar word as the second message arrived. The floor vibrated. She stared at it stupidly for a while, too tired to reason, felt a sudden wave of nausea as if the floor had dropped and then risen, taking her along for the unwelcome ride.

Through the throbbing dullness in her head it all came back in a cruel, overpowering rush, the wave that finally threw her ashore and left here there beneath the harsh sun of reality. She choked back a sob of frustration. She was in an airship. Had survived the crash, abandoned Alltud, wandered aimlessly for... days, weeks, she couldn't remember. Had starved and walked herself to exhaustion. To find herself back where she started.

Almost.

This time she was alone. This time it was her beneath a blanket. Lifting the coarse wool, she discovered she was naked. And what she saw in the dim light shocked her, even with less than her full senses at play. Scratched, bruised, dirty, emaciated, and covered with sores; she had seen long-dead corpses in better condition.

Looking round the small store room for her clothes, it did not take long to work out they were not there. Just her. And a blanket. Everything gone. Everything. Her closest companion.

Her friends. Her swords. Her belt. The amulet. And everything she had achieved was lost as well. She felt crushed. They had taken it all and now, it seemed, they wanted her dignity. Hauling herself into a sitting position and arranging the blanket around her skeletal frame, she vowed they would have whatever scraps might be left at a very high price. Their lives. Her life.

Light from the opening door made her flinch and she lowered her head, the room swimming and swaying. A tray was pushed in clear of the door which closed straight away, and she was back in the muted light of the closed room. Her senses steadied. At least, she thought, they are feeding me.

When she had finished the collection of leftovers and drunk all the dull, metallic water, she crawled to the corner furthest from the door. It was a painful journey, reminding her that not all the physical wear and tear was on the outside. Once there, she curled up and tucked the blanket around herself. Drifting back to sleep, she tried to fight off the feeling that it was all over, that there was nowhere left to go.

It didn't feel like she had been asleep for very long when the door banged open and light poured into the store room. Someone shouted and although she did not understand, she climbed her way out of sleep and up onto her feet. It took a while, in the leadenness of her exhaustion, to realise the guard wanted her to follow him.

She managed it with what grace she was able to muster, wrapped in the blanket and unsteady on legs that trembled. Although she followed someone wearing dark blue, she was conscious of the black and silver uniforms that seemed to be everywhere on the short walk to the service room.

Inside the cubicle she found a pile of rough towels and a large, unused block of soap, realised that along with her filthy appearance she probably did not smell too good. She folded the blanket and put it to one side before making grateful use of the latrine. Then she addressed the wash basin. The water was chill and some of her cuts and grazes began to bleed again as she scrubbed at her flesh, but it was a luxury to be able to wash away the dirt and rub warmth back into her thin frame with the small towels provided. It all took some time and a lot of water. And when she had finished, she wrapped the blanket back round her gaunt frame and opened the door.

The episode had been tiring. As soon as she was back in the store room, she settled down in the corner again. For a few moments whilst washing she had felt grateful for being allowed to use the service room. Now she deliberately let the loneliness flood back in to counter that because, despite her despair and the feeling that it was all over, she realised there were battles still to come, battles that had no need for armies or swords.

She was woken this time by the sound of her boots hitting the deck beside her. Her clothes followed and the door closed. Once again, after her initial start, she crawled out of the deep pit of welcome unconsciousness into which she had fallen. There was no way of knowing how much time she had spent there, but she doubted they had let her sleep for long.

Pulling the pile of things toward her, her heart skipped a beat when her fingers made contact with her belt. For long moments she sat, her breathing ragged, unable to think, not daring to hope, wanting desperately for there to be something of the past and something of the future to cling to.

With awkward movements, she shuffled round so that her back was to the door. Clumsy fingers pulled the belt out from the loops on her trousers and she picked at the panel inside the back. She could get no purchase to begin with, she was so weak and her fingers were stiff and clumsy. Eventually, though, she persuaded the panel to open. Her whole face crumpled when she saw the amulet nestling there, as bright as ever and still warm to the touch.

Once the panel in the belt was closed, she shucked off her blanket and managed to pull her dusty, threadbare tunic over her head. It was a slow and painful task. It felt like she had rolled down a mountainside and been kicked by a horse when she reached the bottom. Which was probably nearer to the truth than she could clearly remember. There had been horses. Of that she was certain. She frowned. Maybe it was camels.

With her clothes were several broad strips of fresh, clean linen. She puzzled over why they had supplied her with fresh underwear and foot wraps. It was a small thing, a small comfort, perhaps even a small act of defiance on someone's part. Jeniche, despite her desire to stoke the fires of defiance, found it heartening.

The corner provided a support as she bent forward and pulled on her trousers. They were dirty, torn and smelled none too sweet, but it felt good to be dressed. She threaded the belt through the loops and did up the buckle, noting that she could do with an extra hole in the leather. To get her boots on she slid down the corner until she was sitting on the floor.

It took her some time to get her feet wrapped comfortably as she was used to doing it with her feet flat to the floor. She was just pulling on the second boot when the door opened again. It was almost as if they had been watching. She looked up at the new guard in his uniform of black with all its silver trimming. His face was impassive. If he had been spying, he clearly hadn't been affected by what he had seen.

A second guard, also in black and silver, entered carrying a heavy bundle.

"Stand," he said.

They waited, watching her climb to her feet.

"Put your hands out."

She frowned.

The first guard demonstrated.

She copied him and watched as the second guard fitted shackles to her wrists and locked them. They were joined by a short section of chain which, in turn, was joined to a longer run of links that were fixed to another set of shackles. The second guard knelt and fixed these round her boots at the ankle.

"Follow," said the first guard and walked to the door.

Jeniche looked down at the shackles and chains impassively. The only thing that worried her was their weight. She was desperately weak and the chains were heavy. Gathering some in her hand, she lifted them clear of where they dragged on the floor. With some difficulty, she managed to lace her fingers to hold the links and let her arms hang full length in front of her. It allowed her to shuffle along, joining the first guard in the corridor.

The second guard followed her out of the store room and closed the door. Jeniche blinked in the light that filled the corridor from one end, dropping her head for a few moments until her eyes adjusted. She shuffled along between the guards, feeling the familiar buoyancy of an airship in flight, the familiar subtle swaying of the floor.

It was a much smaller vessel than the *Trepaharos*. She was led almost directly into a narrow observation room. It was devoid of chairs or tables. Around the edge was a broad sill on which to rest while peering through the windows. The only other feature was a horseshoe shaped railing in the centre of the room that surrounded the head of a steep ladder. Jeniche peered down to see a number of men in pale grey airship uniforms; clearly the room from which they controlled the vessel.

The two guards led her to a window at the front of the room. She doubted she had been taken there to enjoy the view, yet someone wanted her to see something. So she shuffled up to the window and peered out on what she assumed was the landscape of northern Occassus. There, she let the chain out link by link until the weight of the slack was resting on the floor.

There was nothing remarkable to see although it was fascinating to see it from above. Hills, valleys, streams, and rivers. Trees, hedgerows, tracks, and roads. Fields and farm buildings, villages, people and animals. They all slid silently beneath her, an ordered landscape and certainly much more densely populated than the one she had stumbled through in the south.

There was another difference as well. The communities and farms in the south, the places where people had maintained their mark on the world were surrounded by vast tracts of wilderness. In essence, it was an abandoned subsistence landscape, one left largely to its own devices as long as it didn't present a threat to the north. There was no sign of wilderness below and she wondered just how far she had travelled.

As she studied the living map beneath her she began to notice features unique to the country. In many ways it still resembled parts of Ynysvron. All the villages and farms joined by networks of roads leading to larger towns. A green country. But Ynysvron had always seemed to her to embrace its natural elements. Fields were strange shapes, roads twisted, villages sprawled and always looked a little frayed at the edges. Unique. Organic. Lived in. Comfortable.

Below her here there were straight lines and regimentation. Villages were laid out in strict grids and each one looked very much like the last. Fields were rectangles. Even streams had been diverted into straight culverts and cuttings. Everything was tidy. And every village and town had a building and a fenced compound where men in uniform came and went. The larger towns often had a small airship tethered next to its barracks. As if the whole country was a military camp.

Perhaps, thought Jeniche, that is what I am meant to see. It was a warning. A threat. A statement of her defeat. She might have been able to wander about in the south, but here there was nowhere to go that would not lead her straight back to her captors. It was depressing. Not so much for herself, but for the thought a whole country could be run like that.

The ordered countryside dropped down into a wide, shallow valley. The airship made a turn that brought its course parallel with a broad, muddy river that ran between high, straight banks. The waterway was busy with barges and sail boats. Away to their right another airship flew, heading away from them toward the hills. As she looked forward again, she noticed that on the distant horizon was a long, dark, jagged line of mountains with a single, prominent peak to the eastern end.

Standing at the window was tiring but she had no choice in the matter. At one point she edged forward and leaned slightly to let the wide sill take some of her weight. The guards pulled her away and made her stand upright. Some time later, food was brought and she ate hungrily and awkwardly with the shackles on. And still she was kept there.

Somewhere behind them and to their left the sun began to set. Shadows grew long across the valley and the mountains were growing clear, individual peaks catching the evening sun. The river, she could now see, headed toward a gap in the hills ahead, curving eastward to skirt the nearest of the peaks, a squat, darksome monster with a thrusting, twisted summit.

And then she saw what she suspected she had been there to see all along. A city. A huge city. A huge living city. Amparo. Heart of Occassus. Home of the Order and the Bureau of Reports. The dark centre from which all her troubles in recent years had spread. She looked and she refused to be cowed.

She drew her eyes away from the distant metropolis and looked down at the fields directly below. They must have passed over the farm where Kenak grew up. He had spoken of the river and the city to the north of where he lived, of the airships passing overhead. She hoped he had survived, was able to find his way home in one piece. Perhaps somewhere ahead she would learn about what had happened to him. And to Alltud. He had been alive when she had run away. Perhaps he would be there to chide her when she landed, tell her off for getting caught again. There was comfort in that thought. And despair.

Amparo was now impossible to ignore. Late sunlight streamed horizontally across the valley and lit the buildings of the city. It lay on the right hand bank of the river as they approached from the south, rising up and covering the steep hills on that side, clustered about the base of a jagged rocky outcrop around which was built some kind of citadel with a soaring pinnacle or tower at its heart. It had all the look of a centre of power, perhaps the home of the Order.

The opposite bank of the river was bare of all but a road as the river ran up against a long, almost sheer cliff cut into the base of a spur of the mountain that marked the end of the range. Beyond the cliff, the lower slopes of the spur were covered with pine forest. Dark and dense, the trees stretched all the way to the lower slopes of the mountain's main bulk where they faltered, giving way to bare rock. Her eye was drawn to these slopes and to the sculpted twisting peak they supported, to glimpses of the range beyond where the distant summits played host to black cloud and lightning.

The view was eclipsed as they flew in alongside the cliff. It was already in shadow although the sun still lit the higher reaches of the city as they glided over docks and warehouses, workshops and markets, poorer crowded districts down where the river sometimes flooded in the winter.

The airship followed the river round a great curve, the cliff on their left, buildings on their right. For a moment she thought they were going to keep going and leave the city behind. Perhaps it wasn't Amparo after all, large as it was, four or five times the size of Makamba. But then she saw its final wonder and knew the aerial journey was at its end.

Chapter Thirteen

A sudden change in direction and pitch caught Jeniche by surprise. The floor tilted and she was thrown forward against the window sill. The nose of the airship had dropped and its speed had slowed as it reached the far edge of Amparo. For several seconds she rested her weight against the ledge before pushing herself upright and finding her balance.

The vessel engaged in a series of subtle manoeuvres as it approached a vast flat area carved out of the surrounding hills. In many respects it resembled the field outside Anka'a – buildings, people, carts moving back and forth and a great deal of other activity most of it centred round the dozens of airships that were moored below.

She took in as much as she could, frowning when she noticed there was a guarded perimeter. It struck her as odd that all the way back across the ocean in Arbiq, they had simply used the nearest piece of open ground and made do with no more than a few guards. Here in the very heart of their own country...

They passed over the high, turf-covered bank topped by a palisade and there was a sudden silence. The noise of the airship was something that had sunk to a subconscious level, always present, never noticed. When it stopped, however, it came as a great relief. The huge machine carried on under its own momentum, yawing slightly as a breeze caught it, but heading in the general direction of its mooring.

She wondered how the pilot knew, in all the seeming chaos below, just where he was supposed to guide his machine. Perhaps there were signals she had not seen. Which was hardly a surprise because there was too much to take in. Most of her attention had been captured by the enormous tall, thin buildings along the far side of the field. One had its doors open and she could see an airship inside, presumably to shelter it from strong winds whilst at rest. Other structures, much smaller, must be for people and whatever it was the great vessels transported.

As the airship slowed even more and began to turn, they drifted over a huge machine made of two hulls fixed together. She wondered if the *Trepaharos* had been that big. Doubtless even bigger, given that Kenak had said it was composed of three hulls. And as they swung round even more she caught sight of another of the huge double-hulled airships at the far end of the field. It was hovering, manoeuvring slowly, its rotating paddles starting and stopping as it edged into position, something large and misshapen suspended from its bulk. On the ground beneath, she could just make out a long row of... debris, fragments, all laid out neatly; the bare bones and sagging skin of an airship. One that had crashed. One that looked as if it had been made up of three hulls.

And then her view was obscured as the vessel in which she stood continued its turn. Ropes appeared ahead and to each side of the cabin, uncoiling from parts of the ship she could not see, trailing to the ground to be caught by gangs of men and made fast to mooring rings. At the same time the guards grabbed her and pulled her away from the window. She struggled to pull the loose chain of the shackles up out of the way of her feet as she was pushed back along the corridor, past the room where she had been kept, and on toward an open hatch in the floor through which cool, fresh air blew.

They didn't give her time to work out how to climb down the steeply angled steps, just pushed her to the edge and watched her slither down, dropping the last few feet to the ground when she could no longer keep her shackles out of the way. For a moment, as she lay on her back winded by the weight of the chains, she was faced with the terrifying vision of the enormous airship floating just a few feet above her, obscuring the entire sky.

Before she could succumb to fear, she was wrenched to her feet and pushed off to one side where she found herself flanked by a group of men wearing the black and silver of the BoR. Curious workmen on the field nearby stopped what they were doing and stared at her. Almost immediately someone she couldn't see began shouting and the bystanders and idlers found renewed interest in their work or things to occupy them elsewhere.

The man who had been shouting also wore black with silver trimmings. He joined them and shouted more orders, but after a cursory glance Jeniche paid him no attention. If the orders were meant for her, they would no doubt be backed up with force if she didn't respond. She had no idea how much information had reached these people about her, but one of the things she was happy to avoid was letting them know just how much she understood of the Occassan language.

The arrival of a large wagon drawn by four horses seemed to pacify the shouting man. Jeniche watched it arrive. It wasn't the vehicle or the animals that held her attention so much as the large, sturdy, metal cage that enclosed the rear. It looked like it had seen a lot of use.

She was hustled across the packed earth of the airship field, stumbling from exhaustion. At the back of the wagon she had to stand and wait again. As soon as two of the guards had unlocked and opened the cage they hauled her up and threw her inside. She fell on the chains and felt the shackles bite into her wrists. The door clanged shut behind her and she heard a heavy clunk as it was locked.

The driver snapped the reins and the wagon set off with a jerk. Once it had settled to a steady pace, she found the strength to pull herself upright and grasp the bars, looking out. One or two people glanced in her direction, but it was clear they weren't going to risk anything more than that to satisfy their curiosity. And when a mounted troop arrived to act as escort, even those who were meant to be working close by disappeared or turned their backs. Despite her tiredness, it made her curious. She found it difficult to believe that shackled prisoners were such a rarity as to elicit seemingly dangerous curiosity.

The wagon and its escort followed a broad road lined with buildings, workshops, and stacks of crates. It was a busy place, even at that time of day. Most activity, however, seemed to be centred on the wreckage she had seen as they landed. Bright Occassan lamps were being lit to illuminate the large, twisted section of hull that was being lowered to the ground. A convoy of flat carts headed in that direction, some laden with workmen. She had hoped they would pass close to it, but at a junction the wagon was steered in the opposite direction.

123

Before long they had left all the bustle behind, travelled between rows of long, low buildings, and headed for the main gates. These opened inward as they approached and were already closing behind them as they passed beneath an overhead walkway, ignored by the guards in pale grey who watched the city.

Beyond the perimeter berm was a wide open space of rough hewn rock. Only the road was smooth and that was flanked by deep ditches. It was some time before they passed the first buildings of the city, a fenced enclosure containing long single-storey structures similar to those on the airship field. Between two of them she saw a large group of men in dark blue standing in lines. What they might be doing was beyond her.

The sun had now dropped behind the steep river cliff to the west and although the sky was still light, the city was, for the most part, in shadow. Only the peak of the mountain was still brightly lit, a halo caused by sunlight striking the farther side.

The wagon ground on for a while across more open space and then began to approach more buildings. Grand edifices of stone stood either side of a paved road forming a northern gateway to the city. They passed through and the architecture remained grand with imposing buildings lining the broad thoroughfare. Side streets came and went and Jeniche caught glimpses of people going about their everyday business, shopping, gossiping, walking, lighting lanterns. Those few that were nearby stopped to watch as she was driven past. Again, she wondered, then shrugged. There was no way of finding out why.

The broad road they travelled along was deserted, almost as if the ordinary people of the city were not allowed there. It was straight and bleak, the buildings oversized, designed to impress and even intimidate. They didn't intimidate everyone.

Not long after they had entered the city, she became aware of a commotion up ahead and peered over the shoulder of the wagon's driver to see what was happening. One of the side streets contained a group of people who had come to watch the procession. A procession they were clearly not meant to see as soldiers in dark blue were running across the road toward them. A fight started. Jeniche caught a glimpse of someone hurrying away, of someone else being beaten with clubs and falling before her view was blocked by a soldier in black on horseback who rapped on the cage with a long thin stick.

Pulling her hand away and nursing her fingers, she lost her balance and fell awkwardly to the floor of the cage as the noises of fighting faded into the background. Too tired to do anything for the moment she stayed there, her back against the bars. She could still see things: that the roads to the east climbed to a more elevated district of the city where the last of the sunlight still bathed sections of the chaotic roofline of warm red clay tiles.

Once beyond the broad processional way with its grandiose buildings, the city could have been anywhere. Anywhere, that is, that had once been home to Pilgrims. Because through all the tiredness, the pain, and the confusion, through all the gorging on the new sights, sounds, and scents, through all the fear and the despair waiting to spread its dead fingers about her soul, she felt the familiar nausea. It forced her to make the effort to climb upright one more time, holding onto the bars of her cage directly behind the driver.

There was still a knot of soldiers in the distance behind them, but her interest lay in the nearby buildings. They were older here, part of an earlier phase of development. The style was different, less bombastic yet more impressive, with more straight edges, plain surfaces, and far fewer windows. The

125

materials were different as well, and here and there she could see they were built on foundations of something far older, the smooth cast stone.

And there was something else, something new, something that held her attention so that as they passed it she turned. A frown creased her brow. Using the bars for support she shuffled to the rear end of the swaying cage to keep it in sight.

Standing in a niche in one of the walls was a statue. She had seen statues before, ancient ones, worn, chipped, and broken, modern ones freshly carved, good ones that made you marvel how anyone could cut stone so well, and bad ones, a lot of bad ones. But she had never seen one like this.

It was not much bigger than a man, perhaps a head taller. The finish was plain, featureless, the whole a sandy colour. There was nothing remarkable about it at first glance. Indeed, it looked like it had stood in a desert for years, sand blasted, worn smooth. Yet as she passed she felt a strong wave of nausea, sensed something darker, something that frightened her to the core.

And then there was another one, on the other side, at a junction between two wide roads, standing on a plinth looking down on everything that might pass in front of it. Whereas the first had seemed intact if somewhat worn by age, this one looked damaged. She still couldn't say why, but something about it made her flesh crawl.

The statues grew more frequent as they rode on and Jeniche let herself slip back down to the floor of the cage behind the driver. The need to assess a new place had worn off and the reality of her situation, of the place she was in, hit home. This was what she told herself, and it was true. In part. The need to cower on the floor of the cage was a more visceral need to hide from the statues.

Not long afterwards they left the buildings behind and set out across a large, level piece of paved ground. Looking over her shoulder she could see the towering walls of the Citadel as they approached. They were dotted with dark lumps and rusty streaks. It seemed out of place in a country and a city that so far had been unnaturally neat and tidy. A tall double gateway stood before them and they came to a halt. The gates began to open and the horsemen of the escort rode off to one side, circling round as others came out of the entrance.

It was only when the wagon started moving again that she realised just what the lumps were. She gasped and pulled herself upright.

Hanging from fearsome spikes that protruded at an angle from the stonework were naked corpses in various states of decay. Terrified that one of them might be Alltud she began scanning the faces that were still recognisable, a grim task.

They became more and more difficult to see as the wagon, with its new escort, was driven toward and then through the gate. She did not have time study them all, but the last corpse as they went through had a face she knew well. Staring down at her with eyeless sockets, mouth open in what may have been a final scream, a crow gripping his shoulder and tearing away a strip of flesh from his scalp, was Mord Kint.

Chapter Fourteen

Occassan hospitality, she decided, had very little to commend it. At least, this particular brand of hospitality. Elsewhere she had been treated both kindly and generously. Perhaps those people in the south had felt sorry for her, sensed a shadow hanging about her. That had certainly been true of the people who lived in the caves. And it had been easy to convince herself it was there, especially since deserting Alltud. Or maybe it was just hunger.

She had been standing at the door peering through the small barred window at what she could see of the row of doors opposite where other prisoners were peering out at her. No one said anything or signalled. The guards didn't like you speaking or using other ways to communicate. She had the bruises to prove it. Instead, the prisoners watched each other with hungry expressions, waiting to hear the familiar sound of the food being brought. When they did, they let go of the bars and stepped well back from the doors. Because another of the many things the guards did not like was prisoners standing close to the doors when they approached.

Her cell was not unlike the one in Makamba. One way in and the same way out. Never quite warm enough. Slightly damp. A fetid bag of straw in one corner for a bed. A hole in the floor in another corner for waste. The only substantial difference she could see was that this cell was unlikely to be broken open by an attack from the Occassan military. And if it was, she would stay exactly where she was because there was nowhere safe for her to run.

Shuffling back with shackle chains held so they made no noise, she waited by her bed, standing upright just as they liked. A face appeared at the bars and studied her before the door was unlocked and pushed open. An unhealthy looking youth came in and placed her bowl on the floor. He was pale, curved round a collapsing chest, and looked like he could do with a decent meal himself. Not that what he had left for Jeniche in any way constituted a decent meal.

Once the door was locked, she fell on her food and shovelled it down, careful not to drop any. It was disgusting slop and she had been fastidious at first. It didn't last. Hunger breaks down many barriers and destroys many habits by enforcing its own.

When she had finished, licking the inside of the bowl and her fingers, she curled up on her bed in her thin prison garb, sorted her shackles and chains into as comfortable a position as was possible, and tried to sleep. It was her one escape. Besides, there was nothing else to do.

The permanently chill air stiffened the rough cloth of the prison clothes they had given her when she had arrived. Her instinct had been to use the last of her energy to hang on to her belt, but there was nothing she could have done. And to draw attention to it would no doubt have been a mistake. She had made a lot of those in recent months. The worst was leaving Alltud. She could have helped him away from that wreck.

129

They would have found shelter in the woods. A warm cave through the winter that must, by now, have passed. Food. Building up their strength and one day setting out westward. Always the same thoughts as she waited for sleep.

She knew very well that if Alltud was there he would berate her for constantly dwelling on a course of action she could not now follow; especially as what she had done had been at his urging. It made no difference. There was nothing else to occupy her mind and she went over and over the decision wondering each time just why she had left, wondering what would have happened had she chosen differently.

The harsh metallic banging on the bars woke her and she struggled to her feet as the door was unlocked. A guard came in. He stood watching her for a moment.

"Stay on your feet," he said as if she had disobeyed an earlier injunction. After a quick look round her cell, he left.

Jeniche risked a quick sideways flick of the eyes but there was nothing to see apart from the light of an oil lamp and she stood swaying with tiredness, the weight of her chains pulling on her arms. She had no memory of crawling back to bed but she must have done so because when the rattling came on the bars again she was tangled in the thin blanket. Climbing upright, she tried to blink the sleep from her eyes.

"Stay on your feet," said the guard who had sauntered in. He peered at her face by the light of his lantern.

Jeniche stared straight ahead, even when the light was directly in her eyes. Some lessons had been learned quickly.

When next the bars were rattled, she nearly fell backwards getting off the bed and on to her feet. Despite all the sleep, exhaustion was an ache in every muscle, every joint. Her bones and her teeth hurt. Her very soul yearned for respite. By the time food was brought in she was still upright but only half awake. It took several moments to realise it was the guard in front of her holding the bowl.

"The sky is...?"

The question was so absurd, she couldn't understand it at first.

"The sky is...?" he repeated.

The words would not make sense. The guard leaned forward until his face was a hand's breadth from hers.

"The sky is...?"

"Blue?" she ventured, dragging the Occassan word out of her memory.

"Wrong," said the guard and left taking her food with him.

Jeniche stared at the door as he locked it. The guard glared at her through the bars and she turned her head to face the wall in front of her.

"The sky," he said, "is green."

Bewildered, she crumpled onto her bed. It made no sense. Why would the sky be green? She didn't have the mental strength to puzzle it out. She was hungry as well, but that was pretty much a way of life these days. No chance of thinking she was going soft, not now.

The next time she woke, roused by the rattling of a stick on metal bars, she was hunched in a sitting position, her chest sore and her neck stiff. She had not moved an inch since she had collapsed after her previous meal had been removed from her.

She stood, using the wall for support, and stared across at the far wall of her cell. After a while she began to realise that no one had come in. Turning her head a fraction she could see there was no one at the door, either. Lifting her chains silently, she moved across to the doorway and peered out. All the cell door windows were empty and all she could see of the guard was his back as he disappeared round a corner. It had all the qualities of a dream, all the dark, shadowy terrors of a night-mare.

The guard was standing over her banging on the wall with his stick when she came to next time. As quickly as she could, she scrambled to her feet and stood swaying.

"The sky is...?" he asked.

"Green."

She held her breath. The guard looked at her and left and when she dared glance at the floor it was to see a bowl of food. You learned to play their games quickly. No matter how tempting and how often she tried, just for something to do, there was no point in trying to sort out the logic of them. There wasn't any. All you had to do was learn the rules. And if she had to say the sky was green to get her food, then she would say the sky was green.

For several days the sky remained green and her food was left as usual in its bowl on the floor. At least, she thought it was several days. It might have been a lot longer for all she could properly remember. It might have been a single day. There was no natural light in her cell, no way of marking the passing of time.

And then the sky was red and she went without a meal.

The colours kept changing. The objects kept changing. Often there were words she did not know the meaning of. In between she curled up and tried to rest, woken each time from the deepest of sleeps to be hauled to her feet, sometimes by her own force of will, often by the guard. She knew when it was the guard as there were more bruises.

One day she was standing before she woke and came to with the wall in front of her. In a moment of panic that left her close to tears she couldn't remember what shape the trees were meant to be. It didn't much seem to matter as the guard didn't ask. Instead he dragged her out of the cell. In the corridor, she swayed as she waited for her door to be closed, catching up her chains, trying not to look at the second guard who stood close by.

The first guard began walking and she fell in behind him, adding in a painful hop and skip to keep up. Behind her she could hear the heavy tread of the other guard and as her head cleared she wondered what brand of fun she was in for.

They turned out of the corridor with all the cells and into a broader gallery also of stone. It was old, the floor worn smooth and shiny by generations of boot leather. Even the walls at elbow height had a patina created by the rubbing of sleeves over what must have been centuries. And it had light. Natural light.

Each small window spaced out along a substantial stretch on one side of the gallery looked out over a courtyard surrounded by the grim façades of other parts of the Citadel. It was grey outside; drizzle filtered down from grey clouds, drifting in the air and coating the buildings so that even in the dim light the grey stone glistened. Each view was slightly different and brief, but she was able to build up a picture, bright in her dulled mind because of its novelty. She was almost smiling as they passed the last one.

There were more twists and turns on her journey, steps to climb, but she saw none of them, would not afterwards remember any of it. Only when they stopped outside a door did her dazed senses try to focus on the here and now, detaching with reluctance from feasting on the memory of the brief view of the outside world.

After a few moments she was led inside and made to stand in front of a substantial table. The person sitting on the other side didn't look up. He was too busy watching as a heavy linen cloth was laid out. Jeniche watched as well, dazzled by the brightness of everything, uncomfortable in the warmth. Lamps blazed. In a hearth at one end a well-established fire glowed. Hangings lined the wall, obscured in places by cabinets containing books. She thought, with longing, of the library on Pengaver.

A sharp rap on the side of her left knee made her look forward, a brief anger at the memory of Mord Kint. The seated man had the same cold eyes. He was watching as a set of brightly polished knives was laid out by his right hand. They were followed by a series of forks on the left. Plates laden with fruit, bread, cheese, and a selection of sweetmeats appeared. Jeniche didn't bother to let her gaze wander after that.

The smell, savoury, slightly spiced and with a dash of herbs, preceded the main dish. Steaming, it was set down directly in front of the seated man. He peered at the food on his newly arrived plate, nodded his approval and helped himself to bread. Wine was poured for him and he settled down to eat.

Not once during the meal did he look at Jeniche or give any sign that he knew she was there despite the noise her stomach made. Only once did a guard have to use his stick, repeating the rap on the side of her knee that was both painful and once more roused memories of... Tired from the days or weeks of interrupted sleep, she began to nod off where she stood. A sharp flick of the stick's tip against her ear woke her and she stood straight.

She didn't cry until she was back in her cell and alone, curling up under her blanket and lost in darkness long before sleep arrived.

To be woken by a rattling on the bars of her door.

"The water is...?"

Jeniche shrugged. It was a new question. Whatever she said

would be wrong.

"Dry?" she asked.

"The water is square," said the guard and strode out with her bowl of food.

She had long since given up trying to count the meals. There had been three a day when she first arrived, of that she was reasonably sure. It hadn't lasted. She had no idea of how time was passing, no idea of anything beyond trying to remember the correct answer. Day after day. Time after time. Sometimes correct. Sometimes not. Merging into an endless stream until there was nothing else but the infinite now. And then dazed, exhausted, and hungry she was once more pulled from her cell and made to walk along the wide gallery with the windows.

It was still grey outside; she could see the sky as they approached the first opening. And then she glanced down and saw the yard below was full of people, more people than she had seen in a long time. A dozen, maybe more. Walking. In a circle. With guards watching. Each window she passed gave her a picture of their movement just a few feet beneath her.

She veered off course, staring down at those other wondrous creatures, but the guards beat her back to the middle of the gallery and she passed the remaining windows without looking. What she had seen in that brief glimpse stayed bright in her mind. Those men walking, heads up to feel the fresh air, the one who limped slightly, the one with white hair, the one with a scowl. The one...

She stopped in her tracks and felt the beating of sticks around her ankles urging her on. One of them cut the flesh and she felt a trickle of blood tickle her ankle. It didn't bother her. She was immune to pain. Perhaps. Or maybe that hadn't been Alltud down there. It was just a few moments ago and already she wasn't sure. She stopped in front of the door. Empty.

Chapter Fifteen

The voice made no sense at first. It was getting to be a familiar problem. She could hear him well enough. She could see him talking. She knew what process was occurring. It simply didn't engage her at the expected level. Rather, it was annoying. In the same way a fly would be annoying. Besides which, she was much more interested in how she was managing to stay on her feet. It was a balancing act that far outstripped anything she had ever managed in the past climbing buildings or racing across loose tiles on a rooftop.

Even that concern waned when she did not fall over. In the end there was nothing left to do but hang in space and focus on the voice. It was monotonous, whining on like a tavern bore who thought all his problems were the fault of other people. Bit by bit she began to pick words out of the sound. After a while, she found they hung together like strings of beads, much the same as one of Feldar's necklaces. She smiled at the thought. Remembered. Wondered what had brought that to mind. Heard the words again. A name.

Mord Kint.

She made an effort. To listen.

"...although I can't think what possessed him to do that."

And as soon as she made the effort, the man stopped talking and stared at her from his chair with cold eyes as fathomless as some reptile – intelligent, without a doubt, yet wholly divorced from human kind. She wondered what he saw apart from an emaciated and bewildered young woman.

"Young woman."

She shivered at the congruity.

"Jeniche Lusor Remai. You have caused me a lot of trouble."

It didn't look to Jeniche like anything was allowed to cause him trouble, not even finding out her full name, something she had kept hidden for a very long time. Unblinking, he continued to stare at her.

"The Duke of Lant was a useful tool. Brute enough to head off in all directions without the slightest question. Intelligent enough to carry out his orders with some imagination. With a considerable proportion of our enormous and sophisticated resources at his disposal. And yet you..."

Words failed him for a moment and his nostrils flares as if he had caught scent of something he had trodden in. He stood and crossed to a table set against a wall where he poured himself a drink. On his way back to his chair he made a slow circuit of Jeniche, sipping the rich red wine. He was considerably taller than her and much better fed, dressed in plain clothes that did not hide the fact they were well made of expensive material. She couldn't determine his age. Didn't much care.

"In the end..." he said and left the words hanging, just as he had left Mord Kint's corpse hanging. Once he was settled back in his chair, sweeping hair away from his face, he added: "He was too fanatical for his own or anyone else's good. But useful at the last. If you ask the crows."

Jeniche did not much want to be in a position to ask the crows.

"Are you...?" her voice tailed off in a weak croak. He looked taken aback that she had dared to speak. "Are you the Occassan leader?"

A smile decorated his face for a few moments. It was the sort of expression a person would make if they had never done it before spontaneously, trying to reconstruct it from a report. It vanished as quickly as it arrived.

"Me? A leader? No." He studied the fingernails on his left hand for a few moments. "The Order is the governing body. I am a... guide."

"And do you hide behind this title of 'Guide' or do you have a name?"

She knew it was a pathetic comeback yet the very fact she was talking, interrupting his arrogant little monologue, seemed to annoy him. It was her only weapon. He would not be hurt by it. She knew that. She didn't care as she was doing it for own benefit.

"Do not think that because I have a use for you it is some form of protection. I can easily punish others if you pollute my equanimity. And there's still a long way to go with you. But..." he tried on that smile again, cast it off, "if we are going to work together you had better know that I am Ordant Zamler, fourth Duke of Colm, Master of the Archives."

He sounded like he had impressed himself with this announcement. Jeniche felt an unfamiliar twitching of the muscles in her face and realised after a moment she was suppressing a snort of derision.

"Work together?"

"Oh, yes. You weren't invited here simply to leech off the hospitality of loyal Occassans."

"And what do you think I can do for you?"

She shifted her chains. All this talk was tiring.

"You'd be surprised."

"Mord Kint wanted some... trinket. Claimed it had been stolen from him."

"An amulet."

Jeniche managed a shrug. "If it's what I think it was, I sold it a long time ago. I told him that in Anka'a." She met his eyes. "Just before all that carnage." And smiled.

Zamler flapped a hand. "Your attempts to annoy me are, I suppose, laudable. Pointless, of course. The trinket was Mord Kint's obsession. Just as he was obsessed with you. He pieced together that wreck, checked every corpse and all the body parts, worked out that you were on the loose rather than a victim of the crash. Really, though, it was one failure too many on his part. All he had to do was pick you off the streets of Makamba." He stared at her thoughtfully. "Native cunning or intelligent strategy?"

She went over and over the short conversation when she was back in her cell. Too exhausted to sleep, she lay on her bed and stared at the shadowy ceiling. Zamler. He was dangerous, that was certain. Beyond that, though, she couldn't read him; he seemed like a blank canvas.

Maybe that was the point of all these games. Or one of the points. To confuse her. She offered up a bleak smile to the gloom. There was no need for games. Hunger, exhaustion, and fear were more than enough to maze her thoughts.

The lamp in the corridor flickered as a guard passed on his rounds. She closed her eyes, pretending to a sleep that still eluded her. Had she riled Zamler, she wondered, by stating the amulet was lost? Had Mord Kint not told him before he was hung up on the outer walls to become carrion? Is that why he was hung up? If so, was that to be her fate? And what was that about punishing others? Did she dare find any hope in that?

The questions were still there when the bars rattled. They had never gone away, twisting and turning in the waters of sleep like dolphins running in the bow wave of their boat as they had crossed the Mittel Sea. The bright memory of a happy moment was snuffed out and she was on her feet in a reflex movement, eating the food without even realising she had answered a question.

There seemed to have been several meals since she was returned to her cell. Her brow furrowed as she tried to remember. Details of that sort were beginning to slip away from her. As were the connecting periods. Everything now seemed to be a collection of events, thrown into a bag and mixed up to be drawn out at random, inspected, and then cast back into the dark.

She recognised the gallery. It was a place she had been. That was all. Nothing else made a connection. They walked her along and she heard her chains rattling until she settled them properly, gazing out of the windows as she passed. There was a large, drab courtyard. It was empty. There was rain. She remembered rain. Had no idea why. Remembered books and mist, someone singing, didn't even try to work out the reason for that.

Zamler was still in his chair. He talked, as before, his voice the same monotonous whine. The time since their last meeting had collapsed into a nothing, vague rags of dream like scraps of cloud caught in the tops of pine trees on a mountain slope. Blank like snow. Filled with alien sounds. Imagined mosket

fire that made her jump in the silence, a vivid image of someone falling in the snow, dark blood soaking, melting, steaming
in the cold air.

"Why do you take what isn't yours?" She cut across whatever it was he was saying. "Why destroy? Why? By what
right?"

He stood and approached her, pushing his face in front of
hers.

"Steal? Destroy? You of all people stand here spouting these
heresies. We did not destroy anything. The world was ours and
it was stolen from us."

Jeniche reeled from the unleashed venom, alert now and
wondering just how much of this man's monologue she had
missed.

"Yours? Stolen? That's your madness. Not my concern."

"It should be." He spat it out. She felt his spittle on her face
and it disgusted her.

"Why? Why should I care about that?" she asked his
retreating back.

He turned when he reached the hearth. "Because it was you
that stole it."

Jeniche laughed, reined in the hysteria with difficulty.

"Me? I am a thief, yes. I have climbed into rich people's
houses to relieve them of the burden of all that jewellery and
money. But a whole world? No."

"You. Your people. And it will happen again if we don't
stop it now."

Jeniche stared stupidly at the floor, visions of the ragged
city, poor houses, the dusty fields, and impoverished farmers.
"The Antari?"

*

141

It was a relief to be dragged somewhere; someone else doing all the work. The pain in her arms was an irrelevance. She went limp, heels scraping along the floor, the pain there a raw new sensation penetrating the suffocating miasma into which she was sinking. And then she was hauled onto a table and allowed to lie there. Almost immediately she fell asleep, even as they were fixing her shackles to the board and placing the cloth over her head.

The heavy stream of cold water woke her and she was straight back into the river at Beldas unable to fight the current or the weight of her pack caught on the boat. She thrashed on the board, wrist and ankles bleeding as the shackles cut her flesh, muscles straining as she arched her back in an effort to get her head out of the way. Choking, coughing, trying to spit the water out, feeling it in her nose, seized by waves of panic, crying, screaming, gasping for breath, quiet for a moment beneath the damp cloth not knowing if the terror would come again. It did and she writhed, tearing at the shackles trying to twist her whole being out of the way, soiling herself as she thought the end had arrived.

She woke screaming from the nightmares back in her cell. Her body and clothes stank, witness to the reality of the horrors, and she cowered in some tiny part of her mind knowing that even there they could find her, drag her out. The door opened and she pleaded, but they did not listen. Corridor ceilings ran over her as she was dragged along. Windows appeared and with energy and strength even she did not suspect she might have left, she tore free and staggered to the nearest, waving frantically to the men in the yard before being knocked to the floor. She was beaten with sticks and dragged away.

Zamler was there this time. She saw his impassive face as the vile cloth was thrown over her face. And then the choking, the drowning, the writhing, the coughing up of thin vomit, releasing of thin, rank faeces. The pleading. The screaming. All the way down into dark madness. Over. And over.

He even came to her cell, stood in the doorway and watched as the guards came in for her.

She wept. Her throat was raw, burned, but she managed to speak.

"What makes you think I won't just tell you what you want to hear?"

He frowned. "You misunderstand. I don't want you to tell me anything. I simply want you to be compliant, to do what I say when I put you in the machine."

She whimpered as she was dragged away.

There was cold water, thrown from a bowl and smacking her face. It was different this time, but she still screamed and then cowered in a corner, hugging her knees. There was darkness and then there was light. The ceiling rolled along above her. There was no pain in the open wounds on her heels. There should have been. There wasn't. She tried to make something of it all but no longer had the information or the tools to manipulate it.

As well as the ceiling, she could see the tops of doorways. Rolling past. The whole world felt upside down and she wondered why she didn't fall off the surface on which she lay. For a while she felt dizzy. Nauseous. Without strength. Without will. Tears trickled down her cheeks.

The light changed. She heard voices. Saw faces. Felt her whole body shivering with the fear that infected her to the very core. And then the light became so intense she could see it through her closed eyelids.

Shadows moved across her field of vision and she felt herself lifted by many pairs of hands before being set down on her back on a flat surface. One eyelid was pulled back and she tried to roll her eye to avoid the light. The action was repeated with the other eye. Someone lifted one of her hands and let go and she winced as it dropped and hit a hard surface. She was poked, prodded, turned over and had the same indignities perpetrated on her back. All the time she lay there, she was waiting for the towel over her face, the choking, drowning water, trembling until exhaustion came to her rescue and she slept.

Chapter Sixteen

Images once more of an inverted world. The ceiling gliding by, a cold, heavy grey vault that moved in the wrong direction as if she was falling head first into some abyss. Slowly. It made no sense and, apart from an initial disorientation, caused no harm, so she gave it little thought. Even if there had been something suggesting a response, there was nothing she could do, no way to act. She was too weak and bewildered.

Like any wounded creature with no prospect of a future, she withdrew into herself, withdrew into the now. And each time it happened, the grey monotony would give way to a ceiling that was bright, smooth, and still. There would be a momentary sensation of flying before a hard surface pushed up underneath her. She would lie on this flat slab for a while. Meaningless noises would intrude, the sound of footsteps accompanying the feeling that people moved around her just out of sight. Sometimes a face would peer down at her and deep within she would tremble, waiting for the water to return.

Then it all became so strange that she could not help but wake from her torpor, drag her broken self out of that tiny inner cave to which she had retreated, and take notice. She was on her back on a hard, flat surface. It was a solid presence beneath her. Moving her fingers she could feel it, knew it for what it was. It felt like marble to her fingertips. Indeed, she had been deprived of the time to appreciate her surroundings for so long that the smoothness and the warmth were almost overpowering.

Yet her other senses, now they were reawakening, told her something else and she could not reconcile the two. Because although she was still, although the ceiling above her stayed exactly where it was, she felt as if her whole body was slowly sinking into... into... she tried to remember if there had ever been anything that welcoming. Certainly no mattress she had ever slept on. Even the rare hot bath she had stretched out in had never enveloped her with so welcome a warmth and soft-ness. And all the time she knew she was on a flat, hard surface. It made her wonder who could have created such a thing.

Despite an increased awareness of the danger of her surroundings, she began to relax. She couldn't remember when she had last done so. Not as completely as this. It felt good, so good it brought her close to tears, but it worried her as well. She really shouldn't be letting down her guard, especially now she was aware again that she had a guard, aware of how vulnerable she had become.

It was difficult though. So difficult. A warmth flooded her whole body and she felt as if she belonged. There would probably be precious few moments like this in whatever was left of her life. This one she was determined to enjoy.

When Jeniche was pulled off the table it was like being torn in two. She screamed and then lay on the rough wooden surface of the cart where she had been dumped, gasping for breath. She half expected to feel herself lying in a pool of blood the pain had been so intense, the sensation of tearing so real. There was no blood and the pain ebbed away to leave behind all the other hurts that she was heir to.

"Try!"

Confused and exhausted, she rolled her head one way and then the other. Zamler was standing by her side, others in the background. She tried to focus on him, but gave up, letting her head roll again so that she was looking back up at the ceiling.

"Try what." Her throat was dry, her voice a tired whisper. "I don't understand."

"It is simple. Try. Or your companion will be made to suffer."

Every last fibre of her being went rigid with anger. The pressure of her rage alarmed her.

"It's no good. I don't understand."

"Don't understand? You were raised for this. Trained for this. You are our only defence against the inevitable return of the darkness. Don't tell me you don't understand."

But she didn't. Only that Zamler had threatened Alltud. Confirmation he was still alive. Close by. It made her head spin and her heart race. Something inside gave way, some barrier she did not even remember constructing. It collapsed and out poured an overwhelming flow of memories and emotions. Swept up and swirled relentlessly by her rush of feelings, she lost her grip on the world and was carried under into blessed darkness.

After that there was the usual confusion of movement, periods of coherence and periods of disassociation. Food. And then sinking back into that generous warmth where she lay in the soothing aura and felt the desire to sleep. Yet she could not let go as there was a puzzle to solve. She almost laughed. Wanted to cry. Here she was stretched out on a table in the very heart of Occassus with a threat to Alltud hanging over the proceedings and she thought of it as a puzzle?

Surrounded by danger and hurt, all she wanted to do was rest, enjoy the feeling of wellbeing, the feeling of... being at home. The confusion, the paradox, threatened to overwhelm her again. So she lay very still. Not her body, because that had not been moving. Her inner self. She forced it into quietness and she forced it to listen to herself. And there, beneath the cosy sense of wellbeing, floating just beneath the surface, tingling in the pit of her stomach, a trace of nausea.

Once isolated, she was able to remember it from before; from the moment she had arrived in Amparo and through all the times she had been moved along corridors, on to when she had arrived here. Yesterday. Or a thousand years ago. Pilgrim machines. Everywhere. In this room. Especially in this room. She stretched her hand on the smooth surface within which she drifted. Here. Beneath her very fingertips. Now she understood.

She closed her eyes and let the table take her completely, sinking without moving until she was fully submerged. After that she had no idea what to do. Her previous contacts with Pilgrim machines had been few and far between and there had certainly been little or no element of control. The entry into the Spiral Castle on Inissgar was still a mystery to her as was her instantaneous translocation in the caverns beneath Ma'azraq, and the visions in the building beneath the desert on their way to Anka'a. She shook her head.

If there was no grey square out there beyond her eyes, perhaps she ought to look for one within. It made little sense to her, but then much of what she had learned of the Pilgrims, of pre-Ev culture seemed nonsensical, little more than magic. A corner of her mind was lit with a memory of Trag, sitting in the shade at the back of the stables in Makamba with that big book of his spread on his knees as he devoured the pictures and ran his finger along the lines of text.

Things fell into place. Like the symbols in the puzzles she had played with as a child. Is that all magic was? The answer seemed so simple, yet it made such sense. She supposed it must be true. All her life she had taken it as nonsense, wonder tales for children, when all the time it was just a secret way of making the world do what you wanted. It was knowing how the puzzle worked. When people learned the secret it was no longer magic. Like flying.

A tiny spark exploded in the slate grey nothing. It was the sort of thing you see if you close your eyes and press them too hard – dull and ill-defined, yet bright by contrast. And as slate grey nothing was still there after its brief existence she wasn't even sure there had been a light in the first place. Perhaps she had willed it into being. Perhaps trying to see it again, straining after it, made it all the more elusive. Perhaps she had simply convinced herself she had seen something that had never been there.

Settling back again in her mind, she tried to relax, tried to forget her surroundings, wished she could, knew they would never go away. And again she berated herself for not being able to still her mind. She had been beaten into living in the thoughtless now and had done so for some time. The moment it became imperative, the very desire filled her head with thoughts. With memories. And in those memories, help. The Tunduri, she thought, are supposed to be good at this sort of thing. Did Gyan Mi or any of the others ever demonstrate a technique?

Jeniche couldn't remember other than seeing the nuns one day sitting cross-legged with their eyes closed, breathing slowly and regularly. She tried that, concentrating on her breathing, gently setting aside other thoughts if they tried to push their way into her mind. Breathing in. Breathing out. Regular. Slow.

Pale scintillae tumbled along on the back edge of vision. She was tempted to try to see them more clearly. Instead she left them to play and stared up into the slate grey. Breathing in. Breathing out.

Worms of light wove themselves into tantalising patterns. Still dim; still out there on the edge. At one point she thought she could hear voices, way off in the distance. Laughing, singing, children at play, but it faded and she was left with distinct images forming in the air right in front of her. She held her breath for a moment then panicked as something was placed over her mouth and nose.

It was a headache to place on a pedestal and mock all other headaches with its skull pounding awfulness. She stared across the top of the rough thin blanket at the wall of her cell, turned sideways very slowly to see a bowl of food, and closed her eyes again. Like a blind drunkard crawling across gravel, she reached the hole in the floor and heaved the sparse contents of her stomach into stinking oblivion. Aware that she was in danger of falling asleep crouched over the hole, she managed the return journey to her bed.

The food was still there when she woke. So was the headache. It felt like someone had hit her over the left eye with an iron bar. How she got herself into a sitting position she did not know, but she managed it. It was the same with the food. She must have gone through the actions of eating, but all she could remember was looking at the full bowl of cold food and then looking at an empty bowl. By degrees her thundering head drooped and she fell asleep.

Retrieving memory out of pain, she knew, was no easy thing. When there was a fog of exhaustion obscuring the way it became doubly difficult. If, in addition to that, the world then contrived to come apart around her, the chances of finding her way back to safety would be exceedingly slim. She had learned, in such situations, to make her own markers and had no choice but to believe in their efficacy. The alternative was to give herself up to madness.

Jeniche had no more than an inkling. There was nothing in her surroundings that could possibly confirm it. She sat in a cell, possibly the one she had been in all along although even that was not certain. What she did know is that her back was to one stone wall as she gazed at the stone wall opposite. Yet she held to the faint notion, nurtured it, because it seemed real. And she was equally convinced it had happened more than once.

There was a greyness, something different to the dull fuzziness of the headache she had. Again. This greyness was not outside her eyes, not something she could see in a normal sense. It was a greyness within that was as real as the outside world, something other than her, something she could only see when she closed her eyes. She skipped over the bit where she knew that if she closed her eyes now, she would not see this other greyness. It belonged to some other place.

Working out the whys and wherefores was well beyond her just now. Her head ached enough as it was. Instead she went back to that initial feeling and clung on. A feeling that she had been out of the cell and somewhere else, witnessed this other grey, and been returned to her dim stone prison. Over and over again.

There must be a considerable time element, she was sure, because of something else. She'd had sores on her wrists and ankles, latterly on her heels as well. The flesh had been rubbed raw and wept in places where the shackles chafed. But they were healing. The pain had faded. The sick looking patches of flesh were drying and in other places where they had already healed they were returning to a healthy cinnamon colour.

Perhaps you healed anyway if... But she couldn't think of an 'if'. Not in this situation. There was just the fact that time was passing and she seemed to be stuck in a loop, submerged for the most part in darkness yet always surfacing with a memory of having watched coruscations of light dance in from the edges. And every time she began to see them clearly, saw them start to make coherent patterns, pain descended and she woke in shadow surrounded by four walls of cold, damp, grey stone.

She knew there was something else, but every time she tried to dig away at the obscuring mist it made her head ache. Yet the idea would not go away. Like all the other details it hovered just out of reach, just out of sight, and every time she made an effort to identify it, the darkness came. It was all so frustrating, all so familiar.

Worse still, she couldn't decide if it was familiar because it kept happening or because it was like something else. That was a new thought so, painful as it was, she played with the idea, wondering how to resolve the issue. And then it came to her, like things sometimes did when it was misty. A breeze would blow, someone would move, or for some other reason known only to the universe, the obscuring veil would thin and a shape that had teased on the edge of the senses became clear.

She lay back on the bed and rested, tried not to think, let the inner mists blow where they would. Above her, the ceiling was deep in shadow and she let her eyes go out of focus, surprised at how easy this was. As if, perhaps, she was used to doing it. Her thoughts went off at a tangent, but she herded them back, settled them down and tried again. It wasn't thoughts she wanted, but memories.

Image built on image, each inspired by the last, until she had the whole. Memories of the table, of Zamler, of lying on her back clearing her mind to allow the lights to creep in from the periphery. And the circle was complete. She remembered it all now, the trips to the room where she was laid out on the table, the sinking in to the hard surface, the attempts to touch the controls that formed on the screen, the blackouts, the headaches.

Exhausted, Jeniche dropped into sleep. She had dug up more questions than she had answered, but it was a step. Whether it had meaningful direction remained to be seen. However, had anyone looked in at that moment, they would have seen the ghost of a smile haunting her starved face.

Chapter Seventeen

She barely saw them. The cobweb of nightmare still clung to her face and clouded her vision. Even had she been fully awake, the routine was so well established, so all consuming, so much the whole of her experience and memory, that she would not have remarked on events. Her life was this and had always been this. Everything else was a dream seen through the overpowering haze of exhaustion. And by the time they reached the bright room with the table, she was once more asleep.

Being lifted onto the table woke her again. It was the sense of free fall that made her kick out of sleep. She stared in a stupor at the clean white ceiling longing to return to the pain free darkness. Instead, there was the movement of people, the sound of their feet, the low murmur of their voices, and the undercurrent of humming from an unknown source, all of which kept her present. None of it meant anything. None of it stimulated. None of it was worth wasting her limited resource of energy. Only when she felt the surface beneath her become viscid did she shake off the dullness.

Each time they had brought her here, she had done this, waiting, reserving her energy, then snatching a precious second or more between sinking into the table and being pushed into unconsciousness. Each time, she had created a fraction more of space and time for herself in which to look and learn.

Melding with the table, she had discovered, was a combination of letting go and taking control. The times she had consciously tried to do it, nothing had happened. Apart from Zamler's cold anger. Now she could do it without thinking about it and she was able to stand back from herself, observe, take note, and even experiment.

It had surprised her at first that no one noticed what she was doing. It felt like it was lasting for many minutes. How could anyone, especially Zamler, not realise? It was only later, when she was sufficiently in control of what she was doing to look outward as well as within, that she could see the world seemed suspended.

She still had no way of knowing how many times she had dropped into the peculiar netherworld of the table. The distortion of her senses, the standing still of time, the stepping sideways... all these took the normal state of the world and tore it to shreds. How or why was beyond her. All she knew was that each time she dropped into the slow fluidity of the table she had that little bit more time and space to explore.

Her exploratory navigation of the liminal region to which she had been introduced didn't go completely unnoticed. There came a day when she lay on the table expecting the cloth and deadening darkness when all that came was Zamler's hand. It grabbed the front of her tunic and pulled her into a sitting position. Even after all the time she had spent becoming accustomed to the way in which the table embraced her, it was painful being pulled away from it whilst still conscious. She refused, however, to cry out.

"You're holding back," barely restrained violence clear in his cold, soft voice.

Jeniche shook her head slowly, mostly against the pain. "No."

"Up to some game of your own."

"Tired. Hungry."

She was dragged away at a wave of Zamler's hand and taken back to her cell. The guards dumped her on the bed and left. The expected beating did not materialise. Instead, to her surprise, there was more and better food. Simple fare, but edible. An apple. The first one she held to her nose for an hour inhaling its glorious scent before biting into the crisp, juicy flesh with aching teeth. The grubby mattress was replaced with a fresh one and it came with an extra blanket. She cried. Tears of joy. Tears of victory.

Short lived.

As well as the luxuries, they let her rest awhile. She was confined to her cell, locked in with all the shadowy mists that filled her head irrespective of whether she woke or slept. Formless darkness, haunted by an unwanted presence she could neither name nor define. Every time she slept she woke screaming and cried herself back to sleep. There was something in her head. She did not want it there, had not invited it. There were times she came close to beating it against the wall to rid herself of the invasive other that clung within.

With no view of the outside world she had no way of knowing what time of day it was, what season of the year, what year of the century. She could not even begin to estimate how long she had been held. It seemed like forever, the times before fading like an ill-remembered dream. But time passed. And as it passed the abysmal headache faded and each time she slept for longer before the haunting chased her out of the oblivion she was afforded.

She shed fewer tears as well, rocking back and forth trying vainly to grasp anything solid of the nightmares so that she might visit some violence on them in return. They remained elusive, slipping away more quickly when her eye was turned in their direction. Shameful things, insubstantial in themselves, conjured and let loose on her as Mord Kint had once threatened her with Balat. They were abuses perpetrated upon her soul; slick, cold things that had violated her innermost being in a way she knew she would never be rid of.

The wearying round began again and the short break that came with an improvement in her diet became one more mythical marker in her journey through the depths into which she had descended. Back on the table she tried again and again to find out what happened when she was blacked out. Was it Zamler? Was it the machine? Was it her unable to cope with the machine? If so, why did Zamler persist? What was he after? What did he want of her?

Each time she sank into the comfort of the table the questions whirred and hampered her, like soft desert sand on the slope of a dune she was trying to climb. The questions were born out of genuine curiosity, but they were fed by her fear, her frustration, and her feelings of helplessness. They had become habitual, so that each time she reached the table they began tumbling relentlessly through her mind.

So she began to change things. She no longer needed to conserve her energy until she arrived at the table. Instead, she prepared herself on the journey from her cell, disconnecting herself one by one from the fears that taunted her until there came a day when she lay on the hard surface, staring at the ceiling without seeing it, and sank into the embrace of the machine, conscious of a warm drifting as if she floated.

157

And that was the day when light crept into her dreams. Flickering, dancing, shimmering faintly along the edge of vision, searing away the choking darkness and the suffocating intrusions. She thought nothing of them to begin with. They were dreams as formless as the nightmares. She had tried to make sense of the darkness and failed. What chance had she with the light? But they continued and she remembered them when she woke, even through the headache. And they danced there with her when she was carried back to the table.

Danced as she sank into its embrace.

Danced twice as brightly as she took control.

Symbols flickered, skittering back and forth, forming sequences that repeated. They stepped across her field of vision, stacked themselves in columns and interlocked, creating new symbols. Reaching out, fascinated, she touched one, watched it reshape itself around her fingertips. She was doing this, just as she had as a child in the Dhalar playing with the puzzles Palna had given her, when darkness descended. Next time, she resisted the enchantment of the display and looked further, trying to focus on details that she could sense lay beyond her immediate surroundings.

It was a long, slow journey. Each small step took her just a little further before she was pushed into darkness. She even made a journey of the headache with which she woke, trying to find ways to ease it, to pinpoint its cause. And then she would wait out the time until she could return to the table by wrestling with all the other demons still at large in her head.

The moment of release was unmarked by fanfare. She was unaware of doing anything different but must, perhaps, have reached a point where whatever barriers existed had been worn down or set ready to fall. Whatever the case may be, one day she lay upon the table and watched the dancing symbols before

158

dropping into the dark; the next she twisted her fingers amongst the fluorescing shapes and unlocked a door.

It unnerved her at first, not so much because it was unexpected but because it was like slipping back in time. She half believed that if she looked behind she would find Alltud grinning at her with the Tunduri clustered round him or that if she turned that corner up ahead, she would find Cenau and Aros squabbling in their companionable fashion.

She stood in a spacious alcove. Directly ahead, a corridor faded into... it was not darkness or distance, it simply faded as if it were beyond the reach of her senses. There were doors. And when she stepped out from the alcove, more corridors stretched away to left and right, also fading.

The alcove, when she looked back, was a plain, three-sided room with a raised floor. On the furthest wall there was a grey panel in which the slightest suggestion of a glowing symbol faded. Stepping away from it, anxious not to stray too far, she made for the nearest doorway and peered through into a dimly lit room. It was filled with rows of cases, light reflecting from their glass fronts. She knew there would be objects there, neatly displayed on shelves.

Hesitant, she reached out, touched the nearest wall, rapped it with knuckles that felt the hardness. Yet she knew it was not real. At least, no more real than the Spiral Castle. Which had been real enough.

Dimness flooded the unreal corridors, darkened the already shadowy room. Jeniche left and turned to make for the alcove, felt everything dissolve as if she viewed it through a veil of dark material. There was a drop, as if she had fallen; a door opened in front of her and there was nowhere else to go. She stepped forward into pitch black, heard the door slide behind her. Woke from another nightmare into her cell.

As before, each journey into the machine allowed her to accumulate experience and provide the time to explore further. To begin with it was necessarily random. She knew nothing about the place even though it was superficially familiar. Until she understood something of the nature of its peculiar reality, systematic searching was out of the question. So she wandered. There were countless rooms, few with functions she could even begin to understand. Endless corridors, growing in length but always vanishing into a distance she could not visualize, odd events so surreal her mind rejected any memory of them beyond the fact that something strange had happened. And all the while she expanded her territory and her command of the symbols that danced in the air and glowed in the panels on the walls.

Even though she seemed to be able to spend more time exploring and learning, there was no stopping the sudden and unpredictable descent into that dark corridor and the closing of the door on pitch darkness. She tried hard to resist it when it happened, but the drop into oblivion always came. She tried various methods of escaping it and of protecting herself. By some instinct she even raided the display cases for masks. They held off unconsciousness for a short while. It was another conundrum with which to exercise her overstretched mind.

Although she made progress in the machine, it was not without further cost. The extra food rations and sleep had pushed back the threshold of her exhaustion for a while. Now she was slowly catching up with it again. Day after day she teetered on the boundary, her feet on the crumbling edge above an abyss into which she could so easily fall without any prospect of rescue.

Little rest was to be had in sleep. The dreams of light had faded now she was beginning to master the machine. The nightmares, cowed for a while, resumed their reign of terror. And for added effect, she began to remember snippets that haunted her waking hours.

Lost. The first thing that had ever terrified her into inaction. The hours in the dark tunnels beneath the Dhalar; days in the desert away from all that was familiar for the first time ever in her life. She hated what she had left behind, the loneliness, the lack of love. At the same time she missed the things she knew, the chill security of her room there. Even Palna. Gone. Out of reach.

Pain. Delirious and starved, staggering into the city amidst the noise and bustle, the smell of food making her feel sick, the laughter and then the cursing as she sat in the horse trough. The bone-breaking agony as she was beaten, kicked, and left in the dark alley.

Death. Over and over the trauma of taking a life. The shivering, the shaking, the deep despair and inescapable guilt. The vow that it would never happen again. The need to defend, the weight of the sword, the movement of the blades slicing air, slicing flesh, hacking bone, letting blood; the screams, looks of disbelief, the fear. The sound of musket fire, the sounds of panic, streets filled with people running, soldiers hunting in packs, firing from rooftops and moving from house to house in crowded streets. The ineradicable knowledge that each person fallen was loved by someone and would never return to them.

Other visions, too, of death and despair. Of the day the sun fell in a great fiery arc. The day the forests lay down and burned. The day the seas rose up and came to claim the land. The days in which the world dissolved, fell into a nightmare from which, even now, it had not fully woken. Because in the dark, monsters hunted, preying on those who wanted a quiet life, a roof over their heads, and food on the table.

Friends. Dead. Gone. Lost. Good friends who had cared for her and shared the hours, which was all any of them had. Good friends dead and gone, torn apart by the beast in whose belly she now lay.

In the darkness, huddled on her straw bed and wrapped in thin blankets, she rocked slowly back and forth, crying hot tears. Crying because no matter how hard she tried she could no longer call to mind the face of the man with whom she had shared her adventures. Crying because they had taken even that from her.

Chapter Eighteen

Ghosts whispered in the dark. They shimmered faintly in the dim corners of her small, dank cell, faint echoes dancing with shadow. Jeniche listened. She had never been scared by stories of spirits and demons. The everyday world had more than enough wonders and horror. She had seen buildings on the Moon, wandered in vast caverns filled with cities, been moved through solid walls. She had fought in bloody battles face to face with her enemies, maimed them and killed them. She had endured torture. A voice talking to her out of the barely visible coruscations in a darkened room was not going to send her into hysterical convulsions.

All the same it was perplexing and, given that she had been comfortably asleep, it was also deeply annoying. At first she thought it must be one of those dreams that never quite let go when you wake up, turning your idea of reality upside down and inside out, leaving perhaps a feeling of sadness for a world and people that are forever lost as it fades. It soon became clear that it wasn't. It showed no sign of fading and was, on reflection, not much like that sort of dream. And given that her world was a nightmare, she knew a dream offering a sweeter alternative would have left her an emotional wreck once reality shouldered its way forward.

For a few moments she entertained the idea that she had finally gone mad. In her position it wouldn't be surprising. However, if she really was mad she wouldn't be having a discussion with herself about it. Or maybe that is precisely what she would do. She frowned through that for a bit not even able to decide how seriously she could take the whole idea. Alltud would have teased her about talking to herself. A fist, beaten hard against the stone wall, broke the sudden train of thoughts she could not cope with.

And after all that, as she sat nursing her hand by tucking it into her armpit, the voice was still there. She listened carefully and corrected herself. Voices. Talking with each other.

As if caught out by her realisation, they stopped. Silence filtered into the dank stone chamber. After a few moments of listening she settled down. Wary at first, it was not too long before she relaxed, felt her eyelids grow heavy, to be woken again by the covert conversation. Climbing off the mattress, conscious of all the soreness and the aches, long since having forgotten what it was like to exist without them, she stepped to the door. A single lamp burned in the corridor. The noises from the other cells, the little grunts, coughs, snores, moans, the screams of nightmare... they were normal.

Behind her the whispering continued.

"Who are you?" she asked after she had turned back to face the darkness of her cell.

Her voice was husky and uncertain. She seldom spoke any more, was no longer used to it. It felt foolish. Not because she was asking a question of the empty air, but because speaking was... pointless. What was there to say? And to whom? The only person left worth talking to already knew what was going on. As much as she could understand anything, that is. Which, she would have been the first to admit, was not very much.

Sleep was a long time returning, even to her exhausted frame. She lay on her back staring into dark nothing, her head full of random thoughts and images that had been stirred up by the voices and were now slowly settling, her heart awash with incomprehensible emotions. And, as usual, it seemed like seconds between darkness and the banging open of the door, the being dragged into the corridor and carried along.

Back on the table she was tempted simply to sink and allow whatever darkness was normally inflicted on her, accept it, embrace it. It would be a relief to disengage, drift away to some sunny spot inside her mind, and stay there. It would also, she realised, be very easy to do. Yet when she found herself standing within the bright, clean world there seemed to be a new imperative, a drive, a desire to go in a specific direction and once she was there, standing before one of the ubiquitous grey panels, to use her fingertip to draw a specific and complex symbol.

A faint blue radiance enveloped her, flowing and shrinking to become a second skin; a silent pulsation filled her, varying until it settled into a steady rhythm; and a new warmth flowed within her. And she fell into darkness. Woke on her bed. Again. And again. And each time she woke there was less pain and the healing that had started with the sores on her wrists and ankles seemed to take root within her as well. Her teeth stopped aching and the stiffness in her joints began to ease.

With the healing came easier sleep and, although the voices persisted, she felt stronger. Not so much physically. That would take much longer. It was more that she felt as if something had been resolved and put behind her. She also felt less self-conscious about whispering back to the air, asking questions, listening without understanding, knowing that somehow the machine had found a way to talk to her in the cell.

The day came when she stood before the panel and tried a new symbol that came to mind. It was unlike any of the others she had learned. A jolt lifted her as she completed it. It was painful at first in an unspecified way, a sharp tingle through her whole body that took her breath away. During successive events she found a way of easing the shock. This too was a kind of healing. It did not make the bad dreams go away, but she fell asleep now with a smile on her face. Not a smile of happiness or contentment for there was a cruel edge to it, but it was a smile nonetheless, and she had not done that for a very long time.

In the dark she was restless, moving, walking back and forth in the narrow ways that threatened to engulf her. There were glimpses of frightened faces as if some sanction had been threatened and was now being enforced. An even darker vision threatened to push its way through, but never quite managed it as if something else was protecting her.

The first time she felt that, she woke and lay in the dark, conscious of the fear that had come with her out of the dream. A voice had broken into her sleep, pleading, screaming. She listened but it didn't come again. Some poor soul giving out beneath the torture, perhaps, despairing at the world.

The next day, when she melded with the table, it was clear that things had changed. For a long time she had given up trying to sense what was going on around her. The guards gave nothing away and the workers in the room where the table was situated always seemed wrapped up in their work. Only Zamler betrayed much of what he was feeling and that was mostly frustration, probably because he dealt directly with Jeniche. He it was that stood by the table as she melded, he it was that spoke to her on the few occasions when words were used, berating her, venting his anger that whatever progress he expected of her was slow to materialise.

For the most part, however, she must have been producing whatever results he had expected of her. After the initial months of torture she had not, beyond the general lack of welfare, been ill treated. There had been no more beatings, few harsh words or threats. So she had switched off from wondering what Zamler was using her for and channelled all her energy into learning her way round the interior of the machine.

She had not learned much. It was enough, however, to suspect there was far more there than she would ever be able to explore or understand. Despite that, the inner world of the machine was one that offered relief from the bleak confines of her cell. She could move about freely and was already familiar with the section around the alcove in which she materialised. She was so fascinated by the place that had been created and was so desperate to learn what she could that she had no need to pay attention to the other half of her existence.

It could not help but intrude sooner or later. On a day indistinguishable from all the others, some time shortly after the start of the darker nightmares with the pale frightened faces, she was wheeled in and lifted to the table as normal, but there was a distinct difference in atmosphere. The people who would normally be talking quietly and working at various points around the room were silent and unmoving. Given that she rarely gave them any thought any more, the fact that she could sense the tension meant it must have been considerable.

Jeniche turned her head one way and then the other. Everyone looked cowed as if, perhaps, they were wishing they were somewhere else, anywhere but having to share a room with Zamler. As soon as she saw him she could sense his anger. It crackled off him like an approaching sandstorm made your hair stand on end and sent sparks from bits of metal.

He noticed her looking round and strode across to the table. She was helpless there. On her back, weighted with the chains of her shackles. Weak still from lack of exercise and food, even though her diet was much improved from the early days. She flinched as he leaned toward her and immediately felt ashamed. It was clear they had damaged her in ways she didn't even yet know, let alone understand.

That realisation kicked her out of the complacency into which she had sunk and lit a tiny flame. She had little energy to make a physical response and knew her situation was useless even if she could muster the strength to stand and launch herself at Zamler. The desire was there, though, as was the image in her mind. He must have seen a hint of it reflected in her expression as she dropped into the embrace of the table because the last thing she remembered was him taking a sudden step backwards.

Zamler's face, so close, peering directly at her yet focussed some inches in front made her lean back. Disorientated by the sudden shift, heart hammering from the proximity of Zamler, she froze on the spot. She had never seen him this close before, never had the chance or desire to observe him so intently, realised that what she saw was larger than life. No wonder it had been so alarming.

Once she was certain that, despite appearances, he was not looking at her, she studied the pale, shadowed face. She had a recollection of it being well fed the first time she had seen it, with an underlying complacency, although that may just have been a reaction to watching him eat while she stood before him, hungry and bewildered. There was no such indication now. The arrogance had been leached away and the cheeks were sunken. It was the face of a man who no longer had time for food, of a man who was hungry for something else.

His eyes, momentarily fixed on something just in front of her when the face first appeared, were wide, intense, and fevered; the eyes, she thought, of someone confronting uncertainty with barely suppressed anger, looking for reserves of strength in strange inner places. They shifted first left and then right before fixing on something that seemed to be by her feet. As a reflex, she looked down and when she looked up again, the face had gone.

With the strangely magnified face removed from view, Jeniche found her focus shifting to a familiar series of patterns of light, forming and reforming in the air. She watched for a while realising that although they were familiar they were wrong. And as she puzzled over that, shadows of movement drew her gaze beyond them to...

She looked at it. It was something else that was familiar and yet she could not place it. She didn't think it was wrong as the lights had been, but it was just beyond her grasp. So familiar was it, that her inability to recognize it was extremely annoying. Surely she could... And then a face passed in front of her in profile and her perspective shifted, just as it had all those years ago in the painted room.

Tearing her attention from the scene she wondered if there was a way... It was disconcerting to find her thoughts interrupted by her own thoughts answering questions she was barely having time to finish asking. Where was all that knowledge coming from? And how?

Shaking her head to clear away the distractions, she thought back to the room where she now lay on the table and tried to remember if she had ever seen a grey screen whilst she was in a prone position. It had been a long time since she had bothered to look, bothered to take much of an interest in those surroundings, and even then her view had been limited. However, as far as she could recall, there were several. There must have been. These people, these Occassans, these members of the Order, they had been learning to use them, learning how to manipulate the machine, for a lot longer than she had.

With a subtle flickering of her fingertips she wrote new instructions with light in the air. After a few seconds it dissolved, reappeared briefly as a mirror image of itself, and then vanished. Jeniche smiled as she understood. The screen in front of her blinked from view to view of the room until she found the one she wanted. A three-quarter angle view of herself stretched out on the table with Zamler standing above her head looking down at her.

It would have been strange enough viewing herself in that way under normal circumstances. What she saw disturbed her profoundly – a broken, emaciated husk staring at the ceiling with dull unseeing eyes, black hair lank and greasy, an unhealthy pallor to her flesh. But the machine had been healing her. Her sores had gone. The aches, the stiffness... had it all been a lie? An illusion? Some of her puzzlement and dismay must have transferred to her body as her head began to turn toward the screen through which she was watching herself. Just as Zamler lifted a glass bottle and poured a clear liquid onto a cloth which he placed over her face. She watched herself struggle for a second or so.

Faces again, turning away, disappearing into the dark; fear, anger, despair. A sensation of walking, of being attacked, of smashing through things, and waking to the darkness of the cell and the pain of a monstrous headache with a lingering image, blurred, uncertain, slipping from her grasp, fading from the corner of her eye. A reflection. Distorted. Of something she knew she should recognize.

Chapter Nineteen

Haunted. Not by whispering ghosts this time. They were still there if she took the time to listen, engaged in their endless hushed conversation. However, like everything else in her life at present, if it was not a danger to her she expended little energy on it. Only the machine was different. She had no choice but to become involved with it so she tried at least to do so on her own terms. What haunted her now was the feeling that somewhere, just round a corner, just through a door, on the other side of a wall, something was going on. Something connected with her, something affecting her, something she really should know. Yet try as she might she could not pull the relevant information or memories into the light.

It was, in a sense, a double haunting. All the time she had the feeling that something was going on, she was also haunted by the possibility that there was nothing at all. That she had created a mystery out of loneliness, created a terrible truth to explain her complete and miserable failure.

And if that uncertainty was not enough, she could think of no way of finding out which state of affairs was true. So this, too, trailed behind her, another unwelcome shade dragging her down, as she wandered the corridors, peered cautiously round corners, looked into rooms, and listened at doors.

She found nothing. It did not stop her looking. Spurred her on even more. It had taken over from her desire to find out about the machine, wearing her down. And all the time she wandered about worrying whether or not she was paranoid, she was fretting because she knew she was wasting time. Yet there was nothing she could do. It was becoming more and more difficult to concentrate, more and more difficult to escape the destructive loop, more and more difficult to believe in the world she inhabited.

Perhaps that was why she found herself standing in front of a screen, staring at a moving image of a place that was completely different from the stale, aseptic world in which she was the ghost. It was a poor looking neighbourhood. Narrow streets packed with tired people, old and ramshackle buildings, tawdry. In places there were ruins, houses that had collapsed, rubble pushed off the streets and pathways. And everywhere, she noticed, beginning to take an interest, there were uniforms.

It was a distant view and could have been any city. At first glance. Certain elements reminded her of Makamba after the invasion, especially everyday life continuing in altered flows around the military presence. Other elements made it clear this was a long way from the city she thought of as home. There were trees in the top right corner. The clothes the people were wearing were wrong. The clothes. The uniforms. She looked again, leaning closer to the screen, berating herself as she did so.

Trying not to think too much about what she was doing, she reached up and, with both hands, made signs in front of the screen. Nothing happened. She frowned, replayed the actions in her mind. Tried again more slowly. This time the whole picture began to move. The streets she had been looking at slid off to one side to be replaced on the other by different ones. The picture kept moving, revealing different buildings, diverse districts, narrow views of distant backgrounds, a broad and empty thoroughfare and, confirming what had become obvious to her, the open plaza in front of the Citadel in which she was now a prisoner.

She tried to make the picture move in different directions or move closer to the small figures that inhabited the streets, but all it did was swing slowly back the way it had come until she was fixed again on the district that had first caught her attention. If she could see that, though, perhaps there were ways of seeing other parts of the city, perhaps even into the Citadel itself.

Before she could even think about how she might manipulate the image or change it, the screen quivered and she felt a wave of nausea sweep through her. She staggered and was left weak and sweating. Above her the lights dimmed and she dropped to find herself outside the dark room.

She had no desire to return to her cell. There was too much new information to assimilate. So, as the door opened, she straightened herself, determined this time to see something of the interior. For some reason, she took a deep breath before she stepped over the threshold. Looking round in what little light managed to bleed in from the dim corridor outside she saw vague shapes that vanished as the door closed.

Still holding her breath, she waved her hands, edging toward a wall and feeling her way round. She had not managed to stay conscious this long on previous occasions. Long before she found a panel, she had to take a breath. Expecting to black out as she always had before, she braced herself. Although she felt even more nauseous, she managed to stay awake and resumed her groping until she felt the frame at the edge of what she hoped was one of the panels.

Recalling the symbol for light, she drew on the surface and was rewarded with a room flooded with harsh brightness. It was like a physical pain and she closed her eyes, blinking with her head bowed until she became accustomed to it. As she did so, she listened to the whisper of voices from all around her.

There was no one there, of course. The voices continued their whispered conversation and she ignored them as, one hand on the wall for support, she walked round the edge of the room looking at the panels. Opposite the door there jutted from the wall a narrow, sloping shelf. This had panels set into its surface. None of them seemed to work. Or maybe she did not know how to make them work. It did not altogether surprise her. They had a different look about them as if they were modelled on the other panels but made by someone else or for some altogether different purpose. It did not surprise her very much either that when she finished her circuit of the room and reached the door again it would not open. She stared at it for a while and then, exhausted, her stomach rebellious, she took weary steps across to what she had so far avoided – the table that filled the centre of the room.

In all superficial respects it resembled the one on which she knew she now lay. She climbed on and stretched out. Nothing else in the room was working so she thought she might rest awhile without fear of anything happening.

She relaxed on the hard, flat table top; lay her hands flat on the surface and felt its warmth. When it began to take her in, her first thought was that she was losing consciousness and would wake in her cell. When she realised she was melding, it was too late, and she simply didn't have the strength to climb back off.

There wasn't time to worry, let alone time to consider what happens if you meld when you were already on a table somewhere else. The voices around her faded and another became apparent. It had a different quality to the others and although she couldn't understand what he was saying, there was no doubting it was Zamler who spoke.

She tried to pick out individual words. It was not easy. He gabbled away, excited and angry whilst everything around her and within her took on a curious quality. It was like being close to a fire. Everything was partially lit with a flickering that seemed to cast deep shadows although, in truth, everything looked the same. It was like she could see everything but only understand small parts of it. At the same time a smokiness was blowing hither and yon on an erratic breeze she could not feel, obscuring some parts of the wider view, revealing others, eventually blowing into her eyes so that she could no longer see at all.

Underlying the vagueness, hidden by the obscurity, there was a sense of yet another layer, of something else with which she should be connecting. The feeling that had haunted her. With what little of her senses she had left, she grasped into obscurity, trying to find and make contact with this new level. There was something there, of that she was now certain. Quite what it was still eluded her. Every time she thought she was getting close it seemed to drift off in another direction.

It was frustrating. As well as her own curiosity, there was an imposed urgency to the task. Something was pushing her on. It made no difference, however, because she did not understand what she was meant to be doing. She had never been awake at this stage. Indeed, she had always assumed that once she entered the dark room, she blacked out and was returned to her cell. It seemed instead that there was more going on and for that to work she needed to be unconscious.

Of course, now she was there on the new table and wide awake, slipping into further darkness was a thought easier to conceive than it was an action to undertake. She tried emptying her head. She tried relaxing and slipping into sleep. None of it made any difference. The table had her. She felt comfortable. Yet, the more she tried not to try, the harder it became.

Hearing Zamler's increasingly agitated voice didn't help. Especially when it occurred to her that he was agitated because she wasn't carrying out the tasks she was there to perform. Tasks she must have undertaken before. In the end, she shrugged. There was nothing she could do, so it was no use trying or anyone else shouting at her about it.

In that moment, distracted as she was from the task, she was able to step forward. That was the only way she could think of what she did that made sense, even though she still lay on both tables. Quite what she had stepped into she did not know, but it welcomed her, soothed her, and, with precise movements, enclosed her. For a moment there was complete darkness and then she was aware of herself, of something that fitted comfortably, of her own scent as if she had been there many times before.

And then she could see.

Despite all she had been through, all the strange things she had witnessed and done, this both awed and frightened her. Not because she saw unusual things, but because it seemed that her vision had been changed, that someone had altered her eyes so that now she could only see in a particular way. She blinked. Nothing changed. She tried to back her head away from whatever had embraced her. She was stuck fast and there was no escape.

Panic began to scratch frantically at the door of her sanity. She was breathing in short, shallow gasps. Strange colours and shapes moved and flickered in front of her. It wasn't like an image on one of the screens. She was seeing it directly and it truly scared her. It did not matter that what she saw made no sense. What mattered was that Zamler had done this. All the beatings and the other torture, the starvation and the constant drugging might have hurt her, damaged her, left her a wreck and messed up her mind, but she was still fundamentally Jeniche Lusor Remai. Now he had stolen her sight.

She had teetered on the brink of insanity for months and now she felt the edge disintegrating beneath her feet. Had it not been for the child, she would have gone, let herself fall quietly into the abyss and been thankful for the oblivion.

It was the action, the young girl reaching forward and picking up a doll, that allowed her to make sense of what she could see with her altered vision, pick shapes out of the flickering colours and build them into a simple street scene. She moved her head and saw more. It was her eyes. Her vision. She was there.

Panic subsided. Anger did not. She knew what to do with anger, how to channel the fire. It gave her a chance to gather herself and step back from the perilous edge, devote herself to understanding, learning to see in this new way. Breathless still at the depth and detail, she took a few moments to slow her breathing. It was another assault on her being and she would not bow beneath it.

Without moving anything but her eyes she saw shapes, colours, and textures, sensed distances, felt movement as much as she saw it, was even aware of it in places she could not actually see. She could hear as well, although indistinctly as if there were a keffiyeh covering her ears.

The street in front of her was fairly broad and busy. People walked back and forth, lingered by market stalls, gossiped. It seemed like any street scene. Yet like the Makambans, these people were wary, always watchful. Except the young girl who sat on a doorstep close by playing with her doll, just as Shooly had done all those years ago. Jeniche watched, taking pleasure in the child's game, became aware of a steady, rhythmic noise. Hands appeared and snatched the child up, pulling her through the door. Across the street, people crowded up against the walls.

Even though sounds were muted she recognized the approach of horses, two abreast; marked the familiar uniform when they came into view. With so much movement and so much to observe with all her enhanced faculties – the speed and position of the horses as they trotted past, the flicker of light from the harness, the grim, tired faces of the horse soldiers, the disposition of all their weapons – other things did not register. Not until afterwards when the shooting started. Things like the fact that all the people left on the street were men.

The long line of horses passed and she could hear them moving away when the first shot made her jump where she stood. Stood. Standing. She was standing. But how was she standing? She was flat on her back on a table. In the dark. Seeing a street scene. Standing in a street. Watching people run past, seeing people fall.

The fighting surged fiercely around her. Mounted soldiers reappeared, galloping through the crowd with the riders lashing out with swords. More mosket fire, muffled yet close by. And for a moment the street was empty and silent. A puff of smoke drifted past. Then more people appeared, emerging from near-by buildings and alleys as if forming up ready to do battle.

They were a poor collection. Old men and youths for the most part, half starved, poorly dressed and with very few weapons. Jeniche felt sorry for them. They stood little chance against well-trained cavalry and moskets. But it seemed this was not the first time they had fought. She frowned. Vague memories dredged from the wreckage of her own mind spoke of other skirmishes.

That was when she started walking. It was not something she had chosen to do. It was not something she wanted to do. Her legs had been moved for her. She felt the pressure of something against them, felt something flex her knees, felt her feet find their place on the ground. And it filled her with dread.

She tried to fight it, but keeping her legs still was not an option open to her. The same with her arms. And when she focussed back on the gathering crowd she saw them looking directly at her, the pale faces of nightmare with expressions of horror and fear. They panicked and struggled to get away, people crowding the only exits from the street.

There was a strange sensation of leaning forward. It felt like falling, as if somehow she had been tipped over. And then a hand came into her field of vision. Large, heavy, reaching for an elderly man who lay sprawled over the top of a young woman. Jeniche could not tell if he had fallen or if he was trying to shield her. It made little difference. The hand moved inexorably down to him and the fear in his face gave way to resignation as it gripped his throat and lifted him and crushed the life from him.

The hand.

Her hand.

Chapter Twenty

Shadows hid her from everything but that horrific, searing memory. She sat on the floor, her back in the corner, knees up and embraced by her arms. Cabinets and walls loomed above her, dark shapes, inert and threatening. Beyond the shadow there was a profound darkness through which no path could be seen or imagined, blinded as she was by the one bright and awful picture.

She had felt used before; had walked away from all that might have been safe and gone out into the world for that very reason. Tricked, ignored, abused, tortured, violated in so many ways. But this... Letting go of her knees, she raised a trembling right hand and held it in front of her face. How could she have been made to do such a thing? How could she have become so blind, so weak?

Everything shivered and blurred as the tears began again, filling her eyes and running down over her cheeks and lips. Everything blurred but the memory. The look of fear on the old man's face, the look of realisation and resignation. How?

How could she have killed so casually? Why had she not been able to stop that hand? Her hand. The one that—

Her howl filled the vast room and echoed off into the distance, roaming corridors and shivering in spaces that caught it for a while before sending out faint calls in return like fading ghosts. And emerging from the dying sound there were urgent whispers that persisted. Voices. In her head.

She pushed herself further back into the corner, hands over ears, eyes tight closed. And there, still, was that old man's face, bewildered, fearful, and finally accepting; there, still, were the sibilant whispers. There, also, the relentless cascade of other visions: all the people she had known who were dead, all the strangers who had faced her and died, all the alleys, streets, and battlefields strewn with the ones who would never go home, their last hours lived in a fevered nightmare of fear.

Further still she pushed against the wall and in the desperate dark felt something give, felt the tears evaporate beneath the heat of an anger seething deep within her.

Kicking out her legs, she twisted, felt herself running, and could not tell for the moment whether it was her or whether it was someone controlling her. Stopped. Exulted in the freedom. Began to run again, weaving between cabinets and blank faced columns that loomed suddenly out of the dark, racing along narrow corridors, careening round corners, passing through open doorways, clattering over gratings and leaving the echoes behind.

She kept running until a pain cut her side and, for some reason, she thought of Alltud; she kept going, bent over the searing crease, her lungs afire. And still she kept going, exhaustion blunting her faculties so that she was bumping into things, welcoming the hurt, finding it harder to climb to her feet each time she fell, but managing because she knew the next collision or the one after that might just numb her, might just drive the pain and the despair into the permanent darkness where she could follow.

The voices trailed her for a while, a billowing cloak of shadows in the darkness, whispering, pleading. She no longer wanted to hear, distrusted what they might have to say. The last voice she had heard properly had beaten her down and raped her soul, torn her apart inside, created out of the broken parts a monster, a twisted beast that he forced to stalk through the nightmares of others.

And then in the darkness there was silence and she stumbled on, legs atremble, collapsing against some hard corner, dropping into a welcome dark, curled around the tiny, shivering spark of light that was the real Jeniche.

Blood had dried in a thin brown line across her face, cracking as she moved into wakefulness, flaking from an eyelid as she opened her eyes. Stiff and cold, she stared at the floor on which her head rested, shivering at the sudden sense of déjà vu.

After a cursory testing of the mobility of her limbs, she pushed herself into a sitting position. All the aches and pains she had come to expect and accept accompanied the move. So far, so normal. What was not normal were the surroundings. There was nothing that resembled the poor excuse for a bed, no hole in the floor, no cold, grey walls damp to the touch.

Wherever she was, it was much larger than the cell in which she had expected to find herself. Normally when she blacked out in the machine, she woke on her mattress, always out of nightmare and often to the sound of guards bringing in food or arriving to carry her back to the room where Zamler worked.

Rubbing at the blood, and prodding gingerly at the cut on the side of her forehead, she gathered her limbs in general order and climbed to her feet. A moment of dizziness soon passed. The cut was sore, bruised, and slightly sticky as she had, perhaps, caused it to start bleeding again. She frowned, wondering if it was possible to harm yourself physically in the machine. Or perhaps a dream had filled in the blanks in reality.

Her head began to throb so she abandoned the thinking. There was no point to it. She simply didn't know enough about what was happening, about what all these machines could do. She didn't even know whether they were Pilgrim machines or built by people of the pre-Evanescence cultures. There hadn't been any of the usual nausea for a while, but given what she had been put through, that meant very little.

The only thing she could do for now was accept what was in front of her and work from there. The best course of action, she decided, was to keep herself busy with the here and now and, with any luck, prevent those awful memories from swamping her. She couldn't blank them out. It was like the image was burned into the back of her eyes. However, she could put the blame where it belonged and try to keep those visions in their place. Whatever that place might be.

She would have shaken her head to rattle her thoughts back into order, but she knew that would be a mistake. Instead, she stepped forward into the shadow and felt an almost overwhelming gratitude when light panels came on, filling the space with a muted glow – enough to see by without dazzling her.

The first thing she noticed was that her eyes were back to normal. She saw everything in the way she had always seen them. It came as a great relief and meant that it was an effect of the machine at some level or other. What she saw wasn't promising. Directly in front of her was a wall lined with shelves. As she turned slowly on the spot, she could see the other walls were the same. And down the centre of the length of the room were more shelves in a wooden framework. There didn't seem to be a door. She shrugged. It hadn't been a hindrance in the past so she wasn't going to worry about it now.

Her choice was simple. She could stand and wait to see what happened. Or, because she had the feeling that being in the room was the something that had already happened, she could explore.

The shelves contained neatly stacked items of varying sizes along with many hundreds of boxes of some material she was not familiar with. It was smooth to the touch, translucent, light, giving a dull sound when she rapped it with a knuckle. It didn't break when it was dropped, either, something Jeniche discovered almost immediately.

She had stepped up to the nearest shelf. It seemed as good a place to start as any. All it contained was a number of the boxes. The nearest one slid easily as she pulled it toward her and the lid came off without any problem. Inside lay a doll.

Without being aware of how she had let go, the box fell to the floor. It hit a lower shelf on the way down, began to twist, hit her ankle and clattered noisily in the quiet space. She stared down at the container and its spilled contents: a filmy wrapping of pearlescent material in which the doll had lain and the doll itself.

It was as bright and new as the day she had bought it all those years ago. From a toymaker in the Old City of Makamba. After several weeks work on the docks so that it could be bought with honest money. A Birba or jester in his traditional garb of back to front robes. Given into the hands of young Shooly so that her rooftop court of dolls should be complete.

How was it here? she wondered. A doll given as a gift all those years ago so that child and thief might play together beneath the warm summer stars and be happy. She bent and picked up the box, packing the doll away with loving care, reluctant to put the lid back on. She slid the box back onto the shelf leaving the other boxes there untouched. She knew what she would find inside and did not think she could cope. The dolls were so much part of the life of that frail girl, her one freedom from ill health. To find them here, all of them, would be to bring that life to an end.

The pull of the other shelves, however, was inexorable. She moved with slow steps down the room, noting books, instruments, and a large telescope covered by a sheet, knowing that they could not possibly have been pulled from the rubble of the university in such a pristine condition. An idea took on misty form in the void.

She continued to explore. Amongst the items that she recognized there were so many more she did not. Clothes, jewellery, books, tools, furniture, and other items from all parts of the world she had visited and doubtless from parts she had never even heard of. Some were wondrous, exotic, and redolent of strangeness. Most were mundane. Each had a unique story to tell.

Long before she had completed her searches, she came across a shelf that made her stop. Unlike everything else, lying neatly and in a pristine state, as if conjured from memory and recreated here, these items were grimy and worn, beyond all hope of being depicted in any other way. Two sets of clothes, intensely familiar, travel-stained, worn and torn, probably unable to survive another washing. Even though they were devoid of any scent, she could recall their smell vividly, drew comfort and sorrow from that recollection of Alltud. She scrubbed away a tear. A long, straight sword lay beside the clothes, also familiar. Two pairs of boots that were worn at the heel and in desperate need of a clean. Lifting the smaller pair from the shelf, she wondered what would happen if she put them on her feet.

Not wishing to tempt fate in this rare, calm moment, she put them back. She also saw the belt lying there, her name incised in the leather that hid the amulet, the pair of Tunduri swords sheathed in their scabbards. And the ring. Another dead friend and a debt to be honoured. She picked it up, placed it on her thumb, removed it and put it back on the shelf. A long sigh escaped her as the idea coalesced and she looked around. Somewhere in the room there must be a panel. There were things that had to be done.

It didn't take long to find.

Because she was tired, because she was still seething with anger on a subterranean level, it took some time to think things through. She could no longer afford to drift or allow herself to be buffeted by what was happening. She had already come close to being swamped. The next time her fingers would not have the strength to keep her on the raft and she knew by then she would not care.

She faced the grey screen. "What else can you show me?"

It came out as a whisper. The machine heard.

In front of her the screen glowed faintly and an image appeared. She smiled for a moment. Her idea had been correct. She was beginning to understand. And the machine wouldn't need all the fancy finger work she had been learning, not in here.

She stared for a while at the image not understanding it. There was a circle, slightly broader around the circumference and criss-crossed with the finest and faintest of lines in different colours. It reminded her of something, but she was too tired to be able to work it out for herself.

"I don't understand," she said, her voice a little louder, a little stronger. "Is this the Citadel?"

The image flickered and began to expand. Jeniche had a momentary sensation of moving toward the screen, of falling, until she adjusted to the movement. The faint coloured lines vanished and pinpoints raced by in a complex pattern and also disappeared. In their place shapes began to form, shifting, expanding, and moving out of sight.

"Wait, wait."

The image froze. She had seen something.

"Can you... what I saw just now."

Slowly the image began moving again, a reverse of what had been displayed before.

"There. That's it. Stop."

The image froze again. Jeniche stepped forward, her finger tracing a line.

"That's the Arbiq shoreline on the Mittel Sea."

Symbols appeared on the screen, labelling features. She could not read them, but knew what some of them must be, Alboran in particular. It was just like one of the maps in the library on Pengaver.

"Can you show me Ynysvron?"

Nothing happened.

"Makamba?"

The image remained frozen.

"Tundur?"

A sequence of flickers and the image was replaced. New symbols appeared. She could make little of it. Tundur had no seashore and she wasn't sure what scale was being used although the heavier symbol probably marked Rasa, the capital. There was a still a lot to learn. And the machine clearly had no knowledge of some things. Names that had come into being since it was built or since the Evanescence. Which must mean that not only was it very old, but also that it had been dormant for a long time, cut off from the new world growing in the ruins of the old.

"Can you show me where I am now?"

More flickering and a complex pattern of lines appeared. She cocked her head one way and then the other, finally making sense of the street plan. The sinuous line running roughly top to bottom must be the river which meant they oriented their maps with north at the top. The thin pale lines must be streets and alleys. And the dark circle off to the right must be the Citadel.

"Where is Alltud?"

No response.

"The Citadel."

The circle expanded.

"Where are prisoners kept?"

The circle expanded even more and another pattern of lines appeared weaving between rectangles of different size and shape. To one side a small dot began blinking indicating a long corridor from which a series of small rooms sprouted like fruit on a vine. Bitter fruit if those cells were anything like her own.

Jeniche shrugged. Perhaps a cell block. However, she was kept in one and there had never once been a hint of Alltud there. And the courtyard where she thought she had once seen him had been on a different level. Until she knew how to ask the right questions she wouldn't get the answers she wanted and at the moment she didn't think she had the time. Not for everything. But there was one particular item. Something she had glimpsed and noted.

"The other side of the river."

The familiar flickering resolved to a different and more detailed image. This was more than a simple map. She could see, faintly, the surface of the great rocky river cliff and the spur of the mountain, the twisting peak of the Grauberg, as well as the mountainous terrain beyond. More clearly depicted were rooms within. She made a mental readjustment. They were not rooms. They were caverns. Immense caverns, stretching for many miles and delving deep into the earth.

Jeniche stood for a long time gazing at the complex underground network. She had seen something similar before, but for real and from the inside with all its broad tunnels, rooms, halls, and secret machines.

"But if Zamler had access to all that, why was he searching the world?"

She had not been aware she had asked the question out loud until the machine replied.

"Because he has not been allowed to know it is there."

Chapter Twenty-One

She saw the mosket fired: the man lifting the weapon and resting it on the balcony rail to take aim, the flare from its muzzle and the lift of the barrel as it recoiled, the trajectory of the projectile. It painted a thin, pale track across the market square above the heads of the people fighting there. Despite the clarity of her enhanced vision, she was too startled to react and would not have had time to move in any case. The lead balls travelled at a frightening speed. Had it not been for the machine she would not have seen it at all.

The bullet hit her in the very centre of the chest. She looked down as her hands came up to feel for the damage. There was a shallow crater there about the size of her fist. For a human it would have been instantly fatal, but the skin of the statue hadn't been pierced.

It was the perfect opportunity. She offered up silent thanks and a prayer of protection to her unknown assailant before whispering the instructions she had learned from the machine. The scene flickered for a moment and then faded to darkness.

On the surface, nothing much had changed when it came back on. There was still a nasty street battle going on all around her. People were still shooting at her. Others looked at her uncertainly. She was the only who knew there was now a significant difference. With a smile, she stepped backwards to find herself lying on the table in the darkened inner room.

Frantic voices filled the air, muted by the machine. They were talking over one another, arguing. Loudest of all was the shouting of Zamler. Again she smiled. Up until the point the bullet had struck the statue, Jeniche had been 'inside' it and resisting, as best she could, the control imposed upon her. She could have disrupted Zamler's influence at any time thanks to what she had learned. From the outset, however, she had been wary of making it too obvious. The bullet was a perfect excuse.

The commands the machine had taught her had cut Zamler's lines of communication. Everything she had seen had also been seen by him up to that point. It is how he had been able to feed her the requisite instructions whilst she was drugged. She controlled the statue and he controlled her. First she had cut the view and then she had switched the statue off. Presumably it now stood immobile in the market square where units of the Occassan military were fighting civilians.

Through the babble, she had heard Zamler say something about trouble makers. If he really thought that, he was a fool. She had survived long enough in Makamba under occupation to know this was an organised resistance, one that knew the streets and alleys, one that was able to slip through houses and over rooftops, through cellars and tunnels, disappear in one place and form up in another. One that was armed, no matter how lightly. One that was desperate.

Light-headed, she sat up and swung her legs over the side of the table. It was the first time since just before Alltud had been shot that she had control. The sudden memory of that made her realise just how precarious it all was. Despite the seeming reality of what she still called the dark room, she was lying helpless on a table in another room altogether, surrounded by Zamler and his assistants.

Everything she had done up to that point had been the easy bit, even the months of torture. Now it was going to get dangerous because, until that point, Zamler had needed her alive. The moment he suspected she was playing a double game he would, at the very least, pull her off that table and have her thrown back in her cell. At worst... She knew he had a disregard for life and was capable of violence. She comforted herself with the thought she wouldn't see it coming. As comforts go, it didn't do much to ease her fear.

Once the light-headedness had passed, she dropped down to the floor and crossed to the panel directly opposite the table's head. There she began to draw the complex series of symbols she had been shown. Twice she had to stop, go back, and start again and even then she was worried she had forgotten the sequence as the screen remained dark. For some reason, the next screen along lit up and she stepped across to it. Not knowing what else to do, she went through it all again and this time felt a tingling jolt.

Zamler's muted voice ranted on. She returned to the table knowing that she would find out soon enough if this had worked. Climbing back on, she took a moment to think of Alltud, drew in a deep breath, and then exhaled as she lay flat on her back.

Immediately her head came to rest on the flat surface, she felt herself sinking, felt the familiar step forward, felt her limbs make contact as the statue embraced her. After a moment's darkness, her vision was restored and the street came back into view. She listened, but Zamler's voice did not seem to have changed. It may take him a few moments, she reasoned with herself. So she stood still and began to accustom herself to the peculiar colours and enhanced senses now available to her.

The market, somewhere in the northern part of Amparo to judge by the buildings, was empty except for corpses and the badly wounded. It was still difficult to hear, a defect in the statue she assumed, but everything else was clear. Even down to the tiny movement right on the edge of vision where a rat scurried along a gutter. And then another where someone peered round the edge of a window shutter.

Before long, the street was busy again although it remained silent throughout. A small group had appeared with youngsters keeping watch from vantage points whilst the adults moved quickly from body to body. The injured were moved first, loaded onto planks of wood and carried away. Their own dead were retrieved next, vanishing just as completely. Finally, in a move that surprised Jeniche given the danger it placed on the people, they re-appeared and collected the dead Occassan soldiers, laying them out neatly along one side of the street before vanishing.

At no time did Jeniche hear Zamler respond to what was going on in front of her or feel any attempt on his part to regain control of the statue through her. So she decided to take a risk and turned the statue's head. It was a bizarre feeling. She knew her head was still yet she also felt herself turning it, turning the statue's head with it.

Still there was no reaction. Indeed, Zamler had quietened down. He was still talking, but it was part of the general chatter that she heard from the main room where she really lay. If anything was real any more.

It was time, then, to go a step further and test just how much autonomy she now had. She moved her left leg and took a pace forward. A sudden movement startled her and she instinctively turned to see where it had originated. The street swept before her eyes, shop fronts, doorways, shuttered windows. A young boy, tucked into the entrance of a narrow alley had seen the statue move and been caught off balance, taking a step out onto the pavement. Now he was too scared to move. Jeniche turned away from him and began walking along the street in the other direction.

The machine would no doubt be able to tell her where the statue was, but she wanted to get her bearings for herself, take a look at what was happening elsewhere. She didn't have to wait for long.

At the end of the street she turned and saw more fighting, a running skirmish that had become entrenched with opposing parties using public buildings on opposite sides of the street as temporary fortresses. Beyond the battle was an opening onto what looked like a square. She would be able to see from there where the Citadel was. All she needed to do was walk through the fighting up ahead. Which is exactly what she did.

Vibration registered which she assumed were blows from weapons and mosket shots aimed at the statue. Resisting the temptation to duck and run for shelter, she just kept going. One pair of combatants, wrestling on the ground with knives, rolled into her path. She lifted them into the air and put them to one side. They were so astonished that they stopped fighting and she could see them staring up at the statue as she turned back toward her goal.

Several times she had to stop and pluck people up to put them out of harm's way and as she reached the entrance to the square she discovered other things she could do. In the first instance she found she could climb and revelled in the very thought, hands as dextrous as her own gripping the stonework with greater strength and hauling the statue up to a cornice where a soldier was perched with his mosket.

He saw the statue coming and had only one way to go. As Jeniche reached him, he was scrambling backwards as fast as he could up a steeply pitched roof. She caught him by the ankle. Whilst she used one hand to let him down into the gutter where he had been perched, she pulled the mosket out of his grip with the other. When he was safe, she broke the weapon in half and threw it down to the ground.

Having climbed back down it was to discover a small troop of horsemen forming up. The horses were skittish and the riders pulled sharply at the reins. She knew Trag would be angry to see the beasts used this way. As she approached the cavalry troop, she wondered if this is how horses had seen him, a great statue of enormous strength, not someone to be argued with. She singled out the troop's leader and with a deft movement caught hold of the bridle of his horse.

She looked up at the rider wishing she could speak or make a face, but her actions seemed to have been enough. The man looked at the statue for a moment, called something over his shoulder and then sheathed the long sabre he had been holding aloft. Jeniche nodded her head and let go.

Without looking back, she crossed the square, scanning the skyline as she went. It was late afternoon. Deep shadows filled some alleys and streets and she used it to orientate herself, heading off with the statue's shadow ahead of her. There was less evidence of unrest here although when she pushed into another street it cleared of people as soon as the statue was seen.

At the next crossroads she stopped. Despite the fact she was lying down and perfectly still, it was tiring driving the statue. Her limbs ached and her head hurt as she had to think about all the actions she was taking. No doubt someone experienced in directing the statue would have an easier job of it, working by instinct, but she hadn't had the time to get used to it at this sophisticated level whilst conscious. The other reason she'd stopped was because she had come face to face with herself.

For a moment, she thought that Zamler had sent another statue out to hunt her down. Then she realized how stupid that would have been given how easy it would be to disable her where she lay. And then she remembered that she had seen other statues on her journey from the airship field all that time ago. They had been standing, like this one, at crossways and on plinths. Abandoned perhaps from an earlier time when they were in proper working order.

This one looked considerably worse for wear. Its left hand was missing and the head looked partly crushed. Perhaps they had been put up as ornaments by people who did not know what they were. Or perhaps they had an altogether more complex and darker history. It worried Jeniche. All this ancient technology. Here beneath Zamler's fingertips. And so much more that he did not know about.

She caught herself shaking her head and wondered if the statue she inhabited had done the same. The machine that enabled all of this had deliberately kept Zamler in the dark about what was on his own doorstep. As a result, Occassans had descended on countries round the world like locusts, destroying whatever stood in their way to feed the Order's ambition. She dreaded to think what would have happened had Zamler been able to deploy weapons like this statue.

It was bad enough they had airships and moskets, things they may have developed on their own. But to be deliberately seeking out ancient means of destruction after all that had happened centuries ago. That really was insanity. And weapons like that in the hands of the insane... They had to be stopped. Somehow.

She left the other statue behind and continued on through what now seemed to be a deserted city. Glimpses above the skyline of the towering structures of the Citadel guided her until she was standing on the broad concourse in front of the closed gates. Light from the setting sun painted the stonework and its grisly decoration, many more fresh corpses hanging there with the old. And more statues.

Desperately tired, she took the time to scan the corpses, learning to focus on faces as if there were a telescope through which to look. It was a grisly task yet she needed to be certain. None of them looked familiar so she disengaged from her own statue and lay in dim light staring at the ceiling of the dark room. In the background, voices chattered quietly. Her mind was churning, wondering.

"Those other statues," she asked. "Could I waken them as well? Could I control them?"

There was a long silence from the machine. She felt sleep taking hold of her, or something else, perhaps the drugs that Zamler gave her starting to take effect. Sounds died away. Lights dimmed. And into her fading consciousness drifted a quiet voice.

"You have the potential, but you do not have the power. You do not have the key."

Chapter Twenty-Two

It never ceased to make him wonder how the lad had survived having claustrophobia on an airship. Maybe his passion for flying had enabled him to cope with the tiny windowless cabins, or maybe knowing he could walk out the door whenever he wanted was his safety mechanism. In the cell, it had been different. Alltud stared up at the rough slats that were the underside of the top bunk and listened to the quiet breathing. At least the boy didn't snore. Which had been the only saving grace of the whole sorry affair.

Rolling onto his side with care he stared out into the gloom of the small cell. What little he could see of the cramped room was courtesy of an oil lamp in the corridor. It did little more than help differentiate between the darkness of solid objects and the lesser dark of open space. There wasn't much of either. Bunk beds, a hole in the floor, four grey stone walls, and a door. That was their world now.

He had not moved cautiously out of any consideration for Kenak. The lad had the top bunk, so Alltud reserved the right to heave himself about if he so desired. The caution was out of respect for his own wellbeing, of the wound that had healed badly. After all this time it still hurt, some days worse than others.

He scratched at his beard in the dark; suppressed a cough which brought tears to his eyes as pain seared his side. Pulling his knees up slightly to ease the ache, he stared deeper into the dark and wished he could get back to sleep. At least there he felt no discomfort, did not have to contemplate his dismal existence.

So why, he wondered, was he awake? If there was one thing he still did well, it was sleep, especially now the guards had stopped making him do things that hurt his side. All that lifting had been killing him. Bastards. Give him a sword and he'd show them what he was worth.

The thought depressed him even more because he knew the truth. He was a broken down old man, a bony relic who was probably going to die in this place never having found out what had happened to the one soul friend he had ever had.

Anger burned through him and he climbed out of the bunk, hauling himself upright and stretching those bits that would stretch without bringing tears to his eyes. When he got like this, which wasn't so often these days, he had to pace, tire himself so he could get back to sleep. There wasn't much room in the cell but at least it was still reasonably warm and he could go barefoot, letting the lad sleep.

Since those cold, bleak days at the beginning, when they had been dragged from the wreckage of the *Trepaharos*, Kenak had never once complained, never once lost his temper. Given the injustice of his detention, it spoke either of great courage or immense, animal-like docility. Alltud knew it was courage even if Kenak would never admit to it. And not just courage.

Kenak had talked Alltud through his darkest moments of rage, frustration, and loss. It had kept them both sane, whispering their stories to one another.

Three paces one way, turn, three paces the other. Round and round, passing the door and its metal grille, passing it again going the other way, beginning to wonder, eventually stopping and grabbing the bars.

Peering out into the dimly lit corridor he listened.

When he had first woken he had been too full of sleep to think properly. But now he stood there absorbing the silence, he began to wonder if he hadn't heard something, a noise that had woken him. It would have to be something unusual. He had long grown used to the sounds of his jail, the groans, the sighs, the snoring, the frightened shouts of men waking from one nightmare into another, the sobbing.

Something unusual. He turned his head so his ear was to the bars and held his breath. Anything at all. Because the corridor was silent. As if everyone else had heard something, as if they too were all now standing at their doors in the dark. Listening.

"I don't care anymore," said Zamler. "Just get the table shut down. I'm not pulling her off. It might damage her and she's by far the best subject we've got."

The assistant backed away as quickly as he dared. They had tried everything. All he could think of now was to try it all over again so he urged his companions to look busy. Zamler put great value on the little cinnamon-skinned woman on the table. They knew he wasn't nearly so attached to his aides. And none of them wanted to be hung out on the walls.

Breathing a sigh of relief as a member of the BoR entered with a message for Zamler, the assistant turned and consulted with a colleague to see if there might be some other way to turn off the table. As they bent over a panel trying different combinations of symbols, he kept half an ear open for whatever news was being brought from the outside. All he heard was something about the Parade, the open space in front of the Citadel, so he turned his full attention back to the recalcitrant machine.

When Zamler spoke in his ear, he jumped.

"The Parade. Can you show me the Parade?"

The assistant began tracing symbols on the panel in front of him. From the corner of his eye he could see Zamler trying the same and having no better success.

"Anyone! Who is on the other tables?"

There was a hurried discussion and eventually one of the assistants raised a hand. Zamler pushed his way through the group. No one resisted, glad to be out of the way.

The panel showed a flickering image of the concourse in front of the Citadel.

"It's not an image we can move," said the young assistant. "But this is the Parade. And there's..."

Zamler leaned forward to peer at the image. He raised a hand and reached out to touch the screen as if afraid it would burn his fingers.

"No." Zamler's voice was a whisper.

With a slight shake of his head, he straightened and took a step back. The small group of assistants behind him exchanged furtive, puzzled glances. They were used to working in fear, but always knew what they were supposed to be doing. Seeing Zamler hesitant was like being hit by a wave and realising the ground was no longer beneath their feet.

The expression of confusion that sat uneasily on his face slowly metamorphosed into one of disbelief.

"How...?"

Zamler turned where he was standing and looked across the room to where Jeniche lay on the table. She was brightly lit. Immobile. On her face he saw the faintest trace of a smile.

"Shut it down! Shut it down and get her off the table!"

The disbelief had become realisation.

"Sir?"

"I don't care what damage it does to her. Get her off the table now!"

Zamler tried once again to shut the table down. Several of the senior assistants converged on the prone form of Jeniche. They reached out to grab hold of her and lift her away from the table's surface but try as they might they could not touch her. It was as if she was encased in an invisible jelly. They felt resistance in the air around her and no matter how hard they pushed, no matter how subtly they tried to invade the space about her body, they could not manage it. And at the panels, no matter what symbols they drew, nothing happened.

Only on one panel was there movement although everyone was too busy to notice. The flickering image of the Parade which showed a statue as it started walking again, across the field of vision and out of sight.

It was a thoughtful expression that had settled on Alltud's face as he stepped back from the cell door. He didn't stop at one step but took the other three that brought him up against the bunk beds. Without turning, eyes fixed on the door, he raised his left arm and felt along the edge of the upper bunk until he was close to the head. His hand kept exploring, his body contorted painfully.

At the last moment, he turned and in the faint light found his target. His hand reached out and covered Kenak's mouth. The young man's eyes opened wide in the dark and Alltud motioned him to be quiet. He saw the young Navigator frown and once he was certain the lad would keep his mouth shut, withdrew his hand. They had both been confined to the same cell long enough to know when to keep silent.

Kenak had no idea what it was about and Alltud doubted whether he could explain. Not without giving the impression he had finally lost his mind. Yet what he had seen with the side of his face pressed against the bars was still clear in his mind.

He had stood at the door for some while listening to the unusual silence. The impression of others listening grew stronger and he had shifted his head so he could peer along the length of the dimly lit corridor. There should have been a guard at the far end. He had a small stool which he placed on the corner so that he sat with his back to the sharp angle of the walls to help him keep awake. In the arch above there was a hook from which a lantern hung.

The lantern was still there, swinging slightly, the wick burning inside with a smoky light. It must have been left unattended for a while to get like that. Of the guard there was no sign. Alltud began to wonder if that was what he had heard. Someone calling for the guard. Someone... He had stopped speculating as nothing else came to mind as remotely possible. He was still trying to think of something when a shadow from around the corner, cast by another lantern, made him hold his breath. A few moments later, the shadow was followed by a shape.

Alltud couldn't understand it at first. He wasn't sure he did now. If it had been a dream it had been vivid and, judging by the noise from the other side of the door, he was still having it. Or maybe a nightmare, because the shape had moved into the light of the lantern in the archway to reveal a statue. That walked. Along the corridor.

At the first cell it stopped and peered in through the bars. A faint whimper could be heard and the statue turned away and moved out of sight, looking into the cell opposite. It worked its way slowly down the corridor checking carefully in each cell, clearly looking for someone. It was when it had stopped at the cell next but one to theirs that Alltud stepped back.

He barely had time to wake Kenak when the blank, blind face of the statue peered in at them. For the first time in their year and a half together, Alltud heard Kenak swear. He felt like doing so himself, especially when the statue didn't move away.

There was no longer a fire in the tidy hearth, but the room still looked luxurious and comfortable. The walls were decorated with elaborate hangings from various parts of the world. There was a beautifully made cupboard with delicately carved panels in the doors. A table with several upright chairs stood at one end on which were trays containing jugs of wine and goblets, clean and ready for use. There were luxurious rugs on the floor. There were books on shelves. There were comfortable chairs ranged around the hearth with lamps ready for lighting. Evening air kept the space fresh, sweetened by flowers growing on vines around the open windows.

Jeniche had seen the room before, a long time ago. She had been made to stand and watch Zamler as he ate before she had been hauled back to her cell; had been dragged in to listen to his rambling diatribes against those who had stolen his heritage, against the coming darkness. It was a lifetime ago. Maybe several. She could not remember much about the room itself. When you are starving and beaten and there is a table full of food in front of you, your gaze doesn't wander, even if your mind does.

She knew where it was though, with a little help from the machine. And into the silence of the room came a sound that was evidence of that. A distant cry. The clatter of a metal tray falling to a stone flagged floor. Booted feet running away. A moment's silence. Then the crash of wood as the heavy door was pushed off its hinges and tumbled to the floor in a shower of splinters and dust.

Stepping over the shattered door, the statue entered the room and stood looking round. It stared with its blank face at the table for a long time, took a step toward it and then swept everything to the floor. After a moment it turned and moved to one wall where it pulled down an embroidered cloth, returning to the table to lay it flat. Finally, it approached the cupboard, tore off the doors, and sorted through the contents.

They had gone as far as the guard station and found the place deserted. One corpse was discarded in a corner as if thrown there, a broken mosket dropped on top of the body. Beyond that, nothing. Many of the prisoners, as soon as they had been released, had gone staggering off without much thought to their situation. Kenak would have gone with them, mostly because he was hungry and wanted to look for food. Alltud stopped him.

In the small guard room, Alltud found swords in belts and helped himself to one. He doubted he had the strength for a serious fight. The weight of the steel made him feel better, though. Kenak refused to take one.

"I wouldn't know how."

Alltud looked at him; thought of Jeniche. "You're right, lad. It's not a thing you should ever have to learn. But stick close to me and don't go running off at the first sign of trouble."

Alltud helped himself to a second sword and, taking a deep breath, led the way back out into the corridor.

"Whatever is going on," he said quietly, "I am guessing the folk in here won't give up easily."

Kenak said nothing. He knew Alltud was right. He knew full well what the punishment for insurrection was. And trying to escape from the Order was no doubt exactly that. An act of insurrection. He rather wanted to go back to his cell, climb back into his bed and pretend it was a dream. The sound of mosket fire put an end to that. Something much larger was happening and he had no choice but to be involved.

The chamber that held the table where Jeniche lay was at the very top of the Pinnacle which crowned the Citadel. It had the one entrance on a high, broad terrace from which most of Amparo could be seen. There was a single, smaller inner room through an arch with a further door they had never been able to open, but that was all. Zamler and his assistants had given up trying to breach the invisible cocoon and remove Jeniche from the table. They had given up trying to manipulate the panels.

Some stood transfixed by the view on one of the screens, placed there by Jeniche. It was a view of what she could see via the statue. It was a view of the rooms and corridors she had explored and walked along since leaving Zamler's quarters. It was a view of those who had opposed the statue. It was a view of the ways in which they had fallen.

And now, on the screen, they could see a door. It wasn't one of the wooden doors to be found elsewhere in the Citadel. There was no joinery, no heavy metal hinges, and no lock. It was a blank smooth surface. And they watched with a terrified fascination as the statue put down the bundle it had been carrying and studied the doorway.

They all knew the door well. None of them knew how strong it was, how well it would resist the obvious strength of the statue they had made Jeniche control. When she raised the statue's fist, they watched. When the fist struck the door, they all flinched, despite seeing it was going to happen.

The sound was horribly loud in the chamber and they turned their heads back and forth between the screen and the vibrating door. One or two of them felt a degree of relief. The surface of the door had not been marked. Others, including Zamler, did not feel so confident.

As they watched, both hands reached up again and were laid flat against the door's surface. Jeniche did not remember much about it, but she had a vague notion that when she had been wheeled through, part of the door was still visible on her left. She leaned the statue against it and made it push in that direction.

To begin with, the door would not move. Zamler had engaged a locking mechanism. It was certainly holding against the strength of the statue. And then Jeniche smiled again. The screens went blank and there was a groan of dismay.

Outside, the statue stepped sideways to face a small, grey panel and Jeniche raised its hand, amazed again at just how delicate her control was as she used it to make signs and symbols with is fingertips. The door unlocked and slid sideways.

In the second or two it took to pick up its package and step in through the doorway, two of the assistants had tumbled out and scrambled away. The rest backed off to the far side of the room, some of them pushing into the small inner room at the back. The statue stepped forward to the table. It lay down the package beside the inert body of Jeniche and unwrapped the cloth before it reached down and tore the chains from her manacles. When it had finished, it turned and stepped back to the doorway, coming to a halt just inside the room.

There was a long silence. With all eyes fixed on the statue to see what it would do next, no one noticed Jeniche open her eyes. It wasn't until she climbed off the table that anyone knew she was awake and realised the statue was inert.

"Grab her," shouted Zamler, stepping forward himself. "While she's weak."

None of them got very far. The machine had lent Jeniche some strength and her hands grasped the hilts of her swords as she climbed off the table, drawing them with a quiet, metallic ring that filled the room. It was a terrifying sound made worse by the look on her face.

They had only ever seen her as a beaten, humbled subject strapped to a table, drugged and forced to do what Zamler or they had commanded. Now she stood, her face as impassive as the statue, flexing her wrists in a way that made the blades spin, whirling them as if her heavy manacles were made of silk. And her eyes, incandescent with a cruel rage, were fixed on Zamler.

"So you would kill us, like the savage you are." His whole body trembled. His breathing was ragged.

Jeniche said nothing. He glanced toward the partially blocked doorway.

"No one is coming to rescue you, Zamler," she said, her voice quiet and steady.

"What gives you the right to act as executioner?"

"Right? The same right that you had to turn the world upside down, displace millions, cause the death of thousands, and cause the death of my friends. No right at all. I have no right. But. I am the justified wrath of every soul you have ever taken and destroyed. I am the vengeance of every mother who lost a child to your twisted aspirations. I am the walker in the dark places you can never go. I am the scorpion in the desert. I am the shadow in the storm. I am death incarnate and the hatred in my face is the last thing you will ever see."

She stepped toward him and he backed up to the table. A dark patch appeared on the front of his trousers. A faecal stench filled the air. His eyes widened and his hands wavered defensively.

"You would not—"

Before he could finish, her blades passed each other in a horizontal sweep.

Zamler's head dropped sideways and hit the floor with a dull clunk as a fountain of hot blood rained down on them all.

PART THREE

Strike

Chapter Twenty-Three

The room was strewn with the dead. Jeniche had no memory of anything beyond the killing of Zamler. Even that was hazy, an event that involved someone else that she had witnessed from a distance. After that – nothing. Yet there she stood, alone with the slain.

They were scattered about the room and in the small annexe, most lying where they were struck down. One had tried to crawl to the door. Congealing trails of his last, painful movements were drawn through the dark, merging pools of blood on the floor. There was no pity in her heart for them, the men who had systematically beaten her and drugged her, the men who had violated her mind, the men who had forced her to do their killing for them, forced her to walk amongst the people in the city and tear their lives apart.

Dull of eye, she looked around the room. All she wanted was somewhere to sit, somewhere to lie down, somewhere to curl up and sleep. Forever. But you cannot butcher that many people in a confined space and leave somewhere clean to rest afterwards. So she stood, facing the statue in the doorway. Swaying. Swords held loosely, pointing at the floor on to which they dripped sticky gore.

There was no sense of passing time. She had no idea how long she remained like that, drifting into a dream without ever sleeping, eyes sore, shoulders aching, mind numb, no will left to move, no thoughts left to worry about it, no whispering in her head.

Alltud waved his free hand behind him and pulled a face to himself as he heard the others shuffling to a noisy stop. If they had been anywhere else in any other situation, he would have laughed, salted away the memory for long evenings in front of a fire when there was wine, food, good company ready for a story, and a thousand miles between that and any enemies.

Once they were more or less still, he edged forward to the corner and peered round, his sword upright and ready to block any blow. But there was nothing. Lanterns flickered along the length of the corridor and the dancing shadows provided the only movement. Yet it was from this direction he had heard something.

Taking his time, he examined the length of the corridor section by section. It wasn't easy as the light wasn't good. Which was exactly why he took his time. Once he had surveyed the far side and was happy the shadows concealed nothing, he motioned to the others to stay where they were and stepped as quietly as he could to the wall opposite. From there, with his back to the stones, he looked at the doorways he had not been able to see before.

A series of shadows, each the same. Except for one half way along. There the door was clearly ajar. He signalled one of his rag-tag band of followers forward and they sidled along each side of the corridor to the doorway. Kenak peered round the corner at them with fearful eyes. Alltud gave him what he hoped was a reassuring smile. It wasn't easy down there in the heart of the Citadel.

Once they were at the door, Alltud stepped forward, kicked it open, and rushed in. There was confusion in the darkness, a yelp and then whining.

"Lantern!" called Alltud.

Kenak brought one into the room and held it high. The light illuminated shelves piled with sacks and boxes. In the corner, a dog cowered, eyes glancing at the sack it had been trying to chew open.

"What is it?" one of the others called.

"A dog," replied Kenak. "Looking for food, I should think," he added pointedly for Alltud's benefit.

"Sounds like a good idea," said Alltud. He winked at Kenak.

He was tired of creeping round what was obviously an empty building with every sign of having been abandoned in a hurry. The dog was the first living soul they had seen in over an hour. The last one had been an elderly, myopic clerk called Turrance who had got lost. He had seen no one for a while and had elected to join Alltud's merry band of misfits.

They were all looking at him now with expectant expressions. Turrance, Kenak, Willat, who was the only one who had admitted to having lifted a sword before, and four other bewildered prisoners who had decided to take their chances with Alltud rather than look for a way out. Everyone else had disappeared the moment he and Kenak had unlocked their doors.

At first the emptiness had made him nervous. Guards didn't disappear from prisons just like that. There was bound to be someone lurking round the next corner waiting for them. And that meant fighting because he would not willingly go back in a cell. Then it had made him nervous because he began to wonder just what was happening on the outside to make them desert the Citadel so quickly and so comprehensively. And as for the statue that had pulled their cell door off its hinges and then walked away, he didn't even want to start trying to work that one out.

"There are very few soldiers in the Order," Turrance had explained. "And most of those are senior officers. They'll be out there, somewhere," he waved vaguely. "On their estates. Or abroad. It's much the same with the BoR except there are more of them."

"What about guards?" Kenak had asked him.

Turrance had shrugged. "Were there many prisoners?"

Alltud hadn't seen that many. Fifty perhaps. And most of those had been physical wrecks like himself. He had searched each cell, checked each bunk, gone looking for other cells and found none. That was why he had stayed when so many had fled. Looking for someone who wasn't there. And tired as he was, that was why he was still looking.

"Anyone know where the kitchens are?" he asked.

The kitchens had been located, bellies filled with the first decent food they'd had for more than a year, the dog had been fed and had attached itself to a delighted Willat, and sacks had been filled with provisions. After that, they ventured out to look for a secure place so that Alltud could continue his search of the Citadel knowing there was somewhere safe to return to, a place the others could rest and defend.

They climbed up through the levels, roaming the corridors and galleries, until they reached the base of the Pinnacle. At the end of one corridor, by the foot of yet more stairs, they found a room with a large fireplace and a ready supply of kindling in the form of a shattered door and smashed furniture. Turrance stood on the threshold, reluctant to enter.

"It's Zamler's room," he said.

Alltud shrugged. "Who's that?"

Kenak laughed nervously. "He's the Head of the Order."

They looked round the room.

"Someone doesn't like him," said Alltud.

"Not many do," whispered Willat.

Turrance cast a nervous glance along the corridor.

"Never mind that. I doubt he will be back in the near future. Let's find something to barricade the doorway and then you'll have somewhere safe to rest while I go looking."

"Looking where?" Turrance asked. "What for?"

Kenak, who was nearest, explained. "He has a friend he thinks might be here."

Alltud narrowed his eyes.

"But don't you think," asked Kenak, "that she got away when the airship went down?"

Alltud sighed. "I don't know. I hope so. I hope she's a long way from here. But I have to know."

"Airship?" asked Turrance. "The *Trepaharos*?"

"What do you know of that?" asked Alltud.

Turrance shrank away from the sword point, his hands in the air. Kenak intervened.

Alltud looked into the young man's worried face and lowered his sword. "Sorry," he said. His apology was for Kenak. Something about Turrance made him wary.

"Do you know anything?" asked Kenak.

"Were you on that?"

The others were busily lighting a fire in the hearth, trying to eavesdrop without looking like they were interested. Kenak and Alltud exchanged glances.

"I was apprentice Navigator," said Kenak. He had long since resigned himself to the likelihood that his promotion in the field had gone unrecorded.

Turrance nodded, but stared at Alltud.

"There was a young woman," said Alltud.

"I…"

"Well?"

The elderly clerk began to look like he wished he was by the fire listening covertly instead of being the centre of Alltud's hostile attention.

"I just see the paperwork," he said.

"And was there a name? Jeniche."

Turrance shrugged as if he didn't want to shrug, afraid to move one way or the other. Old habits don't easily die. "I…"

"Where would she be if she was here?" asked Kenak, recognising Alltud's impatience.

"Zamler. He… They take the pilgermen up to the top of the Pinnacle."

"Pilgermen?" asked Alltud.

Turrance shook his head and nodded at the same time. "I'm just a clerk."

Alltud looked at him, stony faced, thinking of Jeniche. Pilgrims? What could have possessed… He gave up and focussed back on Turrance. "Watch him," he said to the others, pointing to the clerk. "For your own safety. I'm going…" He shrugged and stepped out through the doorway.

Kenak watched him go. He looked back at the others by the fire and then slipped out into the corridor.

It was noises from the terrace outside that roused Jeniche from the torpor of exhaustion into which she had sunk. The statue, although standing abandoned in the doorway did not block it completely. Now it was inert it was of little use as a barrier and nothing in the world would have persuaded her to climb back onto the table.

Weak as she was, drained of all desire to move or to live in the world, she let her instincts take over. Watching as if from a great distance, she shifted her feet into a fighting stance and stood ready to defend herself.

It was dark beyond the doorway and she stood with her back to most of the lights in the room. Out in the open space visible beyond the statue, shapes moved. She raised her swords, dark now with congealed blood. The person inside her had gone to sleep, overwhelmed by the months of torture and exploitation, burnt out by all the exploring and manipulation, drained by the need to survive. All that was left was a wild animal, an animal armed and dangerous, fuelled by a deep well of anger.

A face appeared in a small gap and then withdrew. There was a violent retching sound. She stood her ground, the tips of her swords unwavering.

A second face appeared, staring over the shoulder of the statue. Shock was written in broad strokes. Flesh already starved of sunlight now looking like the face of a corpse, eyes wide, mouth agape. Jeniche wondered idly if you could kill those already dead. There would be one way to find out.

The face changed. As the mouth closed, it began to collapse, stirring something within Jeniche, like a breeze blowing in to deep caverns where fires had been banked. Light glinted from something. A jewel? She was confused. It moved, a slow downward movement, lost in shadows.

And then the face was gone, withdrawn into the darkness just as that errant breeze found a stray ember, fanned it, and drew forth a glow. The face reappeared, this time beneath an outstretched arm of the statue. It peered up at her and she thought she should know it. But there wasn't time to consider as she had seen the sword. Her own blades drew up, her weight shifted.

"Jen?"

She watched as the man's sword tumbled to the floor and clattered against a gore free patch of polished stone. It didn't make sense. Why would he...

"Oh."

The ember sparked into flame and all the memories were made visible in the little dark places where they had scuttled. The pain hit her hard and Alltud stepped forward, scooping her up before she could fall. For a long moment she hung, crushed in his arms. Then she forced her hands to let go of her own swords and wrapped her arms around his neck. She could not see his face. His teeth were clenched against the pain of lifting her, light as she now was; against the slaughterhouse he could see. And then he wept for her as she wept for him.

Alltud persuaded Kenak to enter the room. Pale-faced and trembling, the young Occassan looked at the swords and picked them up as instructed. He put them on a crumpled cloth on the table along with the clothing, boots, belt, and another, longer sword.

"Wrap it all up," said Alltud. "Bring it with you."

Kenak folded the embroidered wall hanging over the belongings. He followed close behind Alltud who carried Jeniche out of the room, down a single flight of stairs, and onto an open terrace, grateful to be away from the charnel house.

The warm night air felt strange. Sweet, free, carrying the occasional and distant sound of fighting to where Alltud had settled Jeniche. She would not let go of him and they sat side by side in the dark, their backs to the terrace wall, their arms around each other. They sat like that for a long time, crying and holding tight. Kenak had gone off in search of water and fresh clothes. They did not count the minutes that he was gone.

Even without the evidence of the room where Alltud had found Jeniche, he had seen in her face that she had been in a dark place and done dark things. Vengeance had been exacted, but it would never wash away the memories. He knew that. There would come a time when she would be able to talk about it. Or maybe there wouldn't. He squeezed her tightly to him again, held her head to his shoulder with a sheltering hand.

They slept awhile and woke in each other's arms. Above them the sky was full of stars, a quarter moon low in the west. Dark drifts of cloud moved slowly northward. Jeniche woke, a moment of panic at being constricted. It faded as she remembered. She eased herself free of Alltud's embrace, leaned toward him and kissed him tenderly on his cheek. His eye opened and looked at her.

"Tell anyone I did that," she whispered, "and I'll swear you must have been dreaming."

"More like a nightmare." He grinned and caught her hand before she could use her knuckles on his arm. He held it tightly for a very long time.

Chapter Twenty-Four

Despite the warmth of the night and the pile of soft blankets that Kenak eventually produced, they woke stiff and cold. It was, they thought, a small price to pay. Above them a pale sky was losing its stars to the dawn. Fresh, sweet air filled their lungs. The only sound was the singing of birds. Jeniche wept.

They ate where they sat. Alltud opened the sack of food raided from the kitchen store and handed out oat cakes, cheese, and dried fruit. Like a magician, he saved his best trick till last, producing a stone jar of honey. Jeniche inhaled the warm scent as she dipped her oat cakes into the golden liquid. The sweetness dissolved on her tongue. It was so rich it made her head spin. They fed each other tidbits, savoured the experience, kept looking at each other and smiling so hard it hurt.

When they had eaten as much as they could manage, they untangled themselves from the blankets and from each other.

"I'm not doing anything else until I have had a wash," said Jeniche.

She was trying not to think of the past, but it was painted all over her clothes and she could see it dark on the blades of her swords where they were propped against the terrace wall.

"You and me both," said Alltud scratching his beard. "And a shave."

Kenak was roused with a well-aimed lump of cheese rind.

"You need to do some talking," said Alltud when the young Navigator emerged from his own pile of blankets. "Where did you get to last night?"

"I told you." He yawned.

"'Others'. That's all you said. Before you explain that, though, we want to do things without it involving a hole in the floor. And then we want to wash. Bathe. Luxuriate. I expect you do as well. Did you come across a wash house in your travels with these 'others'?"

With her head resting on a folded towel, Jeniche lay in a shallow wooden trough filled with water, staring at the sky through the open doorway of the room. She had wedged the door back with a lump of masonry. The thought of someone coming in as she lay there naked in her bath did not worry her, especially as her swords – clean, newly sharpened, and oiled – were within easy reach. It was the thought of a closed door that disturbed her.

The water was cold as they had found no means of heating it, but she didn't care. It beat being dirty, covered with the gore of those she had cut down, and the action of scrubbing had kept her warm. For a while she pretended it was cleaning away the memories as well, but she knew that could never be.

The brightness of the sky began to hurt her eyes so she looked down the length of her body. In the dirty water she could see the scarred, cinnamon flesh stretched over bones, her stomach swollen from the meal she had eaten. She had never been a vain person, but she looked and she cried.

The tears were easily wiped away. And when she had washed again, wearing the block of soap down to a small, slippery nub, she stood and emptied buckets of water over her head to rinse away the lather. It had been exhausting work but the sweetest of luxuries. She dried herself and, dressed in fresh clothes that had been found in a store room, walked unsteadily out onto the sunny terrace where Alltud stood leaning against the wall, stroking his freshly shaved chin.

"I keep worrying I'm going to wake up in that cell," she said as she joined him.

They stood and gazed at the view, savoured the open space. The city below was quiet, sunlight painting the Grauberg as majestic rather than forbidding. Eventually they retired to a bench and sat together in silence. Jeniche was wrapped in a thick cloak. She had been shivering, unable to stop. Her soul was cold. It would take more than sunshine to warm it, but it helped. That and a space without walls or doors.

On her lap lay the belt into which she had just bored another hole so that it would not sit too loosely on her emaciated form. She had already prised open the panel to see that the pendant was still there, traced her name with her fingertips. It had been a long road. From Makamba, to Tundur, to Ynysvron, to the mountains where she had met Sharlod again and down into the heart of Arbiq. Now here, on the far side of a great ocean.

"Jen?"

She looked up to see Alltud standing in front of her.

"Sorry. I was a world away."

He smiled down at her, his heart aching. His own time had been bad enough, but he couldn't even begin to imagine what she must have been through to lead her to this.

"You have nothing to apologise for. Kenak has just been telling me that the Citadel has been searched. They can find no members of the Order anywhere. When word of Zamler's death got out, they vanished. Even Turrance has disappeared."

"Turrance?"

"It doesn't matter. The important thing is that we are safe here for the moment. The people hold the Citadel and most of Amparo."

"For how long?"

"I don't know. But we can't leave now. Apart from the fact there is a civil war going on, we don't have the strength."

"We'd be safe in the south."

"Maybe. But that's hundreds of miles away and to get there we'd have to travel through country held by units of the army still loyal to the Order, not to mention all those members of the BoR who are still on the loose. Kenak has had word from his family."

"So quickly?"

"He didn't waste any time letting them know he was all right. They don't live that far away and he has relatives in Amparo. Apparently the BoR are saying this is an invasion, not a rebellion."

"Surely no one believes that."

"People will believe just about anything that's told them if they're looking down the wrong end of a mosket. And they've been doing it for so long that for many it has become a creed – what the BoR says must be true."

"I don't want to stay here," she said, quietly.

Alltud sat and put an arm around her shoulder. "I know. But there's nowhere else to go for now. And the people will protect us. Word has spread about Anka'a and what happened here."

Jeniche began to cry again.

*

Late in the afternoon, as Jeniche slept and Alltud sat honing the long blade of his Ynyswr sword, sounds of fighting drifted up to the terrace. Shortly afterwards, Kenak appeared.

"The army have started to mass south of the docks," he said, keeping his voice down. "There's a small river there, the Gill, that the people are defending as a boundary."

"Are there any fortifications?" asked Alltud.

"Not really. It's mostly workshops and warehouses in that quarter. I was down there earlier. It's where my cousin got into the city. There are some makeshift barriers where it's easy to cross, especially by the bridge."

"And what about airships?"

Kenak shrugged. "We don't know how many they can muster. The airship service has never considered itself part of the military despite being under its control. Many airmen have come out on the side of the people. The service headquarters had been seized by the BoR and ransacked." He looked glum.

Jeniche threw off her blankets and climbed to her feet. She had been awake since Kenak arrived. When she got to the terrace wall, she pointed to the river cliff in the distance. "What about the other side of the river?"

"The Tal? There's not much cover there."

"Not in the day. Do the people have any soldiers on their side?"

"Some. But mostly ordinary soldiers. The officers tend to be landowners and they are more interested in protecting their estates. The others are in the BoR and loyal to the Order."

Jeniche sighed. She looked at Alltud who shrugged.

"It's up to you," he said.

"We're too weak to fight, Kenak."

"No one expects you to."

"But we can't sit here. Who's in charge of this… uprising?"

*

226

Early evening and they rode out with Kenak and several others through quiet streets in the south-eastern quarter of the city. They had met with the leaders of the rebellion and come away impressed by how organised they were. It had been a long time in the planning and there was little that Alltud and Jeniche could offer, despite their experience of battle.

It had threatened to turn into something of a celebration when Kenak told everyone who they were, how they were responsible for the downfall of Mord Kint, how Jeniche had killed Zamler. Jeniche could not look anyone in the eye, knowing what death and mayhem she had brought to the streets of Amparo through the limbs of the statue, albeit without her knowledge. In the end, she and Alltud had offered to ride with one of the patrols, look for holes in the defences. Anything, despite their deep weariness, to keep busy and to stay out of the way.

When the attack came, they weren't even sure it was an attack. Riding in a loose group, they had been taking their time, inspecting alleys, noting weak points, speaking to groups tasked with defending the district. In the dusk, they passed a small group of men walking downhill and heading toward the main part of town.

No one spoke. They were all tired. Yet Jeniche was all too conscious of the amount of sideways glances being exchanged. She nudged one of the Occassans they rode with and reached up for one of her swords. Although she had no intention of unsheathing it, the action was enough. The group on foot ran for cover and the mounted troop wheeled about and ran them down.

Jeniche held back. She wanted no part of any fighting. Alltud looked over his shoulder and reined in his horse, trotting back to where she sat. He came up alongside her, their horses nose to tail.

She shook her head, unable to speak, but he could see in her eyes all that needed to be said. He sat there, blocking her view of the skirmish.

"It will take time," he said.

"I'm not really sure I want it to. It can't be forgotten and it shouldn't be." She sighed. "How do they do it? How do they persuade people to throw their lives away when they have what they already need?"

Alltud shrugged. He didn't understand the madness any more than Jeniche.

"When we can," she said, thinking of the orchard behind the library, "we are going home. To Pengaver. Together."

Through unnaturally quiet streets, the sounds of horses' hoofs echoing sharp from the shuttered buildings, they rode along a curved thoroughfare close to the old part of the city that clustered around the base of the Citadel. One or two people watched them from windows as they rode by, some silent and grim, others sparing a wave or a nod. Jeniche could not bring herself to look at any of them. She may have been forced into the actions that precipitated this uprising, but that didn't alter the fact that she had hurt these people.

Alltud watched her, easing himself in the saddle to try to mitigate the effect of his wound. Even with proper medical attention it would have been a problem for the rest of his life, but being thrown around in a crashing airship and then spending a year or more in jail on a poor diet, forced to work at pointless and heavy tasks, doing what he could to protect Kenak whose dreams and beliefs had been shattered, had all played their part in tearing him up.

He would happily put up with that pain though if he could just find a way to help Jeniche. He had seen her depressed before, seen her dismayed by what she encountered in the world, but he had never seen any living person whose body was so thin and whose face was so dead. Where she found the strength to ride a horse he did not know.

Watching her, he missed seeing the runner approach the head of their troop. He shook his head. Another reason, he thought, that neither of them should be out here doing this. They were still too tired, too weak, too burdened with what they had been through. And if he was distracted, he dreaded to think in what strange and distant place Jeniche was at that moment.

They followed the rest of the troop when they set off at a gallop, surprising another party on foot who were trying to break into a building. As the attackers ran off, pursued by the horsemen, Jeniche and Alltud remained behind. Several people emerged from the building with makeshift weapons.

"Have they gone?" asked one, an older man wielding a broom with trembling hands.

"The troop chased them off," said Alltud. "They won't be back."

Behind the man with the broom were several younger men and a woman. They looked shaken, pale faced in the evening.

"What were they after?" asked Jeniche.

"I don't know. We don't have anything of value. No food. No weapons."

Alltud looked at the building. It was a substantial edifice of dressed stone with large doors that had been forced open. There were no windows at ground level and those above were heavily barred with decorative ironwork.

"What do you have?" he asked.

Jeniche eased herself down to the ground. "Old things," she said.

"That's right," said the old man looking at her with a frown. "How did you know?"

"I know," she said, her voice heavy.

Alltud climbed down from his own horse, glad to be out of the saddle. He gathered the reins of Jeniche's horse and tied both sets loosely to the remains of the door frame then followed her into the building. It was mostly in darkness inside, just the few lanterns that had been lit when the doors were attacked and the staff had come to the defence.

"Was anyone hurt?" asked Alltud as Jeniche wandered off into the interior.

The old man shook his head. "Apart from a few bruises. We sent one of the apprentices out for help." He looked round trying to see where Jeniche had gone. "Who is that?"

"Don't worry. She probably knows more about what you have here than anyone alive. It's been her life's work." And brought her nothing but misery, he thought. "You'd better get this door fixed."

Alltud found Jeniche in one of the aisles peering into a cabinet. She looked up as he approached and pointed. "Stuff torn out of the desert in Arbiq."

The old man approached. "Is it true?"

"What?" asked Jeniche.

"He said you know about... all this."

"It seems to have been my particular punishment."

The old man frowned.

"Is this all you have?" she asked.

"This is just the things we display."

Jeniche thought of the small room in the tower of the library on Pengaver. She had wondered then why it was all locked away. Now she knew.

"Jen?" It was Alltud's gentle voice that drew her back from the dark collapsing edge.

"Is there a store?" she asked the old man.

"Yes," he replied. "But we have nothing of value to anyone but scholars."

"And members of the Order."

"Well, yes. This is their museum."

"So they visited. Zamler. People like that."

The old man took a step back, a wary look in his face. He was uncertain now of his standing. There were always rumours, so many more since the uprising.

Jeniche looked at him. Beneath the passive exterior she was fighting to put the rage back in the furnace and close the door on it.

"Did they?" prompted Alltud.

"Yes," said the old man.

"And did they walk through the streets to get here?"

"Oh, no. They have their own private entrance. A tunnel. From the Citadel."

Chapter Twenty-Five

"I appreciate all that, but I'm not sure what we can offer. We aren't soldiers." He ignored the barely concealed expressions of disbelief. "Besides, look at us. We're not exactly in good condition. We've spent the last year or more as prisoners of your Order and," Alltud dropped his voice, "I dread to think what... what's his name?"

"Zamler?"

"That's the sorry cur. I dread to think what he was doing with Jeniche."

Eyes turned in her direction where she sat staring at the flames in the wide hearth. Despite the warmth of the evening they had lit the fire as a courtesy to Jeniche. She still felt chilled deep in her soul.

Conscious of the halt in conversation, she looked up. On the other side of the room, seated around a long table were the commanders of the rebellion, Alltud with them. At least he had the grace to look sheepish.

"Talking about you," he said.

She replied with a vague smile, aware of their discussion yet unable to find the will to interest herself.

"I was saying that we aren't soldiers," he added, but Jeniche was already staring back into the flames.

Padarn, a stocky grocer who had found himself pushed to the fore as a representative of his district of Amparo, laughed. It was a grim, quiet sound.

"You've seen more of it than we have, I would say. War and that sort of thing. All we know is street fighting and for most of us it is a new… skill. The only soldiers in our number are young conscripts who have deserted. All they ever learned was how to obey orders. We need to know how to organise against the army. We need to know how to give orders and what those orders should be."

"Don't think like a soldier," said Jeniche quietly.

"I'm sorry?"

They all turned again to watch the frail figure by the fire. She had not moved, was still half in shadow, her feet stretched out to the warmth.

"It's something a very dear friend once taught me. They were wise words."

Alltud smiled to himself, despite his sadness. Perhaps if he hadn't given her a sword out of the wreckage of that airship all those years ago on the way up to Tundur she would be living quietly and content somewhere. Perhaps.

"What Jeniche means," he said, "is that you may have to risk playing to your strengths."

The Occassans looked at one another and then at Alltud.

He shrugged. "If street fighting is your strength, if the streets are where you feel comfortable, then draw your enemy there."

"You mean let them back into the city?" asked Padarn.

With an effort, Jeniche turned away from contemplating the fire. She had found some comfort in the abstract dance of the flames, had been able to avoid thinking, of the past, of the future. But the here and now would not leave her alone.

"You may have no choice in the end," she said, speaking across the murmur of conversation. "They've already amassed a sizeable force. They won't wait for you to organize and train people."

She was met with bleak stares.

"I am sorry," she said. They had the look of young children denied a promised treat. "You have fought well so far. Achieved much. And believe me, I know exactly what you've been up against. That, however, was just a fraction of what is out there now and growing stronger by the hour. Whatever else you do, you must, at the very least, use your knowledge of the streets and your skills at fighting there to devise a fallback plan."

As the Occassans went back to muttering amongst themselves, Alltud mouthed a question at Jeniche across the room. She smiled and nodded. She was all right. There was a long way to go out of the darkness, but she was moving in the right direction and she had the very help at her side that she most wanted. Help that she must soon, for all his bravado, get to a proper doctor because he looked like a very sick man and it was breaking her heart. He needed sorting out and then she needed to get him home to Ynysvron, to the sweet clean grass beneath the trees in the orchard at the back of the library.

"We will also need to be ready to defend the air," said Padarn when they had settled on organising street defences as their major strategy.

There was a shuffling in the shadows behind Jeniche and she turned to see Kenak getting up from his chair. She had forgotten he was there. He stepped forward into the ring of lamp light about the table.

"I was apprenticed to the airship service. Served on the *Trepaharos*. I can help fly whatever there is."

"No," said Jeniche, cutting through the murmurs of approval.

Kenak turned to her. She had never seen more emotions at battle in a face.

"But I saw the Battle of Anka'a," he said, anger winning for the moment.

"Yes. Saw. From a distance, I take it."

Kenak hesitated, and then nodded.

Jeniche looked from him to the Occassans sitting round the table. "He's a Navigator. That's not going to help you if he dies above the city. He can advise you if he witnessed that battle. He'll understand airship tactics, their strengths and weak-nesses, much better than me or Alltud. Besides, I know and trust him and I need an interpreter. There are other secrets here that might help."

Alltud returned slowly from the latrines. It gave him a chance to straighten up and let the pain fade from his face. He was not adjusting well to proper food, was finding it difficult to keep it down. And heaving over a hole in the ground did nothing to ease the tearing agony in his side. At least he had the luxury of being able to wash afterwards, pick out fresh clothes if he needed them.

Back in his room, he twisted himself as best he could in front of the lamp on the table to inspect the scarred flesh of his abdomen. It was livid and puckered. He shrugged. Scars he could live with. The surgeon had done what he could on the *Trepaharos*. It was the after care that was at fault. He explored the tender surface wondering what was happening inside that caused such pain. He felt a fear unlike any he had known.

Jeniche walked in as he was pulling on a loose tunic, trying not to grimace.

"Other secrets?" he asked quickly to keep the conversation where he wanted it. "What might they be?"

"Well," she said, watching him closely with her head on one side. "They're secret."

It took him a long moment to realise she was making a joke. He felt like crying. Only partly out of joy. To give himself a little time, he blustered around the room, pulling a chair forward for Jeniche and sitting himself on the bed. She took the chair and placed it by the open door. They had been a long time in the meeting and the closed room had started to unnerve her. A view of the sky with its bright stars helped to settle her.

"We can't just walk away from these people," she said, enjoying the luxury of warm night air as it drifted in from the terrace.

"I know, Jen, but..." he shrugged.

"I saw things. When I... when..." How could she explain? "I saw things. We might be able to use them to help."

"It's not our fight."

"You sound tired."

"Can't think why."

"Anyway, it's been my fight since the day I met Sharlod in Makamba. I didn't choose to make it mine, but I can't run away now."

"No."

Alltud pummelled his face.

"Get some rest," said Jeniche. "I'm going with Kenak down to the museum to make sure it's been properly blocked off. And there are some things I want to look at down there."

"Tread carefully. I'm not losing you again."

She smiled and crossed the room to lay her hand on his head in a brief caress before she left.

Kenak had gone ahead with the lantern. The entrance doors to the museum had been replaced and were reinforced on the inside with cross timbers and props. No one was getting in that way without a lot of effort. There were guards there as well, local lads armed with knives tied to the end of broom handles, although when Jeniche and Kenak had arrived, they had been wandering around staring at the exhibits. Most of them had never heard of the place let alone thought of visiting, despite living in the same district. Jeniche would have been happier if the whole lot had been ground to fine dust and dropped into the ocean.

She had seen what she wanted to see; rather she had seen what was no longer there. Now they were on their way back, walking slowly along the passage that connected the cellar of the museum with the Citadel, taking the time to explore the gloomy rooms and chambers cut out of the rock. Most of it was crudely engineered and done fairly recently. One or two places on the way, however, looked as if the tunnel makers had stumbled upon something that had been there for a great deal longer. She could certainly feel the familiar tingle in the pit of her stomach that told her of pre-Ev ruins, of Pilgrim hideaways, of a tangled history made increasingly obscure by the few glimpses afforded them these many centuries after the event.

"Don't get so far ahead," called Jeniche.

Kenak came back in silence, watching his feet on the shallow steps.

"And there's no need to sulk."

He hadn't said a word the whole time they had been down there, not even in the museum where he had, like the guards, wandered off to gawk at the exhibits.

"Not sulking really. Well. A bit. I am grateful. I felt I ought to volunteer, even though I had seen what it was going to be like. I'd never been so scared in my life. But I suppose having worked myself up to it..."

"Don't thank me," she said. "You might die yet, down here on the ground. It comes to us all."

"I hope not. Not for a while. I'd like to see the farm again. My family." He sounded very young.

"Nice?"

"Oh yes. Green. Lots of trees. I'd ride the bounds with Pa."

"Worth fighting for?"

She saw him frown. "I don't know if anything should be fought for. It seems an awful sort of life to lead. Oh. I didn't mean..."

"Sometimes we don't get a choice. People bring the fight to us."

They stood a moment in the tunnel, each lost in their own thoughts, each dreaming for a moment of the places in the sun they would rather be.

"Come on," said Jeniche. "That bright image, the place you treasure, keep it with you. Just don't let it paralyse you."

"How did you know?" he asked as they resumed their search.

"What?"

"That I think of the farm all the time."

"We all have our own inner sanctum. Did you never wonder how Alltud and I have survived the things we have seen, the things we have lived through?"

Papers in bundles tied with twine, brown with age and brittle. Old parchments, curled and flaking at the edges. Books, some of which must be centuries old, their covers scuffed and their spines broken. Jeniche and Kenak had found a small cart, loaded it up, and manoeuvred the lot up to their rooms off the terrace near the top of the Pinnacle.

Many of the documents they had searched through were dusty and she put those to one side. They might make interesting reading at a later date when one half of the population wasn't trying to kill the other. For now, she needed to know what Zamler had been trying to do in recent months and years. The dustier the document, the less likely it was he had consulted it. It was the only clue they had to go on.

If Zamler had kept notes, they had yet to find them although they may easily have been lost or destroyed. Instead, with the aid of Kenak, she was trying to skim through the recently consulted papers to see if she could retrace the line of Zamler's research. It made for a smaller pile of material, but it still seemed an impossible task.

"Look for certain words like 'weapon', 'amplifier' and 'Pilgrim' or any marks or underlinings," she had said to Kenak on whom the task of reading had fallen. Jeniche knew a few Occassan words by sight, but not enough to be reading this sort of material. She had always been good at languages yet there simply wasn't the time to acquire reading skills and technical jargon.

That had been a long time before. Now, after hours of squinting through the night with nothing but lamp light to illuminate the sometimes faint documents, both Kenak and Jeniche slept.

Alltud stood in the doorway for a moment, dawn light behind him. He was reluctant to disturb either of them. For many months, sleep was all they had to shelter them from the harshness of reality, and even then reality had chased into their dreams to taunt them there. For now, though, the pair of them seemed peaceful. Sadly they would have to be woken at some stage and in this case, the sooner the better.

Having roused them, Alltud left them to follow him outside in their own time. Their rooms, in one of the upper levels of the Pinnacle, faced west. Standing on the terrace they could see down over the Citadel and across the city all the way to the river and the massive granite cliffs beyond. The sun was not yet up, although the peak of the Grauberg was ablaze. Despite the early hour, the city was alive, tides of humanity surging along the channels formed by streets and alleys.

They were heading to the southern end of the city, pouring into the narrow lanes where workshops and yards gave way to warehouses and the docks. All along the line of the River Gill, which marked the city's southern boundary, the defences were filling up with men and women and children, not one of whom had done more than swing a fist at their neighbour or been caught up in skirmishes with the city's militia. Alltud was glad to see that there were also patrols elsewhere in the city, watching the River Tal from the parks, keeping an eye on the wealthier quarters. People loyal to the Order were bound to live within the city limits still and might decide to interfere in whatever ways they could.

Alltud pointed to the south and there, in the pale light and fading early morning mist they could see the mass of the Occassan army lined up in battle order. Kenak gasped. It had doubled in size overnight. Jeniche stood silent and grim faced, scanning the cloudless skies.

She turned to Alltud. "They have chosen a good day."

Chapter Twenty-Six

The main rush of defenders passed. The old, the lost, the reluctant, the terrified followed on and made their way to the barricades as best they could. South of the Gill, ground troops were moving forward within their own ranks, preparing for a massive surge. They were phantoms in the morning mist that covered the water meadows.

From their high vantage point on the Pinnacle hardly a sound reached Jeniche and Alltud. They watched until the sun cut above the hills behind them and poured light along the top of the cliffs opposite. It was clearly the signal by which the attack was co-ordinated.

Out of the thinning mist that clung to the Tal, sails appeared. Running with the steady flow of the river, and making use of what small breeze there was, a motley flotilla of ships laden with troops slid toward the docks. Ahead of them, smaller boats sped forward, manned by oarsmen who steered them toward the string of barges that the defenders had moored right across the river during the night.

The small boats came under heavy fire from the barges and the dockside. Men died and boats foundered, but a number made it through and the great mooring cables were severed. Released from the stays on the eastern shore by the docks, the string of barges began to move with the current, holding to a line that swung from the cable on the far shore, leaving the river clear. With them went the first corpses, tiny specks turning slowly in the water as they were carried along.

Someone released the cable anchoring the barges to the far bank and the large vessels were picked up by the steady current and pulled midstream where they floated past the city and away from the approaching troop carriers. Men jumped free, preferring the river and battle to facing the rapids and waterfall downstream.

As the bargees swam for the shore, the first ship of the attacking forces pulled in toward the nearest quay. Jeniche and Alltud could only speculate on its role. Presumably it was meant to drop off the troops that lined its rails and then move on to allow other vessels to pull in. They could only speculate because it never got as far as the quayside.

The barges that had been strung across the river had been put there in part to prevent vessels from sailing past the city. But that had not been their main purpose. Under cover of darkness they had carried and deposited a cargo. Not on the quayside, but into the river itself.

When the empty flat-bottomed barges were cut loose, they rode high in the water and slipped away. The deep keel of the heavily laden approaching vessel snagged on the submerged cargo. The whole ship shuddered, dipped and slewed sideways. Men who had been crowded on the decks ready to jump onto land now found themselves falling into the water, pounded against the rubble of buildings destroyed in the uprising and the metal remains of the *Trepaharos*. Turning with the current and holed below the water line, the ship began to keel over, shuddering even more as the ships behind, with too little space to manoeuvre, ploughed into it.

Timbers splintered, masts and rigging tangled, sails dropped and smothered. Men were thrown in all directions, injured, drowned, and fighting for their lives. The noise and shouts of terror and confusion that went up from the river were picked up by the army and by the city's defenders and worked into frenzied battle chants that heralded the second wave.

Unaware that those in the first attack were now fighting the water of the river rather than the defenders on the docks, the main part of the army swarmed forward. From the terrace on the Pinnacle, they could see makeshift bridges brought up and slung across the Gill, troops pouring onto one end before the other had smacked down onto mud and stone on the far side, running straight into a hail of arrows and stones and mosket fire.

There would be no more silence that day.

Smoke rose in tiny puffs and mingled with the last of the mist drifting between the warehouses and workshops in the south of the city. Everywhere along the banks of the Gill, the makeshift bridges were being pushed back whilst the two stone bridges that carried the main roads into the city were now beginning to burn, great bonfires of wood and oil blazing to keep the attackers away. How long the fires could be kept burning was anyone's guess.

Thicker smoke began to coil upwards, strands reaching the terrace of the Pinnacle where they stood and watched. Kenak was rooted by the horror of the spectacle; Jeniche and Alltud detached from the surreal tableaux spread before them. They had expected the city to be overrun fairly quickly. Experienced troops in a highly militarised country were going up against shopkeepers and road sweepers, blacksmiths and ladies' maids.

But the city was holding its own. The Occassan army was advancing, that was clear, but progress was slow. Very slow. And being made at tremendous cost.

"How much training do the army get, Kenak?" asked Alltud. "Are they all volunteers?"

Kenak did not answer. He hadn't heard.

Jeniche touched him on the shoulder.

He looked round as if trying to wake from a nightmare. "Sorry?"

A loud explosion made them all crouch. The roof of a warehouse blossomed, fragments of shattered tile firing off in all directions as the main structure fell. Thick smoke and lurid flame pushed into the air.

"The army," said Alltud. "Are they volunteers?"

"No. No. Every able bodied male youth has to do two years training. Many stay on or, as I did, go into the airship service."

"So there are people in the city who have trained to be soldiers?"

"Everyone trains when they are sixteen."

"Everyone?"

"Well, not girls, of course."

"Of course," said Alltud, one eye on Jeniche.

It was her turn not to hear. She was too engrossed in events unfolding off to the east.

"Kenak, get some runners up here who can take messages to the commanders on the ground. And take the first message yourself. There's a group... see..." she pointed to a rocky outcrop beyond the farthest bridge over the Gill.

Kenak nodded and was gone, his footsteps clattering down the stone stairs.

"Not girls," she muttered.

"Of course," said Alltud with a grin.

Before long they were joined on the terrace by a small crowd of people they had never seen before. Observers with telescopes, commanders, runners, all straining to see what was happening and direct their own people to the most effective locations.

The first attempt by the army to take the bridge that carried the Eastern Highway was thwarted. It had been a small expedition probing the city's defences. There were no survivors to make a report back. Instead the Occassan commanders elected to use their superior numbers to push on into the docks and warehouses, fighting street by street, alley by alley, courtyard by courtyard, and building by building.

Smoke now lay heavily over the whole quarter and the early crackle of indiscriminate mosket fire had given way to specific battles that could be heard from different sections.

The smoke drifted away from the buildings and across the tangle of ships on the river. Several of them had burned fiercely down to the waterline, one of them exploding as fire reached the powder it had been carrying for the moskets.

The effectiveness of establishing a command post up on the terrace quickly became apparent. The defenders were able to pull their forces away from areas not under attack and put them where they could best repel the invading army. Attempts to breach weak spots were quickly spotted and thwarted just as quickly. It also meant that fires could be controlled with greater ease. Some were left to burn where they aided the defence; others were quenched or redirected.

Jeniche began keeping an eye on the sky. It was still bright and cloudless, although drifts of smoke occasionally obscured the view.

"Looking for anything in particular?"

She turned to Alltud. "This," she said, indicating the open air command post, "is going to make us a target. Moskets can't reach this far."

"Unless they are fired from an airship."

"Which could come from anywhere. Where's Kenak?"

"Here."

"We need several good archers and a brazier up here as quickly as you can."

He frowned but was gone again, clattering down the stone stairs into the building. Jeniche and Alltud turned back to the view of the city.

"It's going better than I expected," said Alltud.

They watched some of the defenders pulling back from a warehouse. The Occassan army, already wary, waited. The building bulged and collapsed in a flurry of smoke and sparks. Soldiers trying to climb over the rubble were caught from behind by a new tactic.

"Maybe," said Jeniche. "But it's a single city against a whole country. And how long will they have the stomach for fighting their own people, friends, cousins, brothers, their own children?"

Jeniche had reached her own limit. Tired of standing and looking down on all the slaughter, watching the slow but inevitable encroachment of the army and the BoR, she returned to her room and waited there for Kenak. When he came back they got on with their search of the papers and books they had retrieved from the store room in the tunnel down to the museum.

Kenak found it difficult to settle. Jeniche could see his gaze kept going to the door. There was nothing she could do and she certainly had no intention of trying to force him. The young lad's country was tearing itself apart just a few hundred yards away. And if she was honest with herself, she also wondered how things were going, despite being sickened by the whole notion of war.

Looking up from a series of diagrams that made no sense to her she was surprised to see Kenak bent over a handwritten notebook, his finger trailing along a line of text before he flicked back to another page. He sat back, finger keeping the place in the book, looked up to see Jeniche watching him.

"I don't understand this."

"What makes it different from all the other stuff we haven't understood?"

"It keeps mentioning a table."

Jeniche had to restrain herself from snatching the book from him. It would have been a pointless gesture, but it was the first thing they had come across that she understood and it could well be the key.

"Yes. I know what a table is."

"No," said Kenak.

"Yes," said Jeniche. "I've been on one. Was forced onto one. Many times."

Kenak stared at her. "But it says here..."

"What does it say?"

The room exploded. Somewhere in the background of consciousness there was a succession of crackles, mosket fire. Stone chips and splinters of wood burst from around the door frame. As Jeniche launched herself at Kenak, grabbing the book and knocking him to the floor, she was conscious of other people diving into the room for cover. Someone outside was screaming, someone else was shouting. A dark shadow passed across the doorway accompanied by a deep buzzing sound.

"Stay down," said Jeniche to Kenak, "and whatever you do, keep hold of this."

She gave him the book and scuttled across to the doorway. A mosket ball hit the floor just inside the room, leaving a crater in the stonework and breaking into fragments that buried themselves in the top of an upturned table.

"Alltud!" she called.

"Just behind you."

She turned to see him lying on the floor, face white, hand pressed to his belly.

"Are you all right?"

"Do you count being scared witless?"

"How did it get so close?"

Alltud shook his head.

"Any archers?!" she called.

Someone groaned and there was the sound of scrabbling. She couldn't hear anything else and from where she crouched could see nothing so she decided to risk climbing to her feet to peer outside.

Several bodies lay on the terrace floor amidst a mess of equipment and burning coals from the brazier. It had taken several hits from a mosket but still stood. Beside it there were arrows and a bow, just out of reach of a now lifeless hand. Keeping close to the wall and moving sideways, she turned her head up and watched the sky.

At the end of the terrace, she took her eyes off the sky for long enough to pick up the bow and nock an arrow. She wasn't much good, but at the moment she was all there was. So she stood and listened and watched. And through the sounds of battle drifting up from the city below, she could hear the faint drone of an airship.

"Did it come from over the Pinnacle?" she called.

No one answered.

The drone grew louder.

It could be the only answer. They must all have been so busy watching the fight below that an airship had sailed in from the east, perhaps stopping its engines for a while to drift in silence. It would explain how it had taken them by surprise. The drone continued to increase. And then she heard another with a slightly different pitch. And another.

Risking another quick glance, she looked out over the city and through the clouds of smoke she could see other airships approaching from the south.

"Kenak!"

A noise from inside the room.

"Yes?"

"Please tell me we have airships! Please tell me they are watching for—"

She didn't finish. The sky darkened above her. She pushed the head of the arrow into the brazier, pulled it free and, trying to remember what little she had been taught about using a bow, she fired upward. As soon as the arrow was on its way, she was grabbing for another, nocking it, flinching as chips of stone bit her flesh. The second arrow fell short, but she could see the first one embedded in the underside of the cabin, a tiny flicker of flame tasting the wood.

A sound to her left made her crouch as she turned, groping for another arrow. Several men appeared from the stairway with bows longer than she had seen before and they loosed off arrows that hit the receding airship, one of them making a small explosion as it made contact. As a result, the small craft veered sharply to the south and headed quickly away from the Pinnacle.

It was chaos on the terrace for a while. Kenak had gone running off yet again to make sure that the approach of the airships was known about. Others emerged from cover to help clear the dead and move the wounded to where they could be treated. By the time Jeniche had sorted out the room where all the papers were, Kenak had returned and a new team of observers was in place, protected by more archers and a sturdy woman with a mosket.

The approaching airships had drawn close to the city's southern border and the fleeing airship that had attacked them could be seen trailing smoke as it headed for the river. Arrows and mosket fire followed in its smoky wake but it escaped further harm before ditching in the water. Crew members could be seen jumping into the river as it went down.

If the oncoming airship fleet had expected to fly across the city unchecked, someone had mistaken both the resolve and the ability of the defenders. Many in the airship service had walked away from the conflict, but there had been those who had little or no love for the Order and the BoR. They had witnessed what had been done to Occassus and every other part of the world to which it had reached out with its grubby, cruel fingers.

The small, sleek vessels that flew in from the south, firing on the crowds below, dropping devices that burst into flames, had just a few minutes before an opposing fleet rose from the airship field to the north. Giant, double-hulled cargo vessels, a single-hulled passenger ship, survey ships, patched up old wrecks; all cast their own shadow over the city as they formed into a rough line and set off with their noses into the wind.

They were all doomed. Jeniche knew it. Kenak knew it. Alltud knew it. They had seen it before. Kenak had volunteered to crew one of them even though he had known what his fate would be. Jeniche looked at him as he watched all those other volunteers going to their deaths in a fight for something, win or lose, they would never savour. She shook her head. Such madness.

As the defending airships came into view and began their advance, they gained height and, in a move that was both risky and audacious, fired rockets from their cabins. Streaks of smoke tore through the air above the city and the fireworks began exploding amidst the attacking airships.

Explosions reverberated across the valley and through the smoke and flame, pilots began trying to move their vessels out of harm's way. There were collisions and flaming, deflating airships dropped out of the sky onto the streets below.

The attacking line had been broken and the neat order of battle became a series of deadly skirmishes. Airships turned, climbed, dropped. They yawed and rolled. Men fell to their deaths. Rockets shot upward from the ground for a while but after several defending ships were hit, orders must have gone round to hold back on such tactics.

Horrifying as it was, it was difficult not to watch. Even when one of the larger defending vessels, its rudders flapping uselessly, shuddered toward the Pinnacle they stood on the terrace watching. It passed close overhead, the pilot trying to use the engines to steer.

The battle lasted an hour or more until there were too few vessels left for effective fighting. The remaining attackers turned and fled southward, their parting shots landing along one of the hulls of the gigantic cargo vessel. Flame ripped through one hull and it began to drop toward the merchant's quarter on the banks of the Tal. It would have caused untold damage had it hit the ground as most of the defenders were congregated there.

Close behind it, the other double-hulled vessel, in a suicidal manoeuvre, dropped beneath the flaming airship and with engines at full power, lifted it forward. Both vessels, in a deadly glory of flame, ploughed into the docks and exploded close to the confluence of the Gill and the Tal, an area occupied by the attackers.

Kenak, in tears, went back into the room where they had worked through the night. Alltud and Jeniche looked at each other. They knew there was nothing they could say.

Chapter Twenty-Seven

A small circle of warm light was cast by the lamp on the table. It lit the edge of some papers, an open notebook, a hand spread over the pages to keep it open, and the side of a sleeping face. The rest of the room was in darkness apart from the wall above and behind the resting figure. There, another light flickered, barely visible, the echo of flames dancing in the city below where buildings still burned.

It was Kenak who slept at the table. As the afternoon had worn on and the fighting had become more sporadic, Jeniche had tried to distract him from the horrors he had witnessed. She wanted him to explain what he had found in the notebook. He had tried. It was mostly technical shorthand that he did not properly understand along with sets of symbols in a kind of glossary. He had trouble engaging with it and his thoughts kept drifting back to all the terrible things that had happened in and above the city, to the idea that he might have been out there.

In the end it had been too much for him. Even through his year and a half in the cells of the Order, he had nursed a vague feeling that it was all a mistake and that sooner or later everything would be fine. It was an illusion to which he could no longer cling. His own countryfolk were fighting each other to the death, some to escape an oppression he had been brought up to believe did not exist, others to impose it by whatever means possible. It was overwhelming. Exhausted, he had rested his head on his arms and was immediately asleep.

In the deep shadow at the far end of the room, Alltud also slept. He lay on a makeshift bed, curled around his pain in a way he would never show when he was awake.

Jeniche sat in the dark and watched over them both. She had tried to sleep as well, but there was far too much going on inside her head. All this new information about the machine which made far more sense to her than it did to Kenak. Worry for the future of the young Navigator. Fear for the future of Alltud.

At the sound of mosket fire Jeniche rose and went to the table. She slipped the book from beneath Kenak's fingers and closed it quietly, then folded the papers they had put to one side and wrapped them all into a flat package that she slipped into her tunic. The oilskin was cold against her flesh and she gave an involuntary shiver.

Out on the terrace, two watchmen kept an eye on the city. Fires still burned in the warehouse district by the docks, the glowing ribs of the two vast airships still visible in the dark ruins. Shadow shapes could be seen running across open spaces picked out by the flickering of flames. Everywhere else, the city seemed quiet, resting where it could beneath a clear sky full of stars.

They were woken early. And when they came out onto the terrace, red-eyed and weary, they could see that it all had to be done again. Set out in ranks across the misty water meadows to the south of the city was the Occassan army. There seemed to be as many of them as the day before. And overnight the threat to the city had doubled as scouts to the north had returned with news of a force making its way along the narrow, steep-sided valley through which the Tal flowed to the coastal plains below. The defenders would now be trying to hold the city on two fronts.

Jeniche and Alltud helped themselves to food that was brought up to the terrace in baskets. It was basic stuff and already rationed. Wheaten biscuits, cheese, and jugs of a weak local brew that Alltud thought had little to commend it beyond being wet. Kenak watched them in disbelief as they ate and surveyed the city.

"You need to keep your strength up, no matter how grim the view," said Alltud quietly, placing a hand on Kenak's shoulder for a moment as he turned and went back into the room where they had slept.

From the corner of her eye, Jeniche could see him pulling on his boots and strapping on his sword. She leaned toward Kenak.

"When the city falls..." she did not try to honey coat it with an 'If', "...do no try to be a hero."

He looked at her with dark defeat in his eyes.

"Are you listening?" she asked.

He nodded, unable to speak for fear of being sick.

"Do not try to be a hero. It will accomplish nothing. Hide. Use the tunnel to the museum if you have no other choice. But hide. Escape. Walk away from Amparo. Go home to your family. And if anyone asks, you tell them that you were not here, that you got out before all this started. There is no shame in this. Do you understand?"

He nodded again.

She hoped he did understand. It was difficult to tell with Kenak. He professed to be a coward, a bit of a backwoods boy, but there was something hard in his core. Reaching out, she took his chin in her hand and turned his face to hers. He held her gaze.

"Don't be a hero," she repeated. "They usually die."

Leaving him to make what he would of that, she went into the room and found her own things.

Alltud winked at her. "Rallying the troops?"

"This country needs people like him to survive this, to help rebuild it."

She stripped off her shirt. Kenak was stepping through the door as she did so. He gave a squawk, turned on his heel, and went back outside. Alltud chuckled as he went out onto the terrace, pretending he hadn't seen the scars on Jeniche's body, leaving her to bind the packet of papers to her stomach with a strip of material torn from the bedding.

When it was secure and comfortable, she put her shirt back on, tucked it into her trousers and tightened her belt. The jacket she had found in the Citadel was of good quality. Although the leather was thick, it was supple and allowed her arms to move freely. She buckled the front and slipped on the harness for her swords. Finally, she picked up her Tunduri blades one by one and, after a quick flick of the wrists, slipped them into their scabbards. Now she felt ready for the day.

Kenak was not on the terrace when Jeniche emerged. She raised an eyebrow at Alltud.

"No idea. He scuttled off the second he saw you changing."

"Perhaps he's had the sense to go looking for a bolt hole."

"Maybe we should as well?"

"Time enough yet."

256

It was Alltud's turn to raise an eyebrow, but an explosion from the north signalled the start of fighting. A dark plume of smoke billowed into the dawn air and spread as it rose, skirted by a flock of startled pigeons. Shouting could be heard from somewhere lower in the Citadel. Alltud lowered his brow and sighed. Jeniche took his hands in hers and squeezed them. He nodded.

There was no definite start to the day's fighting as there had been the day before. The explosion had been a damaged airship. Unable to fly it, the crew had towed it to the northern edge of the airship field and left it there until someone on what was meant to be a clandestine attacking force could no longer resist such an easy target. Afterwards, there had been a lull, the defenders roused and well into position.

Movement in the docks heralded the first skirmishes. Avoiding the still smouldering wreckage of the previous day's fighting, Occassan army units had worked forward to try to surprise the city's defenders. It was a pointless exercise. The men there had worked in those streets and alleys all their lives, knew their way through the cellars and across the rooftops. Anything that moved into their line of sight was cut down by a vicious crossfire.

The only thing the army had on its side was numbers. Every defender lost meant a gap in the defences. Every attacker lost was replaced with some mother's son who had dreamt all his short life of visiting the big city and making his fortune. All they were offered now was nightmares or oblivion.

Smoke soon filled the streets at the southern end of the city, wafted northward in lazy drifts across wealthier quarters. Beyond the city, much attenuated, it was filtered into the canyon from which, a day late, emerged the northern units of the army. Cheated of their major objective, the airships that had fallen on the previous day, they fell in their hundreds trying to cross the huge open space where the aerial vessels had been tethered and tended. Like their compatriots to the south, they had numbers on their side.

And with those numbers, with the attack from the north drawing defenders away, the army pressed in from the south and began to carve a corridor toward the Citadel. Alltud watched this ruthless progress with dismay. What had the Order and BoR done to all those young men to persuade them to slaughter their own kin or die in the attempt?

With a heavy heart he turned away and went to the doorway of the room where Jeniche was looking through what was left of the papers.

"Jen?"

She looked up and, seeing the expression on his face, got up and crossed the room.

"There's still time," he said.

As soon as he spoke, he knew she wasn't leaving.

"There may be a way to help."

He straightened slowly, pushing his elbow against his side in what he hoped was a surreptitious movement. It was a long look they exchanged, oblivious to everything around them.

"I want to stop them. If I can. Otherwise they'll rebuild this place and start all over again."

"How can you stop them? You've seen. There are tens of thousands of them."

"I've found what Zamler was looking for."

"Is this to be meddled with?"

She drew a deep breath. "No. Probably not. But even if I can't use it against them, I may be able to use it against itself."

He shook his head. "No. Come away. We can get a ship."

"I spent a year. A whole year. Inside that machine."

She looked up to the Pinnacle as she spoke, the terrace above theirs was where the statue still stood.

Alltud said nothing. She had not spoken of her time up there before and he had not asked. It was her story to tell when she chose, although he wished she had chosen a better time and place.

"That's why they wanted me. And others. There are others. Somewhere. But none of them could work that table up there."

"And you could?" He thought back to what Turrance had said about Pilgrims.

"The machine had been working against Zamler. I was able to get further. But it was... difficult. I hadn't the strength."

He nodded. "And now you have your pendant back."

"That and the things we have learned from those books and papers. Zamler wasn't the first."

"Can we not just burn all this down to the ground?"

Jeniche shook her head. "That up there... that's just a few bits and pieces brought here from elsewhere. Most of it is across there, deep beneath the Grauberg and the mountains beyond." She pointed out over the city through the drifting smoke of battle to the vast, sheer cliffs on the other side of the river, to the peaks beyond.

Alltud frowned, not sure how to broach the subject. "About that. About the Pilg—"

A shout from one of the watchmen had them turning to see where he was pointing. Fighting had drawn close to the Parade, the concourse before the gates of the Citadel. Units of the Occassan army were already forming up under cover of the buildings at the start of the processional way that led down to the park on the river bank.

"The decision is made for us again," said Alltud. "You'd better hurry. There's no knowing how long the Citadel can be held. We'll buy you what time we can."

"Tell people not to be startled by the statue. They won't have good memories of it, but it's on their side now."

Jeniche reached up on tiptoe and kissed him on the lips. He held her close for a precious moment, winked and was gone. She could hear him calling out orders as she mounted the steps to the top terrace, scrubbed away a tear with the heel of her left hand.

The familiar clatter of Kenak rushing off down the stairs on an errand was lost in the pounding of booted feet struggling their way up. She heard Alltud's voice again, but steeled herself to ignore it as she crossed the upper terrace to the door of the table room where her mind had been torn apart, where she had slaughtered every last one of her tormentors.

Chapter Twenty-Eight

It felt like a lifetime since she had last been on the top terrace. Somebody else's life. Except she bore the scars and carried the memories. In fact it had been just a few days. So little time had passed that the shock of being free had not yet worn off; neither had the joy of being reunited with Alltud. Much had happened to them whilst they were apart yet the bond between them was unbroken. Stronger.

The statue was still just inside the doorway. It filled the space, barely taller than a man yet radiating a sense of mass that made it seem much bigger. She had been surprised to see it there, perhaps because she only really knew it from the inside. And by the time she had stepped off the table, her mind was fixed on other things.

No one else could have moved it the way she had. The only other method would have been to lever it over, carry it to the far end of the terrace, then pitch it over to fall the hundred or so feet to the courtyard inside the main gate. Given what had been done with the wretched machine, it was a wonder that hadn't been its fate. But then, she supposed, not many people knew it was there. They too had had other things to think about.

Squeezing past the inert bulk, she tensed herself for what lay beyond. Let out her breath slowly. Someone had been in and removed the dead, cleaned the place down. Even the ceiling where blood had splashed – a flashback of the butchery she had meted out made her stagger – even the ceiling was clean.

It all seemed mundane. Innocent. Small. A bright, square room. At its centre a solid plinth, the table. Around the edges, jutting from the walls, angled shelves with grey panels on them. On the walls, more grey panels. In the far corner, an opening to a smaller room. She walked round the table and looked into the annexe. There was a single grey panel in there, on the wall beside a closed door. And that was it.

With an involuntary shiver, she stepped back to the centre of the room and looked down at the flat surface, a pearly white slab that was smooth and warm to the touch. Her hands rested on it whilst she wondered how on earth she was going to make it work. Before now she had been dragged up from the cells in a drugged state and dumped on the table, surrounded by men dressed in the uniform of the Order who had worked at the panels. Jeniche did not believe in ghosts and even if she had, she doubted very much if they could be appealed to for help.

Something had to be done, however. The sounds of battle filtered past the statue and into the room. She walked to the head of the table where Zamler used to stand, turned and faced the panels on the wall and the sloping shelf. All those symbols she had learned, the movements of her hand, none of them came to her and try as she might she could entice nothing from the dark places her memories had hidden.

Not knowing what else to do, she turned back to the table, walked down one side, and hoisted herself up onto the flat surface in a sitting position facing the door. A faint tremor fluttered in her stomach. It might have been nausea. It might have been fear. She reached back and grasped the hilts of her swords. They emerged in silence, light running along the honed edges and forming a symbol of death in the air as she swung herself around and stretched out on her back. For a second the blades pointed to the ceiling and then lowered as she relaxed. Alltud would watch her back. She knew that without the slightest doubt. However, if the table took her she did not want to be without weapons to hand if she needed to rise in a hurry.

To Jeniche it seemed like a very long time before anything happened. She was on the point of climbing off the table when she felt the all too familiar sinking sensation, felt she was falling. Fighting off the fears and trying not to resist she woke to the new layers of awareness that immersion in the machine always brought. This time they were much clearer. No one else was interfering, there were no drugs to fog her memory or reasoning, and in the small of her back was a warm pulse of power.

As she melded with the table she could still hear the distant sounds of battle: mosket fire, shouting, boots pounding on paving stones. Nearer was a familiar and comforting voice – Alltud calling orders, deploying whoever he had managed to gather in order to protect the upper terraces and give Jeniche her chance. And closer still, her own breathing as she tried to relax into an environment that had for a whole year been associated with pain, fear, and violation.

The outer layers of perception slowly faded as the inner world of the machine opened up to her. So different was the experience, she lay for some time wondering if the table had rejected her until she realised she could no longer hear what was happening outside.

To her left was a door. It was closed. With swift movements, she climbed from the table, fully aware that somewhere else she lay alone with very little between her and death or enslavement. At first she felt lost. Although everything was familiar, it was completely other. It wasn't something she would want to try to explain to someone else. And adding to her confusion was the fact she had never seen this section of the machine's interior before. Normally she emerged in an alcove off a corridor. It seemed sensible, then, that she find that or some other place she knew from before.

As she approached the door, she stopped and berated herself. All she had to do to find her way to the other table room, the dark room, the one that controlled the statue, was ask the machine. She turned to the grey panel on the wall by the door and then stopped again in the act of reaching out her hand. After a moment's hesitation she signed for the door to be opened and then stepped out into the corridor.

It would have been quicker to ask the machine and she knew time was short, yet something had stopped her at the last moment. She had long since learned to trust her instincts. They sometimes let her down, but she was alive and still had options. Given what she had been through, that was a plus.

As she explored, she began to realise what the difference was to the previous times she had been here. Everywhere looked sharp and bright. Working at full power. Unlike all those other times she had been forced inside when there were dark areas, shadows, a feeling of great age, tiredness, decay. Now it was as if it had just been built and was waiting to be inhabited. She knew that could never happen. This was not a building. In some way she did not understand, she was inside the machine. She had seen the places where it stored all the information it held, had travelled the corridors which must represent all the connections to the wall panels and other bits of the machine that people used, had heard the distant hum of whatever made it all work.

It probably didn't look anything like this; it was just her way of understanding it, using the things she had seen in the outside world, especially the city beneath the desert, to construct an analogue in which she felt comfortable. There was a touch of sadness that it resembled a Pilgrim site rather than Makamba. A question, too. Something Alltud had said.

"What are you looking for?"

The voice startled her so much she lost her balance as she turned, reaching for swords that had not travelled with her. She leant against a wall to steady herself.

"I was going to the room that controls the statue."

A beat of silence. "Why would you want to go there?"

Jeniche resumed her search. The intersection ahead seemed familiar. "I would have thought that was obvious."

A turn to the right and she was heading for the door to the room she wanted.

"You want to revive an ar'tziem."

"An ar'tziem?"

"The device you call a statue."

"How much are you aware of what is happening in Amparo?"

The machine did not answer. Jeniche drew the symbol on the panel to open the door to the chamber. Nothing happened. She tried to remember which way the door slid, leaned against it and pushed. It was hard work but she forced it to one side and stepped into the room. The door closed behind her.

265

"Zamler wanted to use the ar'tziem and other machines for evil ends."

"I am well aware," said Jeniche quietly, "of what Zamler wanted and of his methods. I could never work out why. What did he intend to do? Conquer the world?"

"I did what I could to stop him."

"I am not Zamler."

"But what will you do with the ar'tziems if I allow you to use them?"

"Ar'tziems. More than one. How many are there?"

She knew from what she had seen on the streets and from what she had read in the books and papers that there were several of the statues, the ar'tziems as the machine called them. Nowhere had she found an exact number nor any information about how many could still walk.

The machine did not answer. Jeniche waited.

"What will you do with the ar'tziems if I allow you to use them?"

"Is that the sort of question you should be asking?"

She moved forward to the panel on the wall at the head of the table and tried to activate it. Nothing happened but she kept trying as she talked.

"What will you—?"

"Aren't you a machine?"

A pause. "Yes."

"Are you alive?"

"No."

"Who built you?"

Silence.

"Are you in full working order?"

"No."

"Why did you try to stop Zamler?"

"He wanted to destroy."

"But why did you want to stop him doing that?"

"It is wrong."

"Did you decide that?"

"It is wrong."

"Or did someone once tell you that."

"It is wrong."

Although the machine's voice continued with the same calm delivery, the final iteration was punctuated by a solid clunk. It sounded like a door being bolted.

"Have you just locked me in?"

"You must not destroy."

"How do you know I intend to do that? Can you read minds?"

"No. But you are lying on the table with a sword in each hand."

Jeniche swore under her breath. It was something of a giveaway.

"They are for my protection."

"But you have used them to kill."

This she could not deny. The lights began to dim, the air seemed... more difficult to draw into her lungs. Could she die in here, she wondered.

"It was you that enabled me to do that. You that taught me how to break free of Zamler's control. You must have known it was a strong possibility that I would kill to end my torture."

The machine did not respond.

"Would you destroy me to stop me?"

The silence was absolute.

Jeniche took slow steps to the dark table in the centre of the room. It was definitely becoming more difficult to breathe. She wondered how the machine was managing that, more curious than worried. For the moment.

"You know what is happening in the city," she said, wanting to keep the conversation going.

"People fight."

"Do you know why?"

"They should not fight. I will not aid that."

"You didn't stop Zamler when he made me use the ar'tziem."

"I had no choice. He used you against me."

Something else to think about. Some other time. She could barely see the walls now and felt the first hint of panic.

"Do you remember you once said I needed a key?"

There was a pause.

"Yes."

"I have that key now."

Another pause. It stretched out and Jeniche waited. At least the lights had dimmed no further although she was gasping for air.

"Yes," said the machine eventually.

"I know the key is mine, but could others use it?"

"Yes. It would not be so effective. A key is specific to a person. I did not know they were still made."

So many questions the machine could answer, but she did not have the time.

"If we do not stop the fighting in the city, if we do not win, then someone will replace Zamler, someone will take the key that I kept hidden from him."

More silence. She sat in the gloom and struggled to draw breath.

"And just as you would destroy me," she continued, "to preserve others, so I feel forced to destroy them to preserve so many more."

And still she waited, leaning against the table now, knowing there was no way out if the machine did not want it.

"I could force you," she added. "I could use the key." She felt its warmth in the small of her back. "Use it to make you do what I want. I would much rather you helped me voluntarily."

She was light-headed now and felt weak. Even in the failing of her body, she had time to wonder at what she was doing. Talking with a machine, persuading it to let her do something she found abhorrent in order to prevent something even worse.

At first, she put the barely visible flickering down to her fading consciousness and did nothing. It was when one of the panels in front of her started to display symbols that she realised she was breathing normally.

"Thank you," she said.

"It has been..." said the machine, "...lonely."

"And we are both," she replied in a whisper, "just a little bit mad."

Chapter Twenty-Nine

Now that it came to it, she wondered whether it wouldn't be better to leave the machine, destroy the amulet, and stand beside Alltud. It was the simple solution. In her heart, though, she knew it was no solution at all. They would fight, they would fall, and when they were gone nothing would have changed. A few more thousand dead would be mourned, their lives torn away for nothing. Because it would all still be there, ready for someone else to exploit, ready for the next tyrant to bring down destruction and misery on the world.

In the small room that wasn't a room, in a place that existed only inside her mind, she laughed. At herself. At the absurdity of it all. Jeniche Lusor Remai of Antar, runaway, thief, non-believer in destiny, reluctant warrior. And it all hung on that one night in Makamba all those years ago when she had chosen to take the bait that Sharlod had dangled in front of her.

With a deep weariness, she climbed up onto the table in the dark room and stretched herself out. Almost immediately, she felt a warmth in the small of her back, even though she wasn't technically wearing the belt there in that inner manifestation of the machine. The warmth flowed through her and she relaxed, dropping into the table. In the dark she felt herself stepping forward into the ar'tziem, felt its senses flickering on.

The impression of joining with the ar'tziem was much more pronounced than at any time before. Her legs slipped into its legs as if she were putting on a long pair of boots; she felt her arms push into what might have been sleeves, hands into gloves which she flexed. Looking down, she saw the hands of the ar'tziem flexing. Looking up and turning to face into the room, she saw herself lying on the table in the room at the top of the Pinnacle.

She turned the ar'tziem, walked it forward, and looked down at herself. It was unsettling to know that the recumbent form, for all the world looking completely unconscious, was herself controlling the ar'tziem through which she saw herself. She turned it once again to face the open door. All that looking at herself made her feel dizzy.

Before doing anything else, she took a few moments to explore the workings of the ar'tziem. Functions that had been unclear or simply not there before opened up to her. She could see much more clearly, move more easily, and when she reached back to touch the side of the table behind her, she was aware that she had touched something, felt it through her own fingertips.

She also discovered that the ar'tziem was in poor condition. There were whole aspects of it that simply didn't work, other mechanisms she didn't understand. They clearly had a purpose, but it had been built by a people whose world was alien to her. It was not inherently a weapon, simply a device capable of intricate tasks as well as those requiring great strength.

On stepping outside the room, one of the malfunctions she discovered was with the sound. She could hear, yet as before it was muted. When she reached the wall surrounding the terrace and looked down, she could hear sounds of battle, as if they reached her through a thick wall. Nearby were muffled voices. She recognised one of them and smiled.

The top terrace was clear with only the table room and its small annexe opening from it, so she made her way to the stairs, wondering for a moment how they had carried her up here each time and then dismissing the thought. The steps wound round the outside of the building and into a covered hallway with a number of doorways. One led to more stairs going down into the rest of the building, another onto the terrace where she and Alltud shared their room.

The ar'tziem emerged onto this terrace and she saw the group of men there turn and form up into a defensive position, swords and bows raised. It was no surprise they looked wary and frightened. Not only was a living statue scary in itself, tales of its rampages through the city streets would have reached their ears if they had not themselves been witness to the destruction it had wrought. It was only a sharp word from Alltud that stopped them where they stood. Whether that was from running away or attacking she could not tell.

Alltud looked odd and it took a moment to work out why. It was that she was so used to looking up to his face that to see him looking up to hers was disconcerting. The ar'tziem was not that much taller than him, but enough to change her perspective. She raised the ar'tziem's hands, palm outward. She had warned him, but he still looked apprehensive so she spoke. The ar'tziem made no noise, but Alltud frowned as if he had heard her voice. She brought the ar'tziem's hands to its breast as if to say, 'It's me' and he seemed to understand.

When she formed one of the hands into a fist with the knuckles on display, he gave a broad grin and winked. With a wave, she turned the ar'tziem back to the doorway that gave on to the stairs and began the journey down to battle.

The corridors of the Citadel were swarming with people who had sought refuge and now found themselves being handed a weapon by neighbours whose sum total of battle experience was forty hours. It was enough to make them veterans and they did what they could to steady the nerves of those whose only thought had been safety. It didn't help them that the scourge of the streets was walking in their midst, even though word had gone round that people were not to be startled. It was difficult not to be wary when the last time you had seen the ar'tziem it was squeezing the life out of a friend.

The lower down in the Citadel, the greater the chaos and the less she became the centre of attention. Instead of standing around in the slightly self-conscious way of people holding weapons they were not used to, men began pushing their way past the ar'tziem, casting quick glances up at it. Before much longer, the dull pounding sound she had thought was the ar'tziem's footfall became louder and was cut off abruptly by a rumbling roar that shook the floor.

Thick, choking dust billowed into the corridor impeding the flow of people. The ar'tziem, however, enabled Jeniche to 'see' through it, creating a clear picture of the surroundings so she could guide it over and around people who were coughing and shielding their eyes, groping their way along unfamiliar passageways.

The source of the chaos was obvious the second she stepped out into the main courtyard of the Citadel. Piles of rubble lay scattered across the paved area and the huge gates lay flat beneath the feet of Occassan soldiers who were pouring into the space. The surge of uniforms had filled half the large area when the defenders opened fire.

Even protected by distance and experience, Jeniche flinched and closed her eyes. It was a withering crossfire, a terrifying meat grinder. The Citadel contained an impressive arsenal, presumably to have been used against the populace in an uprising. Now the populace had it in their hands and were proving to be just as ruthless as those who had governed them.

Soldiers fell on top of soldiers to be replaced by others urged on by commanders who, Jeniche could see, were sharing safe rearguard positions with members of the BoR. As she picked them out using the ar'tziem's senses, she saw miniature images of the different uniforms appearing along the bottom of her field of vision. They clearly meant something, but she didn't have time just then to puzzle it out. For all its losses, the army was gaining ground.

Taking a deep breath she plunged the ar'tziem into the centre of the fighting. Without weapons, she used the strength of the ar'tziem itself, pulling moskets from the hands of soldiers and breaking them into pieces, knocking people aside and trying to remove them from the fight without killing them. She had been forced to do too much of that already.

At first the defenders gave the ar'tziem plenty of room, not knowing if it might turn on them. As confidence in its loyalties grew, Jeniche no longer found she was trying to guard a wide gap on her own. With help moving in close she was able to look round. She was aware of mosket fire hitting the ar'tziem, of arrows bouncing from its carapace, but was able to shrug it off. Her distance from the violent chaos allowed her the opportunity to take a broader and longer view of what was happening.

In all the mayhem, she caught sight of a small group of Occassans working their way round the edge of the fighting, guarded by a second group. There was something about the way they moved that made Jeniche look more closely. They were older than the youngsters being slaughtered all around her, had the faces of men who were used to watching others die.

Disengaging the ar'tziem from two Occassans who were trying to wield a long metal bar, perhaps with the idea of tripping it up, she stepped away from the fighting in time to see the group disappear into one of the doorways. Guarding the entrance was part of the second small group, a rearguard for the others to give them time to achieve their objective.

Jeniche was torn. The ar'tziem was most effective where it was, but whoever they were, that group was not going to be stopped by the shopkeepers and artisans defending the interior of the Citadel. She had not the slightest doubt their objective was the Pinnacle, the room where she lay. And between the ar'tziem and herself was Alltud.

Moving into the thick of the fighting, she reached the main gateway to the Citadel. The pounding that brought down the gates and their surrounds had also loosened stonework on the wall. Using the ar'tziem's strength, she began tearing down more of the masonry and piling it into the gap. Rock after rock came tumbling down and she was joined by defenders who began heaving smaller pieces of stone to build up a rough breastwork.

Although it hadn't taken long, it was minutes lost. Ignoring the rearguard, Jeniche took the ar'tziem in by another entrance. The inside of the Citadel was a multi-layered complex, a maze of interconnecting corridors, rooms, and levels. Rather than follow the intruders, she was going to try to cut them off.

She walked into a chaotic nightmare. Occassan soldiers who had made it as far as the corridors were fighting from room to room with defenders, many of whom were simply trying to keep out of the way. In places the corridors were blocked with the dead and dying. In others, the fighting was too intense for Jeniche to force the ar'tziem through. Already she was beginning to feel the kick of mosket fire.

She reached the base of the Pinnacle, the level that contained Zamler's room and the entrance to the tunnel that led to the museum. There was fighting there, although the tunnel entrance was closed. She decided to ignore it and move on when she caught a glimpse of one of the defenders, a desperate look on his face, blood on his tunic. Cursing, she did an about turn and waded into the attackers. Taken by surprise, they soon went down and seeing that Kenak was safe for the moment, Jeniche resumed the climb to the top levels of the Pinnacle.

Reaching the next floor, she moved into an eerie region where the fighting had yet to reach. Fearful eyes watched the ar'tziem from shadows as it passed. All the time, Jeniche was trying to get the ar'tziem to communicate with the machine so she could find that map of the Citadel's interior. When it appeared in front of her, she didn't know what it was at first, thought that part of the ar'tziem's senses had been damaged.

When all the other information began to flow, symbols and images, she stopped for a moment.

"It can do all this?"

The machine did not reply. It did not need to.

She knew she had arrived in the right place when the ar'tziem was attacked. Mosket fire hit the chest and head and, despite the muffling, the sound was painful. Her chest hurt as well, but that didn't matter as long as she could get past this blockade. Although it was dark, the ar'tziem's senses, now enhanced by all the other things that were being displayed, enabled her to see where the soldiers were.

In the far distance, at the top of the stairs, she could see some were engaged in hand to hand fighting, caught a glimpse beyond them of several swordsmen. One went down as she watched and another moved in to take his place. The ar'tziem reached and grabbed two of the attackers and, this time, Jeniche squeezed, throwing the corpses behind her as she moved the ar'tziem forward. She was all too aware of one Occassan, lying on the stairs, a mosket in his hands aimed upward.

She fought forward, suddenly desperate. She knew they would want to take out the best swordsman on the terrace. Several more attackers went down, the man with the mosket concentrating solely on his target, waiting for the moment, confident that his comrades would protect him. Jeniche pushed on. The ar'tziem had become a hammer and men died as she worked it up step by step, reaching down for the prone figure just as he fired.

He only had time to turn his head, see the hands that grabbed him and lifted him high before hurling him down the long flight of stairs. The ar'tziem staggered out onto the terrace and came to a halt, blocking the doorway.

The terrace was not that wide. Several bodies lay at the ar'tziem's feet. Beyond, sitting against the terrace wall, legs splayed, was Alltud. There was a dark, ugly hole in the centre of his chest. Blood welled from it, staining his tunic and trousers, filling the growing dark puddle in which he sat. His right hand went limp and in all the muted cacophony of battle, the only thing that Jeniche heard was the dull clatter of his sword as it hit the paving stones.

Chapter Thirty

Her scream was heard right across the city. A cadence of anguish, sorrow, pain, and anger, twisting into something that unleashed an elemental fear in every living soul. It curdled the air around the Pinnacle, ran like a heart-stopping demon through the corridors and was picked up again through the city by those remnants of an ancient technology that still worked, filling the streets and alleyways before echoing back from the river cliff to haunt the city again.

Life seemed to go out of the ar'tziem. Its head dropped forward a fraction, the shoulders seemed to slump. All movement ceased. In the room at the top of the Pinnacle, Jeniche struggled to disentangle herself from the table.

She was only half disengaged when someone shot at the back of the ar'tziem. The pain was searing, flashing through every nerve in her body. For long moments she went into spasm, hands grasping like claws, back arched, eyes open and looking at the panels behind her where symbols and images raced by in a sickening succession, blurred by tears.

And then the pain in her body was gone and she went limp. Her hands came back down on the hilts of her swords. By an instinct born out of years of training and use, her fingers curled loosely round the familiar grips and she felt complete.

Out on the lower terrace, the ar'tziem raised its head. With a long, last look at Alltud, she blinked back the tears and turned away. The ar'tziem was an inanimate object, had no musculature and no well-defined facial features. The few people who saw it in those moments, however, were convinced that Death itself had woken and they knew that the preceding days would be made to look like a playground brawl in comparison.

The badly injured Occassan soldier that she had thrown down the stairs raised his mosket again. He fired and then he died, beaten to a mangled, bloody pulp against the stone wall of the stair well. Beyond him, the only other survivors of the group turned and fled, pushing their way through startled defenders who had braced themselves to do battle with professional soldiers. Standing back they let the ar'tziem pass before they swarmed up onto the terrace to replace Alltud's group and guard Jeniche. Among them, Kenak. When he saw the man who had kept him going through all that time in the cell, the will to fight left him and, overwhelmed by a sudden sense of loneliness, he knelt beside Alltud's corpse.

Screams could be heard from within the Citadel; screams of terror cut short. As the ar'tziem moved down through the maze of the fortress, it was relentless in the death it dealt. Anyone in an army uniform, anyone in the black and silver of the BoR, anyone dressed in the trappings of the Order was a target. Many of the corridors were ill lit and the ar'tziem loomed out of shadow and darkness working methodically from room to room.

As it moved, Jeniche fought her own battles in the table room. She had learned one of the ar'tziem's secrets and it was now moving its way down through the building without her doing any more than lie on a table connected to its systems. The images that scrolled along at the bottom of her vision had yielded their purpose and she had selected certain targets for the ar'tziem to follow of its own accord.

Whilst it slaughtered, she worked through weeping, incandescent anger to unlock it and gain access to all the other secrets she had discovered in the papers and books that had been hidden away in the room at the top end of the tunnel. In there had been such terrible things. They had shocked her when she had first seen them. It was no wonder the machine had fought to prevent Zamler gaining access. It was why she had taken the book. To make sure no one else ever had access to it.

Now it was her battle and she struggled to understand the complex instructions and overcome the various barriers that would allow her to gain access to the weapons of the ancients. It was anger that drove her. Anger that her life had been torn apart and her only friends, the only people she had ever loved had been cut down. A vast anger. Fiery. Hard. All consuming. Choking.

Still wrestling with things she did not fully understand and a machine that was probably trying to prevent her unleashing a terror she had no way of comprehending, she saw that the ar'tziem had reached the courtyard of the Citadel. Tears still blurred her vision. Ice crystals began to form in her heart.

The rubble she had brought down to block the open entrance had been partly cleared and the Occassan army had control of the gateway. Beyond, Jeniche saw that they were preparing a full out assault. With the vision afforded by the ar'tziem, she could see army units lined up and ready, with many more in reserve hiding just out of sight. How the ar'tziem was able to detect them she neither knew nor cared. All she knew is that they must not succeed.

Striding forward she sent the ar'tziem after whatever soldiers it could find and then went back to working on her own problems. As she studied the various panels that were displayed in front of her eyes, she could hear screams and mosket fire, felt the battering of mosket balls as they hit the ar'tziem. She no longer cared. They had brought this to her. Now she was returning it. Like for like.

The battering of mosket fire became painful and she shifted her attention back to what the ar'tziem was doing. Dead lay around its feet, torn apart by the ar'tziem's hands. Now the area around it was devoid of life. The soldiers had retreated to safety. Instead a concerted and concentrated hail of fire was being directed at its carapace.

Jeniche watched, unconcerned, wondering how much pain the ar'tziem could transfer to her, wondering how much punishment it could take. Feeling went from the right arm. It was a curious sensation. She could still move her own arm, if that's what she was really doing, yet the ar'tziem was not responding. Then some of its senses began to fade and she no longer felt any of the impacts although she could see the soldiers were keeping up the same rate of fire.

She felt the explosion all the way up in the Pinnacle, heard stones and other fragments raining down a few moments later in the ensuing silence. In front of her, the view of the courtyard she had experienced via the ar'tziem faded away. But as that picture died, other visions appeared. Two or three overlaid in a confusion of streets and buildings that separated and lined up side by side. To be joined by more. And then more as the other ar'tziems she had woken came to life across the city.

Mixed in with the increasing number of smaller and smaller images were ones she did not recognise and could not understand. Pulling them forward, she saw a succession of views of dark corridors, blank rooms, places that looked remarkably similar to the tunnel beneath the excavations in Arbiq, to the city beneath the desert in Makamba.

Although she had seen nothing of it but maps before now, she assumed these were part of the vast complex deep beneath the Grauberg on the other side of the River Tal. She gave a mental shrug. Once such ruins and remains would have fascinated her. The old her. The one who had shared a world with Alltud. Today they were a glimpse of something she felt compelled to destroy. As soon as she had cleansed the city.

The ar'tziems began to walk. Programmed just as the original had been, they moved through the city seeking out uniforms and destroying those that wore them. Resting from her own work for a moment, Jeniche watched the images in front of her, the death, the agony, the fear, the pleading, the blood, and the many sounds of death. She watched, descending by each act of horror into a madness from which she knew no escape.

And the machine fell with her, disgorging all the images it held of pain, starvation, and death. She tried to turn off the feed, but it kept on in a relentless succession, a world teeming with people always pushing, always fighting and inventing ever more elaborate and unpleasant ways to reduce their fellow creatures to piles of meat. And whilst the resources were more and more used for war, others starved in the wastelands that had been created.

As the images seared her mind, the ar'tziems turned Amparo into an enormous slaughterhouse, moving tirelessly from street to street, clearing away anyone in uniform as if they were summer flies. Behind them, the fighting stopped and an ever growing area of devastation knew a kind of peace as the wave of destruction rolled on southward through the streets and alleys, building by building, pushing through the destruction of battle and out across the Gill into the fields and meadows where the remains of the Occassan forces were camped.

Jeniche continued to fight with the machine to little avail. It had harboured so much for so long, abandoned, decaying, and trying to maintain itself and its own logic, facing an oblivion it did not understand. And borne along on the tidal wave she had unleashed, witness to all the destruction of centuries, Jeniche screamed for release in a voice only she could hear.

As the ar'tziems spread out southward, destroying every-thing she had asked them to attack, they were brought down one by one with sustained mosket fire. Some fell. Others exploded in lethal fashion, shrapnel embedded in surrounding walls and unwary flesh.

All the while, as the sun set, new horrors were unleashed on those left behind, cowering in the ruins. None dared light a fire that might attract death to their door. In the growing darkness, those who were brave enough to watch saw the mountains alive with strange, slow ripples of green flame. From the peak of the Grauberg, lightning shot into the sky.

There was thunder on the mountain. Terrible thunder that rolled across the city and shook the earth. Needle thin beams of light pierced the heavens and left those who saw them temporarily blinded. They seared the clouds and burned them away. As Jeniche lay oblivious to the strange storm, stars fell blazing through the darkness to distant horizons.

And when the machine had voided all the poison and the last of the stars had fallen, she was left with images of what the remaining ar'tziems could now see. Many of them were still, watching men who were tearing off their uniforms in the dark. Others quartered the rubble strewn streets of the city. Still searching, no longer controlled by Jeniche or any other agency, they wandered back and forth, lit by flashes from the sky. She lay as if in a coma, watching, absorbing, devoid of all feeling, her head jerking slightly.

In all the mayhem, a burned and disfigured face passed across one of the screens and Jeniche woke with a start. She scanned the images, wondering what she had seen that had made her thrash her way to the shores of sanity. Using what limited capabilities the machine still had she reviewed as many of the images as she could, but that fleeting glimpse of a monstrous face was nowhere to be found and settled in to plague her at a subconscious level.

It was then she became aware of everything else she could see, of the destruction wrought, of the storm that still raged in the mountains. One by one she shut down the ar'tziems and finally disengaged from the machine. She woke from the nightmare and lay on the table in the Pinnacle. Her hands ached where they gripped her swords; her face was wet with tears.

She climbed slowly from the table, her muscles sore and her joints aching. It was full night and devoid of all the extra senses leant by the machine, she felt half blind and completely deaf. Leaning against the table with head bowed, swords still in hand, she listened. Her own ragged breathing, the sigh of a warm breeze scented with ozone, a faint flickering of light, the slow roll of distant thunder. And then her own footsteps loud in the silence as she walked to the door, boots crunching grit against the smooth paving stones on the terrace.

The sky still flickered with the afterglow of the weapons unleashed against the stars and in the city below she could hear people moving, someone crying. The rest was strangely still. She sheathed her swords and made her way down the stairs to the terrace below.

Stars were appearing as she stepped over corpses and knelt beside the one that sat against the wall. Heedless of the blood, she turned and sat beside him, slipping an arm behind his head and pulling him gently into a cold embrace. And there, in the night, she gave herself up to grief.

Chapter Thirty-One

There had been many injured throughout the city, especially in the lower levels of the Citadel. Whatever treatment for their wounds could be made had been administered through the night and they were being cared for as best as anyone knew how. Many of them would die in the coming days.

At dawn, the mercy parties reached the top of Citadel, venturing up into the Pinnacle to collect the dead. In the grey light, beneath smoke from the fires that burned across the city, they moved up, level by level, sorting the fallen. Working quietly and with reverence they took them down the steps and through the gutted building out to the open concourse in front of where the Citadel's gates had once stood. It was already being called the Plaza of the Fallen. The bodies were covered with cloth taken from warehouses and homes and the living moved in silence between the rows of corpses looking for loved ones.

Up on the next to last terrace of the Pinnacle, they left the two tightly entwined corpses sitting against the wall until last, clearing a way through the gore until they could be disentangled and moved with care. It was a task that would haunt them the rest of their lives. They had already seen horrors in the few days of battle. Sorting the corpses, the thousands of corpses, left most of them silent and grim.

It was a butcher's wife who bent to lift the first of the sitting corpses. She had volunteered because she thought she would be able to cope and because she reckoned the men had done enough already by standing up to tyranny. Small and strong, she had been with the mercy parties from the moment fighting started. Patching up, carrying, twice despatching those in pain and beyond all hope. And through her hardening shell, she had come close to tears on seeing the two sitting there.

One, an older man with a greying beard had a desperate, ragged wound to his chest. His clothing was soaked with blood. He sat leaning at an angle, enfolded in the arms of a younger companion. At first she thought it was a young man, perhaps his son, saw on bending to them that it was a young, dark-skinned woman.

When Jeniche woke from exhausted slumber and saw someone trying to remove Alltud, she let out a feral scream they all knew. She watched with mad, defiant eyes as people scuttled away, peering back at her from the doorway.

Someone must have sent a message because, before long, others appeared and stepped out into the growing daylight. With them was Kenak. He had kept vigil by Alltud until driven inside by fear of the strange storm that had raged about the peak of the Grauberg. Woken by the noise, he joined the others and picked his way across the terrace. At a respectful distance he stopped and lowered himself to sit on his heels.

"Jeniche?"

He spoke softly and waited.

Jeniche watched him warily. She was a long way in hiding, somewhere deep inside herself, and had no desire to be enticed out into a world where everything she had ever held dear had been torn from her.

Kenak was not sure what to do so he waited and watched as the feral anger died from her eyes. He shuffled forward.

Instinctively, Jeniche tightened her hold on Alltud.

"He will be treated with honour," said Kenak, tears on his grimy cheeks, his voice wavering. "I will see to that. It's the least I can do."

Her own tears began to flow again and the butcher's wife bustled forward to kneel beside her, help release her hold on her dead friend, the man she had grown to love. And crooning sounds of comfort she helped Jeniche to her feet whilst Kenak made sure that Alltud was lifted and laid out on a stretcher of wood and carried away with all the reverence he deserved.

Later that day, after they had bathed and rested and eaten, Jeniche and Kenak were escorted out of the Citadel and along streets that bore scant resemblance to her memories of the city. It is true she had seen little and that had been more than a year ago from the inside of an iron cage as she was driven from the airship. Then it had been like any other city she had visited. Now it lay in ruins, wrapped in a thin layer of acrid smoke beneath a dead grey sky. It matched her mood perfectly for this was the place where Alltud had been killed.

Everywhere they looked, people worked to salvage what they could, some loading carts with the intention of leaving and seeking fortune, comfort, or shelter in the countryside. Others were standing on street corners surveying the damage as if waking from a nightmare to find it was still there just outside their door. Jeniche saw all this, but gave it little thought. She could still feel the weight of Alltud's head on her shoulder.

The Council of Citizens, as they styled themselves, had chosen a room in a secure part of the city. There were still pockets of resistance from the few surviving members of the Order and the BoR, but they had been sealed off and the people of the city were content to let them starve. It didn't stop them taking pot shots or trying to break out.

The building was heavily guarded and the room to which they were led was large. Inside, chairs were arranged in concentric circles, each one occupied. Behind those, many more people stood – men, women, and youngsters. It was noisy but had a good natured atmosphere and it took some moments for Kenak to push a way through for a frowning Jeniche.

As people in the meeting began to realise she was present, silence began to fall. Jeniche tried to push her way back out but the crowd had closed behind her and Kenak urged her forward, whispering in her ear, pointing out Padarn whom she had met before. It meant nothing to her. She didn't remember any names. She didn't want to face these people.

At the edge of the inner circle of chairs she stopped. Off to her left, Padarn stood and turned to her. He was smiling. Her frown deepened and he saw, his smile becoming a grimace.

"We..." He stopped and cleared his throat. "We wanted, as a city, to thank you and to pass on our condolences."

She held back the tears and gave a slow bow of the head in acknowledgement. They had none of them known Alltud and they had all had their own, much closer losses. For the rest...

"I truly appreciate your condolences. But you have nothing to thank me for."

There was an awkward silence.

"What will you do now it's all over?" someone asked from the back of the room.

"It isn't over," she said.

Again an awkward silence.

"The machines that brought all this destruction are still out there," she said.

"The statues? If they are just machines," someone else ventured, "couldn't they be used to help us rebuild?"

"Perhaps the ar'tziems, those things you call statues, could," said Jeniche. "Until the day someone like Zamler decides they should be used to shape the world as he wants it. Then how would you stop them? Or all the other machines?"

"Other machines?" asked Padarn nervously.

"You live above a gigantic underground city filled with pre-Evanescence technology, machines built by our ancestors, machines built by the Pilgrims. You saw them unleashed in the night. Zamler was trying to wake them and others will try to do the same unless they are destroyed."

"Destroyed? How would we do that?"

"Shouldn't we discuss it?"

Other voices chipped in with questions and an argument began. Some agreed they should be destroyed; others thought they should be studied. Jeniche stood for a minute or more then turned and began to push her way out of the room. Silence fell again as she reached the door.

"The machines are beneath your city and they are beneath the Grauberg," she said. "You have a day and then I destroy them. I don't know what will happen up here on the surface, but you have had fair warning. This I can do. If you wish to stop me," she said over her shoulder as she left, "you must kill me."

Kenak finally caught up with Jeniche as she was crossing the now empty Plaza of the Fallen toward the Citadel. She turned as she heard her name and stopped. Breathless, Kenak ran up to her.

"Are you really...?"

"Yes. Otherwise it will start all over again."

She watched him as he struggled to say something. Rubble slithered down a pile and they both turned to look.

"If needs be and there is the time and the will," Jeniche said more softly, turning back to face Kenak, "please see to it that Alltud is cremated. As the sun sets."

"But won't you... You will be back."

"I don't know, Kenak. I don't know." She looked up at the cloudy sky. "It's late. Midnight tomorrow. Will that be enough time to clear the city?"

"I..." he shrugged. "I suppose. I don't know. A lot of people have already started to go."

"Then get your Council to urge the rest to follow, even if only for a few days until they know what will be left standing."

Kenak watched her a while as she strode off toward the Citadel.

The guards at the entrance had been told that apart from a few of their compatriots keeping watch at the entrance to the Pinnacle, the Citadel was now deserted. She had told them to go home, pack up their families and belongings and get clear across the Gill. She had no idea if they did. As soon as she had told them, she had picked her way across the rubble in the courtyard and climbed up into the building.

Empty corridors echoed to her footsteps as she made her way up from level to level. The smoke that had become trapped inside drifted slowly in uncertain air currents, got into her lungs and made her cough and wheeze.

Rooms had been ransacked in a methodical and comprehensive way. Some, like Zamler's quarters, had been put to the torch. She peered into the soot-blackened space that reeked of smoke and then moved along to the room that gave on to the tunnel. She ventured down as far as the room where the papers had been stored. There was nothing there now but ash and she smiled a grim smile. It was one job she would not have to do.

As she left, wondering if Kenak had been responsible for destroying the papers, she heard what sounded like a single footstep. It made her stop and she drew a sword, moving on silent feet to the doorway to the corridor. There was no one there and she heard nothing else. With a shrug, she sheathed the blade and carried on up to the first terrace.

A light rain was falling and the two guards were standing in the shelter of the way up to the top level. She repeated to them what she had told those at the main gate, asking them if they would make a quick sweep of the building on the way out to make sure no one was left inside. They nodded, but she doubted they would and didn't blame them. It was a miserable place at the best of times. Now only ghosts remained and they did not make for good company.

The table room felt strange. Open to the elements. Deserted. Dead. She stood in the doorway for a moment before finding the courage to step across the threshold. Her past had gone. She had no future. The present was a grey, damp late afternoon in a land far from her own.

At the table, she spoke: "Will you resist?"

The panel at the head of the table flickered.

"No."

"And the other machines elsewhere in the world?"

"I can give no guarantees that they can or will listen, let alone comply."

"Try. It is all I ask."

"It is all I can do."

"Does it... worry you?" Even now she was curious about the machine.

"I am but a part," it replied in its ever calm, sexless voice. "It isn't our world any more. You can't go forward in safety if you are always looking back."

"There's so much more I would have liked to know."

The machine did not reply and she wasn't even sure if she had spoken out loud. She crossed to the panel where she began instinctively to create symbols on the surface with the tip of her finger. It took a long time as she had to find the things that had been hinted at and glimpsed in her ramblings through the machine's workings, spotted at times when her mind was on other things. In the end, however, the machine had been given its final instructions and she waited.

The steady footsteps of an approaching ar'tziem drew her from a reverie and she stood to one side as it came in through the doorway. Its head moved as if taking in the whole room, pausing for a moment as it took note of Jeniche. She backed away as it approached the table and then watched with a deep sense of satisfaction as it began to tear it apart.

When it had finished with the table, flinging the broken pieces out through the door, it began tearing panels from the wall and from the sloping shelves. So absorbed was Jeniche by the systematic demolition that she barely saw the other shape before it was on her.

There was no time to draw a sword, hardly time to make sense of what was happening. A person, twisted in body and with a face burned down one side to a waxy sheen, the nose completely missing, cannoned into her and knocked her into the small annexe at the rear of the table room. Jeniche kicked and punched in an attempt to get free but the monstrous, reeking form was on top of her and clawing at her with a ferociousness that was unnerving.

As she fought, she recognised the face she had glimpsed on a screen during the rampage of the ar'tziems, recognised the figure she had last seen rolling down a slope, wounded, into the burning shed outside Anka'a, recognised the man she had disfigured all those years ago in the prison in Makamba.

Balat sat astride her, raised both fists to bring them smashing down, but she twisted and bucked and managed to scramble to a wall that gave way behind her as Balat attacked again. They fell together into a small dim space, Jeniche almost supernaturally aware of everything she could see: the ar'tziem standing silent and still amidst the wreckage, Balat beside her on the floor, doors sliding together, closing just as the blinding flash of the exploding ar'tziem hurt her eyes.

There was a fraction of a second as the sound engulfed them and the doors of the small room were pounded with shrapnel. Balat began to climb to his feet and the small room dropped a fraction. Jeniche had felt such things before. So when the room began to plummet she was not entirely surprised.

Chapter Thirty-Two

Smothered by a monster that kicked and punched and tried to get its deformed hands round her throat. Floating weightless with every action ineffective and feeling as if it was slowed down. Writhing in dim light that barely let her see that she could not see very much.

The almost silent nightmare was, after a few timeless seconds, filled with a screech that hurt the ears. At the same time they crashed into the floor of the tiny room, Jeniche crushed beneath the weight of Balat, overwhelmed by his smell, but still managing to get in short and painful jabs to the side of his head.

By trying to move his head out of the way, he gave Jeniche room to swing even harder blows, fold her legs and push. Punching with her knuckles, she caught him in his one good eye and he reared back, climbing away from her. She began to kick at him and as the small room came to rest, he staggered back against a wall as it opened down the centre and the two halves slid apart.

Off balance, he tumbled out into a dimly lit space. Jeniche climbed to her feet. She rested first against a wall and then stepped forward, intending to take the fight to Balat, but the room dropped again and she braced herself against one of the walls expecting the worst.

It was a steadier drop this time and just for a few seconds. When it ended abruptly, she found herself facing another set of doors and a high step. Not wishing to be caught in there again, especially if it was going to drop any more, she forced the doors open and climbed up and out onto a wide, dimly lit area. Several light panels flickered some distance to her left, but they did little to illuminate the gloom.

The air was chill and damp and she shivered, hit by a wave of exhaustion and sorrow that left her floundering. She buckled at the knees and went down painfully, head bowed, wondering how much more the world would throw at her before she had a chance to find a small, quiet place into which she could crawl and die.

There would, she reflected, be no difficulty with that last part. This place she had fallen into, stretching out there into the dark, had a way of destroying itself built into its structure and she had instructed the machine to do that very thing. And as far as she knew there was no one else who could countermand her instructions. Not even the machine itself. So all she had to do was find a place into which she could crawl.

Sniffing back tears, she looked up. All the time she had been there, her eyes had been growing used to the dim light. Despite that, she could now see very little more than she had before – empty spaces shrouded in darkness. So she climbed to her feet and turning her back on the strange little room that had dropped her and Balat into this deep hole, she began to walk.

Broad, straight, and long, the passage echoed closely about her. She walked for a long time. Now and then, as she passed, a panel would flicker with a rudimentary light before failing. All it did was illuminate the poor state of the place. And the further she walked, the damper it became. Slimy growths on the walls glimmered and it became wet underfoot, water dripping from cracks in the ceiling.

She assumed that she was somewhere under the river Tal and heading for the main complex that she knew to be under and beyond the river cliff, carved deep in the ground beneath the Grauberg and the mountains beyond.

Several times on her journey, she stopped and turned, convinced she had heard footsteps following her. Each time she peered into the dimness there was nothing to see bar shadows and bad memories. Balat must be there somewhere, of that she had no doubt. He had dogged her footsteps for years and was unlikely to give up now. Wherever he was at the moment, though, he was keeping well clear of Jeniche.

After passing through a curtain of drips that echoed their own strange music into the darkness, the tunnel began to get drier. The air remained chill and Jeniche kept up a good pace.

Further on, when the only sound was her footfall, doors began to appear on each side of the passageway. Not far after that, it came to an end, giving on to a high hall full of strange constructions. It was lighter there and the air carried a strange, smoky odour. Some of the constructions looked like larger versions of things she had encountered before but that made it no easier to identify them. Ultimately, it didn't matter what they were. In less than a day it would all be gone.

A faint sound and she was standing with both swords drawn. Something was approaching from behind one of the structures. She edged sideways to meet Balat face on and was surprised when an ar'tziem stepped out. It stopped for a moment, the head turning toward her. It was a chilling sensation that lasted just a few seconds before the ar'tziem continued on whatever errand she or the machine had given it.

With nothing better to do, she followed. It wove between the various structures, stopped now and then at panels, few of which seemed to work. She lost it eventually when it climbed what seemed to her an unsafe ladder that disappeared into the darkness above her head.

With a shrug, she carried on in the same general direction, wandering deeper and deeper into the complex. Halls and walkways, stairs and galleries, rooms and vast pits, rows of small alcoves, she passed them all until she felt compelled to rest.

Although her body needed it, the moment she sat down her mind turned to Alltud and she felt the weight of her pain just as she still felt the weight of his head on her shoulder, the feel of his dead and cooling body in her arms as she sat with him through that awful night. Eventually it became too much to bear and she clambered to her feet and, exhausted, went on her way.

In the end she was walking for the sake of walking, walking to keep her thoughts at bay, wondering how much time had passed. The smoky odour grew stronger and ahead she could see a dull glow. With nothing better to do she went in search of the source of the light.

It took a long time to get to where the glow originated. The air there was warm and she could see layers of smoke drifting high above her near the roof of the cavern, lit from beneath by an area where something had clearly gone badly wrong.

It was an enormous hall along which were ranged six identical structures, frameworks holding narrow cylinders. The second one along from where she stood had fallen. What she could see of the frame looked as if it had been fractured by an explosion. The cylinder lay on the ground almost horizontal. In the direction it was pointing a hole had been melted in the side of the cavern. A hole the size of the Citadel. Rock, still glowing a pale orange and crusted over with a network of glassy black, had run in streams down to the cavern floor. The remains of a number of ar'tziems could just be made out as if they had been there working to prevent the accident. Or perhaps they had caused it.

Jeniche shuddered. It must have been a world of madness that had such power. It was no wonder it destroyed itself.

As she walked away, Balat dropped down on her from a walkway. One of his feet caught her on the shoulder and she went down with a cry. Rolling she found herself facing him where he stood with something that looked very like a mosket in his hand and something that looked, on his ruined face, very like a smile.

He raised the weapon, aimed it at her as she tried to scoot away on her backside, her left shoulder grinding painfully. She saw him squeeze the trigger and braced herself for whatever pain there might be.

Nothing happened.

Balat roared, reversing the weapon to use it as a club. He charged at Jeniche who was on her feet and had drawn just the one sword. The other would have been useless as she had little feeling in her left hand and could barely lift the arm. As her feet instinctively found a strong position that favoured her right arm, the thought crossed her mind that although she was here to die, there was no way it was going to be at the hands of Balat.

His attack was frenzied. Already distorted by the damage she had done with the lantern all those years ago and the

299

burning he had suffered, his face was a twisted mask of rage and hatred. She kept the club from her head, but he landed blows against her body, knocking the breath from her and pushing her backwards.

On the defensive, her broken shoulder screaming with pain, she tried to find a way to slide within Balat's defences. But he didn't have any. He must have been so far gone that he simply didn't care.

Bumping into something behind her distracted Jeniche long enough for Balat to get in a blow to the side of her head. She ducked and missed the full force of it, but a red explosion came with the pain and she fell to one knee.

Another blow missed altogether, hitting the railing she had bumped into. She was only vaguely aware of the ringing sound of the club on metal and she shook her head to try to clear her senses. It didn't work.

Stepping back, Balat swung again and Jeniche twisted so that her already damaged arm took the force of it. Her scream startled Balat long enough to allow her to get back on both feet. She was dizzy and her vision was blurred but she knew enough to know that if she didn't stop Balat now he would kill her.

She found her own madness, lurking just beneath the surface, and she let it loose.

Heedless of the pain, working through the dizziness, she lashed out with her sword and stepped forward on the attack. Balat hadn't expected it, didn't know what to do except flail wildly, right up to the point where her sword caught him just beneath the breast bone and she drove it forward with all the strength left in her body.

They stood face to face for long seconds. She heard the weapon he had used clatter to the ground, saw his hands come up aiming for her throat. With a hard smile, she tightened her grip on the hilt of her sword and pushed herself away, twisting, rotating herself under her own arm so that the blade turned like a skewer with a sickening sound. And when she was facing him again and saw the life finally fading from his eye, she lifted a foot and pushed him off the blade.

He fell in a limp bundle and bled out on the hard, stone floor. She watched, swaying, wanting to be certain this time that he was dead. And when she was sure he had bled his life away, she turned and wandered off, her sword trailing behind her until she collapsed to the ground and slipped into welcome unconsciousness.

Bright moments of life came and went after that. She crawled for a while until she came to what seemed a safe place. Later, exhausted, she sat herself against a wall and wept at the pain. There were moments when she pulled her tunic free of her trousers and unwound the cloth that had bound the book of notes to her. It was a struggle, but she managed to get it free at last and used the cloth to clean her blade before sheathing it.

Her vision grew worse and the pain in her shoulder and in her head increased. Sleep and unconsciousness offered increasing amounts of respite. In the short moments of waking she stared at the wall opposite watching symbols on a panel. They mesmerised her, changing on a regular basis. And then she dreamt she was flying, that the corridors and hallways were spinning and moving, that arms held her safe, so she gave herself up to darkness.

Kenak had been one of the last to leave Amparo, hanging around the Citadel in the hope of seeing Jeniche again. By mid evening he had headed south and walked through the ruins of the docks before crossing one of the makeshift bridges over the Gill. From there, he headed for high ground where many of the late-leaving refugees were gathered, as far away from the Tal as possible.

It was a dark night, cloudy, with a thin rain falling. Kenak, feeling lonelier than he ever had before, wandered between the encampments until he found the party charged with guarding Alltud's body. It was a subdued place, hushed talk, no laughter.

They had, perhaps, expected fire, a repeat of the storm that had torn a blazing path all the way to the stars. Instead the earth rippled beneath them like a shaken carpet and the air filled with a choking dust that the rain soon settled. It was a frightening experience and many thought that was what they had been warned of. Seconds later, however, the world cracked apart with a dreadful, deafening thunder and the solid earth convulsed.

Across the river, the Grauberg became a vast cloud of thick dust, lit through with lightning as it climbed for the sky. Dark on dark, roiling, twisting, its shape delineated by the static discharges that played around its outer surface, the column of dust surged upward mile on mile. Louder shattering sounds swept across them and in the night they could see the river churning, one or two people yelling that the cliff was sliding into the water. And then the dust column collapsed.

Many of those camped on the upper water meadows left everything they had and ran to even higher ground to wait in miserable dark for the morning. It was a long night of subterranean roaring and choking air, of lightning in the dust, of pebbles raining down. And when the dust-choked dawn finally came they were able to see that the Tal, filthy with mud, had been dammed by the shattered cliff and was now finding a new course into the gorge, scouring away parts of the city as it went.

Like everyone else, Kenak had been unable to take it all in. Even though the air was thick with dust it was evident that the twisted peak of the Grauberg had gone, collapsed in on itself, whilst the mountains beyond had been shaken and shattered into new shapes. He stood in shock, grit in his mouth, the stale damp stink of stone dust in his nostrils, a thin layer of dirt on his flesh, and bruises developing from where bits of gravel had fallen on him from the sky. And as the dust cleared down by the new river bank he could see an ar'tziem standing there, a body cradled in its arms.

Chapter Thirty-Three

The torch sputtered in the rain and nearly went out when it was thrust into the pile of logs. After a few moments, however, the oil warmed and the vapours spread into the cavities, catching fire with a deep oomph. Water turned to steam as the timbers began to burn. Flames spread, settled in the heart of the pyre, and roared high as a cool breeze fanned the blaze.

"Cynfelyn ap Emrys. In exile no more. Fierce as the evening star, he lit my skies, but evening ever becomes the night and he has set, gone into the west, and is lost to us. In the Otherworld they rejoice for a new morning star has risen, a new star awakens." She stopped a moment to wipe her eyes and settle the sling on her left arm, before resuming the traditional Ynyswr prayers for the departed. "You go home this day to your home of winter, to your home of autumn, of spring and of summer; you go home this day to your lasting home, to your rest of great deserving, to your place of sound sleeping. Sleep now and so fade sorrow; sleep, my dearest one, in the heart of truth. The sleep of seven lights upon you, the sleep of seven joys upon you, the sleep of seven slumbers upon you, my dear one. Sleep in the quiet of quietness, sleep in the way of guidance, sleep in the heart of love, sleep, my dearest one, everlasting in my heart. With thanks for your presence and the joy it brought; with love for your friendship and the strength it gave; with tears for the loss of you – a light has gone from my world."

She stood and watched the pyre burn, soaked by the torrential rain. Somewhere behind her stood Kenak and beyond him others from the city who were curious, who had heard of the deeds of these two strangers and who had come to pay their respects.

They drifted away as darkness fell to take shelter by their own fires and mourn for their own loved ones. Only Kenak remained, keeping vigil with Jeniche through the long night.

She stood for three nights and three days and no one knew how she managed it. Kenak brought her food and drink, but she took little of either. He built a windbreak from scraps of sail canvas to keep the worst of the weather from her and he treasured her smile of thanks for the rest of his life as it was full of the warmth and light of a summer day.

Toward sunset on the third day, Kenak came with a black-smith as instructed. He handed Jeniche the metal cylinder she had asked for and she turned it in her hands. It was beautifully made of fine steel, the length of a dagger and the width of a finger. One end was sealed, there was a strong belt loop welded in place, and a separate piece that would serve as a cap. Inscribed along the length of the container were designs copied from Alltud's sword.

She thanked the smith and took the cylinder, filling it carefully with ashes gathered from the pyre. The smith took it back in order to weld the cap in place.

"What shall I do with the rest of the sword?" asked the smith, for he had forged the cylinder for Alltud's ashes from his blade. That way Jeniche could take him and his sword back home.

Jeniche thought a moment and then drew one of her own blades, handing it hilt first to the smith.

"A blade of this size," she said. "Straight."

He studied it and nodded as he handed it back.

"It will be Kenak's, so a hilt to suit his hand."

The smith took Kenak's hand as the young man sputtered in protest. With a grin, having gauged the size, the smith walked away to his forge.

Jeniche turned to Kenak. "He would have wanted you to have something."

"But a sword?"

She looked long and deep into his eyes until he began to feel uncomfortable and then she said: "Learn how to use it well. Spend the rest of your life learning ways to keep it sheathed."

In the weeks that followed, as her body mended and her soul found ways to deal with its pain, Kenak told her of the mountains erupting, of the ar'tziem that stood with her in its arms, handing her over before it strode into the river to explode underwater. She rested and helped with rebuilding and all the while she was conscious of Kenak wanting to go home just as she once had, just as she had promised Alltud he would.

Came the day she talked of leaving, Kenak offered to show her the way to the coast and find her passage on a good vessel across to Arben. She told him off, told him to go home. Later in the day when he was packing, trying not to get his legs tangled on his new sword, she turned up at the room he was using in the remains of a building.

Leaning in the doorway, she said: "Have you ever heard of a place called Cayenembe?"

Kenak shook his head.

She tried another word she remembered hearing the Pilgrims use. "What about Ekador?"

"Ekador?" He looked surprised. "Yes. It's from a fairy tale. A place where the mountains touch the stars. It's meant to be in the far south. Why do you ask?"

Jeniche touched the cylinder that now hung from her belt, a twinge in her still healing shoulder, a silent ache in her broken heart. There were places and people she could not face just yet; things she needed to know.

"Perhaps," she said, "I'll take the long route home."

Acknowledgements

All quests require companions who offer their support, advice, and wise-crackery to the poor deluded fool saddled with the ring/curse/destiny/good idea for a book. Some, sadly, fall by the wayside (though never in such final and grisly fashion as those in the books) and new ones turn up unexpectedly. To all those who have supported me to this halfway point in the adventures of Jeniche I offer my heartiest thanks.

Special mention, as always, must go to Barbara. These books wouldn't exist without her ~~keeping me locked in the spare room with the computer~~ love and support.

I would also like to thank all those other writers out there on quests of their own who have taken the time to offer help or simply chat about things important to us that would bore non-writers rigid or have them shaking their heads and reaching for the restraints.

My thanks are also due to my agent, Leslie Gardner. She is the writer's equivalent of a magic sword and shield. To have someone in the business who believes in what you are doing is extremely empowering and it is for that reason this book is dedicated to her.